PROTECTING HISTORY

PROTECTING HISTORY

B. J. CHATFIELD

iUniverse

PROTECTING HISTORY

This is a work of fiction. All of the characters, names, incidents, organizations, and dialogue in this novel are either the products of the author's imagination or are used fictitiously.

iUniverse books may be ordered through booksellers or by contacting:

iUniverse
1663 Liberty Drive
Bloomington, IN 47403
www.iuniverse.com
1-800-Authors (1-800-288-4677)

ISBN: 978-1-5320-1257-0 (sc)
ISBN: 978-1-5320-1259-4 (hc)
ISBN: 978-1-5320-1258-7 (e)

Print information available on the last page.

iUniverse rev. date: 02/02/2017

This book is dedicated to my friends, family and to my many students who over the years have kept me young at heart longing to look to the future. I also want to thank three dear friends: Sue, Helen and Veronique, ladies I know would walk through that door with me if I was to ask. Thank you one and all for a great adventure.

CHAPTER 1

If anyone had glanced at him, which most people never did, he or she would have said that he was an excellent guard, manning his post in the strictest tradition of the British soldiers. The problem was that he knew better; he'd had one gin and tonic too many the night before, and he could feel it clogging up his mind. Yet what did it really matter? He was guarding air, or at least that was how he viewed his life and work. He stood there day after day, nodding to people who walked past him without ever seeing him. He would smile at the tourists who growled at the man in uniform, and although he knew it should bother him, it never did. He was a part of the furniture in the grand museum, a part of the wall, and so if they were not growling at him, they ignored him.

People came to the British Museum to see the mummies, the pots from Greece, the coins of ancient Rome, and the famous Rosetta stone that dominated the main hall. No one thought about the people who worked down in the basement cleaning and cataloging the vaults of material, and they certainly did not think about the man who stood sentry at the front door. He had been told when he took the job fifteen years earlier that he was supposed to be ignored and that unless someone walked in drunk or attempted to break the cases covering the museum's treasures, no one was even supposed to notice that he existed.

The most fun was when school groups came in. The little ones would run up and ask him all sorts of nonsensical questions, mainly because no one had told them that he was a simpleton, a guard who knew very little about the mummies or armor that filled their eager little minds. He enjoyed chasing the children around the hall as they raced from floor to floor, playing hide-and-seek with their teacher until something would spook them and they would scream.

The building was a tad spooky at times, especially the mummy chamber where the stiffs covered in four-thousand-year-old bandages were laid out. Hell, they spooked him, so he could only imagine what they did to the overactive imaginations of schoolchildren who wanted to be scared. Terror was one of the real joys of childhood, or at least that was how he remembered it.

On this crisp September Friday there were no school groups, and really the only people who had come in by noon were a tourist group from America. He tried to smile when they passed him, but they ignored him, which was just as well because he and many of his mates hated Yanks. They had such a superior air about them, as if they and they alone could save the world, which, as his friend Clancy had pointed out over another gin, was ridiculous since it was the Americans who usually got everyone into trouble in the first place. He knew that it was odd, considering the history books, that he preferred the French and Germans who made their way across the channel. They were actually friendlier and not as insulting when they came into the pubs.

He had been told that they were shutting down the museum that afternoon for a private showing, which was not uncommon. Dignitaries often had the pleasure of wandering through with the director and some of the academics without the unnecessary burden of having to deal with other guests. He had not been told who was arriving, and in his gin-addled brain he really did not care. He was simply told to announce at noon that the museum was closing for maintenance, and after a sweep was done to make certain all the visitors were out, he was to lock the main doors. He had done it all before and knew the procedures; there was nothing new here.

"Ladies and gentlemen, the museum will be closing in fifteen minutes for a maintenance overhaul. We will be closing the main doors in fifteen minutes. Please make your way out of the building. We will be reopening tomorrow at 9:00 a.m. Thank you for your cooperation, and have a nice day." As he spoke into the intercom system, he heard his voice boom out across the massive halls. The first time he'd had to make an announcement using the system, this had startled him, but now he was used to the loud baritone voice that bounced off the walls.

He had told the people arriving that morning that they would be closing for the afternoon, so there was no one grumbling or complaining about the inconvenience as the tourists meandered out past him at his post. He had half-expected some of the visitors to ask for their money back, but no one had, although one group, when they were told the museum was closing for half the day, had debated the amount of time it would take to do a real tour of the building. They then had decided to head off to Westminster for the day and return to the museum on Saturday.

He waited the fifteen minutes and then did a walk-through, noting that other than some personnel left behind to help with the tour, the building was now empty. It was at these times when the old place really did take on a spooky quality, and it was when he hated being there the most. He actually dreaded doing a buzz through the mummy hall because that was the room he was the most freaked out by. He stuck his head into the room, waited for a moment, and, when he saw no one was there, retreated back to the main hall.

"George, is the building secure?" The director smiled at him, a nervous twitch causing his left eye to wink.

"Yes, sir." The guard felt like saluting but decided that the man was in no mood for a joke.

"Good." The director rubbed his hands together and walked away.

George shook his head and wondered who was coming for the guided tour that had this normally sedate man so on edge. He had seen the director remain calm when Her Royal Highness came through, so today's visitor had to be someone the director was unfamiliar with. Security was an issue in this old place, and when heads of state had arrived in the past, the security team had actually been told to sweep for a bomb, which to George's way of thinking was ridiculous since not even the press had been informed when prime ministers or presidents of some other land were coming to see the ancient wonders.

He glanced around the room again and headed for the main doors. He took out a huge set of keys and locked the doors from the inside. The keys were older than the queen herself, or at least that was what George told his mates down at the pub. He had told his boss that they needed to change some of the locks, but the main door was such an ornate monster of a structure that many people considered its facade to be far too impressive to mess with. They had built a restraining door on the outside that was closed at night, but during the day, the director did not want people to miss seeing the grandeur of the place, even when it was locked. It was ridiculous, but that was England for you: ancient wonders and old architecture were not to be destroyed by security issues.

George went back to his desk and waited to be told what to do when their guests had arrived. When they were in the building, he was to do another walk-through to make certain that no one, including the press, had sneaked in with the VIP party. He was used to all these precautions, and none of it was news to him. He tapped a console on a computer screen and brought up a display of the building, which informed him that all the outer doors had been locked and the security codes had been entered. Everything was exactly as it should be, so he leaned back in his chair and waited.

He had almost dozed off when he felt someone approaching his station. He did not want to get into trouble with the director, so he bolted awake and sat up straight.

"The party has arrived," the director's secretary whispered to him as if it was some major secret that she was afraid to tell.

"Fine. I will do another check of the doors," he said in a normal tone of voice, which seemed loud and harsh against her nervous, squeaky whisper.

He sensed the woman in the ill-fitting tweed skirt and beige blouse watching him as he walked to the main doors, and that convinced him more than ever that whoever this VIP was, he or she was someone of note. The entire front-office staff was on edge, and that rarely happened. The British Museum was of such grand importance in the London scene that people in politics and the entertainment industry often requested guided tours, and the director was always willing to oblige them. George had seen the tours, the director looking bored and contrite as he explained for the millionth time the importance of some of the exhibits.

George shook the handle of the front door and checked the security codes on the newly installed keypad lock. He liked that he was one of only three people who knew the codes to lock the doors. It made him feel important.

He turned back to the front hall in time to see a group of people being led by the director to the main hall entrance. George gulped in some air, and for the first time in a long time, he was impressed. The VIP was someone of note: the president of the United States, his wife, their three teenage children, and a small entourage of tall men in dark suits were all listening intently as the director of the museum described how the museum had acquired some of the more famous artifacts. George had heard the line of bull before, and he tuned it out. He stared at the famous man and his equally famous wife and took note of every little detail, from how they stood to what they were wearing. After all, how could he impress his mates down at the pub if he did not have all the fine details?

"Would you like to begin the tour in the main hall or the mummy room?" the director asked, gulping hard.

"Oh, please, can we see the mummies first?" The First Lady almost squealed with delight at the idea of seeing four-thousand-year-old dead people. "I have been looking forward to seeing them all week."

Her children laughed at her enthusiasm, but George could see the glint in the eyes of the two younger girls and the boy, who George knew was all of fifteen. They were anticipating this encounter more than their mother was, and it showed in the way they walked and the way their eyes darted about the room. George had once told Clancy that in some ways everyone who walked into the place was a small child when it came to the first time they saw the mummy cases. They all were waiting for the ancient dead to rise and walk around with their arms stretched out.

The director heaved a sigh. "Fine. We can start upstairs and work our way down to the main hall." He gestured toward the large staircase.

George sighed and went back down to his desk. He was not expected to tag along with the VIP party. He was to stay one step ahead of them, clearing rooms as they went, so he grabbed a clipboard and headed to the service elevator, which would allow him to get to the mummy room ahead of the group. He would check to make certain no one, living or dead, was walking around before heading to the artifact rooms, where Egyptian relics waited to be studied. The director had told him exactly which rooms they expected to visit and the order in which he should clear them out. It was always the same with these groups, and George knew where he was supposed to be and when.

He did not want to be in the mummy room for very long, but he did walk through to the other end, making some check marks on the clipboard as he walked. No one alive was in the room, and the dead were all sleeping peacefully. He chuckled and wondered if he should add that thought to his tally sheet. He glanced into one of the cases, into the empty eye sockets of one of the deceased, and shuddered. He really did hate these things.

He passed into another room where more of the dead waited to be viewed; these seemed even more animated than the ones in the other room, and they disturbed him. He made another check mark and picked up the pace, almost running out of the room as the main VIP party made its way into the first mummy chamber. He heard one of the curators begin the usual lecture on how the ancients made mummies. It was a disgusting and distasteful procedure, but for some reason people were fascinated to hear about the way the priests used hooks to pull the brains out through the nose of the newly deceased.

George did not stop to listen; after all, he had heard it all a million times before, and he could probably give the lecture himself if they let him. He walked briskly into the relics room, where statues and jewelry that had been found in some of the tombs lay in ornate display cases. He didn't even look into the cases; they were all wired, and if someone without authorization tried to open them, a thousand alarms would ring out through the building, so he knew that all the little baubles were exactly where they were supposed to be. He made another check mark and strolled onward toward ancient Greece and all the lands that lay beyond it.

On every step of his journey, George could hear the group behind him, President Harold Carlson and his family asking questions and the director directing them to the individual on his staff who might know the answer. That was what the tours were mostly about: discovering who might have answers rather than actually providing a bunch of information people might or might not want. Over the years George had been told that a good guide allowed questions to determine the direction of the tour rather than just expounding his or her knowledge. George had learned a lot about the museum that way, and it had kept him interested in the place.

He had just stepped into the ancient Greek period when he heard a crash and a muffled scream. He froze and glanced back the way he had come. He waited to be summoned because if all that had occurred was someone knocking over a display case, then he really was not needed. However, something in his soul told him that whatever had happened behind him was more than the destruction of a glass case. His blood ran cold, and a thousand horrifying images raced through his mind, each more gruesome than the last. He stood there undecided for only a moment before he made a decision. He ran back to the mummy room, his hand on his cell phone.

He stepped back into ancient Egypt and utter chaos. Three teenagers stood transfixed in a corner, their mouths contorted into screams of terror. The director and the curator knelt beside the First Lady, whose husband lay crumpled on the floor. George stood for a moment, confused by what he saw before him; how was any of this even possible? There was blood pouring out of a wound on the man's side, and his wife was trying to stop the flow with her hand. The other people were already on cell phones and radios, screaming madness at empty air, trying to summon help to the still form of the commander in chief of the American people.

Sirens were already blaring as someone in uniform ran in from the side door. Where had he come from? George guessed that they had been outside, waiting for the party, and had raced up here when the call for help went out. The building was now blaring with sirens and alarms from every corner, and the sounds seemed to be pounding into his head. George backed out of the room and stood in a corner, wondering how any of this was possible. No one had been in the room when he cleared it, no one except dead Egyptians, so what was he to believe—that one of the dead had risen and shot the president?

He glanced back into the room, where emergency personnel were now leaning over the still man while his wife hugged her terrified children in a corner. George saw the director and the blood on his jacket. He walked over to him and stared at the shaking hands of the man who had already been unnerved by his guests. "What happened, sir?" George finally asked.

"You ... you were to clear this room," the director stammered.

"It was clear." George shot a glance at the blood. "I swear to you, there was no one in here except dead people."

"The dead can walk," a shrill teenage voice screamed from across the room. "One of those mummies killed my father."

"Now, honey," her mother said, patting her head, "it was not one of the mummies."

The curator pointed to a side door. "Someone came in from that room, used a silencer, and then went back out."

George was studded by this revelation. "Sir, that door was locked this morning." He walked over and tried the knob; it held fast. The only time that door was ever unlocked was when they were moving some of the mummies around, and then it was locked again.

"It was opened a moment ago," one of the American Secret Service agents screamed at him. "We all saw it, so where does it lead to anyway?"

"It opens onto a service hallway that we use to move artifacts around the museum," the curator said, his voice soft and barely above a whisper.

A radio on the agent's vest squawked in protest. "Sir, we lost the suspect."

The Secret Service man's face froze in disbelief, and he grabbed at the radio. "How is that possible? The maniac was in this room not a minute ago, and this building is on lockdown!" He glared at George, who shrugged his shoulders in dismay. "You better tell me how someone can get out of this building that fast."

"I have no idea." George was so confused. He really had no idea how any of this had happened on his watch. "I keyed in the alarm codes when you entered the building. The only way out is with the codes, and only the director, the night watchman, and I know all of them."

The emergency crew pulled in a gurney and then hoisted the still form of the president onto it. They wheeled him out, with his wife and children trailing along behind them. The two girls had not stopped crying, and the boy seemed numb. George watched them go and wondered what their world would be like now that their father was shot or even dead. He shook his head and solemnly turned back to the American agent, who seemed to be shaking from head to toe.

"Now you better answer some questions," the agent said, his voice suddenly shrill. "If you are the only ones with the codes, you know who this was or at least how the shooter got in and out of here so fast."

"I can assure you," the director said, shaking, "Mr. Marsh and I are above reproach, and I do not like your accusation."

"Well," the officer said, pointing his finger at the director, "there will be a great many accusations, sir. The assassin got into this building, and according to your man here, only three of you know the security codes, so it stands to reason, either he let the man in, or you did."

George took a deep breath; he knew that even though he had done nothing wrong, he was still in a world of trouble. Security was his department, and it had been broken. He had not even seen the attack or the person they had said pulled the trigger, so he had no information to give them. He closed his eyes and focused on breathing, keeping himself as calm as possible. When he finally did open his deep blue eyes, the other people in the room were all glaring at him, waiting for him to speak. "Sirs, maybe it would help if we reviewed the security tapes for this floor."

"You have cameras around here?" The agent glared at the director, as if this should have been offered long ago.

"Of course we have cameras. It is 2020," the director sneered. "We are a museum of antiquities, but we are not in the Stone Age."

George wanted to laugh at the absurdity of the reference, considering they did have Stone Age tools down the hall. However, he knew that laughter was completely out of line in their present circumstance, so he quietly headed for the door and waited for the rest of the group to follow him to the security room and the camera feed. The tension was so thick it could be seen in the very air around them. Not one of them knew whether the president was alive or dead, and none of them knew how any of this had happened.

The small security office was in the basement, and it was there that the group filed in in complete silence. Harry Tumble, the tech man, was already pulling up the camera feeds from the mummy room when they entered. His face was ashen, and he did not even bother looking up. He simply cued up the image on to the screen. The director sat down beside Harry while the rest of the group stood around the room staring at the small screen, waiting to see something to explain what they already knew.

George watched the screen with deep interest because he had not been present when the incident occurred, so this would be the first time he would see the possible death of the world leader. As the video played, George watched himself come into the mummy room, glance around, and then leave. A few minutes later, the VIP group entered, and the curator began to explain in some detail how mummies had been created four thousand years ago. It was all very normal until suddenly the side door that had been locked burst open and a hooded figure came into the room with a gun drawn. The killer fired once at the president and fled out the side door once more. The whole thing took only seconds, which explained the stunned look on the faces of those present in the mummy room, including the president, who stood there for a moment before collapsing onto the floor.

George turned and stared at the Secret Service agent. "I swear to you, that door was locked; it is always locked. There was no reason for it to be open."

Harry nodded in agreement. "I have checked the cameras, and George never went near that door, so he did not open it, and it was locked when I was up there this morning."

"What the hell were you doing up there this morning?" the director shouted, exploding in a momentary fit of rage. "Harry, you are to remain here at all times."

"I took Mr. Meitson a cable for his computer." Harry sighed. "The mummy wing is a shortcut to his office, and I tried that very door since it would have made my journey a whole lot shorter, but it was locked."

"It is never unlocked," George said, nodding again. "There is no reason to open it. Honestly, sir, in all my years at this museum, I have never once seen that door open except when they are changing the exhibits, and that particular area has not been altered in two years."

The agent lowered his gaze to the floor and then raised it to meet the eyes of the director. "That door is never open, and yet we all saw it open and close. You and I were in that room when it opened and figure walked in to shoot my president. Minutes later, when this idiot"—he jabbed a finger at George—"tried that same door, it was locked again. Can you explain any of this?"

"No more than you can explain how that hooded figure got away from your security team," the director sneered. "You have people on every floor and in all the halls. You tell me how this individual got past your people."

"I can't!" the agent screamed, pounding his fist against the door of the office. "I am going to have to explain it, and I can't."

"It is a massive complex," one of the junior agents standing behind them whispered. "There is no way we could have eyes on every nook of the place."

"I know that." The senior agent lowered his gaze again. "But it does not change the fact that my watch was the one that lost us a president."

CHAPTER 2

The young woman sat at a desk munching on an apple, feeling lost and alone. She had wanted to make the boss feel that she could take on any assignment, but the last column she had written was so bad that it had to face three rewrites and an editorial reboot from the legal department. She was a newbie and in the trenches of a large metro paper, which meant she was at the lowest rung of the totem pole. Everything she did and said was put under a microscope for analysis by everyone.

"Jenkins!" a voice screamed from across the room.

She jumped to her feet and bolted across to where a large, rotund man stood, his hand on the door. "Yes, Mr. White." She tried to smile, but it came out all wrong. She looked more like a schoolgirl afraid of the principal and the scolding she was about to receive for something that she was not even certain she had done.

"Get over to the British Museum." He banged his hand against the door. "This one is hotter than a firecracker, and I have no one else to send. Everyone else is out covering the G-20 leaders' summit."

"The museum?" Her heart sank. She really hated that place. It was boring, and nothing new ever came out of there worthy of page one. She wanted a page-one lead more than anything else, being sent to the antique department.

"That is what I said!" he shouted. "Someone just called in 'shots fired.'"

"Wow," she said, her voice going up an octave. Maybe this was the story she had been waiting for her entire career to cover. "Shots? Are you certain?"

"No," he bellowed, "I am not certain about anything, which is why you are hightailing it over there to check it out. And if anything is happening, call me, and I will send a team to cover it."

"Oh." Her heart fell again. White was sending her there to make certain that it was worth sending his better writers.

"If it is worth something, get a quote from someone who the channels are not interviewing." He headed back to his office. "I do not want to rehash what they have already covered on the six o'clock news. Is that clear?"

"Yes, sir." She raced back to her desk, grabbed her bag and a coat, and then headed for the elevator.

As the elevator headed for the basement parking garage, Shelly Jenkins mentally ran through a thousand questions that she could ask about shots being fired at the British Museum. White had told her never to do that, but she could not help herself; she always rehearsed the interview in her head before it ever began. The boss had warned her that having a preset bunch of questions limited you and caused you to direct the interview instead of allowing the story to develop on its own. "There is no formula to all of this, and if you think there is, then you have missed half the story. Sure, the who, what, where, when, and why are the beginning, but the rest is never cut-and-dried."

Shelly knew she should listen to the old man; he was a veteran and a real professional who had won awards for journalism. However, try as she might to be more organic in her interview skills, she was always too damn nervous to not script it out before hitting the pavement. Gary Melman had tried to help her develop her skills by running scenarios with her. He pretended to be witnesses and victims who she could practice on, but her approach always came out dry and forced. Gary had told her to calm down as she posed her questions, but she was too green and nervous. The questions she asked were always the same, and that meant the answers would always be the same.

"I have to get better," she whispered as the elevator door opened and she walked over to her little green car parked at the end of the floor. "If I can't even ask one question right, White will toss me out with the trash."

She settled into her vehicle and turned the key. With her shoulders hunched forward, she backed out slowly. She was, in fact, a terrible driver, and she was always terrified—not afraid of being in an accident as much as afraid of causing one. Her father told her she drove too cautiously, which meant she was always in the way of the traffic flowing around her.

She turned on the radio, praying that there would be something on the service about the shooting at the museum that might help her with her first round of questions, but so far there was no report. She was not really certain what that meant except that White always seemed to know what was happening in the city before anyone else did. Gary had told her that White was part bloodhound and had eyes everywhere. If there was a story about to break, the old man heard about before it had actually happened. Shelly was not clear on how a reporter developed that particular talent, and she was almost afraid to ask.

As she turned toward the museum, her heart began to pound harder and harder. There were emergency vehicles everywhere, and the police had roped off the entrance. Whatever was happening in that massive building, it was a huge story, and it might even help her make the page-one byline that she craved so desperately. She pulled onto a side street and pulled out her press pass. It was not always useful for getting into the heat of the moment, but it helped get her past the ropes if they were allowing anyone in.

Shelly Jenkins adjusted her blue blazer over her skin-tight low-cut T-shirt and tight blue jeans as she casually walked over to the first police officer she saw. Gary had told her to use her female wiles as much as possible. "It is not very twenty-first century, but it still works on most males," he had told her. "And if it gets you past the front gate, then all is fair in love, war, and the news game."

So she adjusted her low-cut T-shirt and flashed that schoolgirl smile at the officer. Initially, he growled at her, but then she saw his eyes lower to her ample cleavage.

"What do you want, Miss?" he finally asked, his eyes still below her neck.

She hated doing this, and when she was in journalism school, she had vowed never to use her feminine wiles, but the real working world had changed her mind quickly. Is there no way I could get closer?

The police officer tried to keep his eyes averted, but the closer she moved to him, the more he gave ground, and finally, he opened the rope and allowed her into the area where the emergency vehicles stood like sentries to whatever was happening.

She saw an EMT standing next to an ambulance and made her way over to him. She ignored the older woman on the side of the truck because for the most part women ignored her, seemingly thinking that she was too young and too pretty to be anything but a distraction for the men. Women hated when someone like her rode in and turned the head of every man in the room, and so Shelly had learned to give most women a wide berth. They were always hostile and antagonistic toward her, so most of her quotes and interviews were with the male members of the community.

"Sir, can you tell me what is going on?" She smiled at the EMT, who blushed at the pretty news reporter. Shelly held back a sigh. She knew that if she asked him to give away state secrets, he probably would.

"Well, we are not supposed to, Miss."

"Of course not." She lowered her gaze and patted her eyes as if she was about to cry, which was ridiculous. "I understand, and I will tell my boss that."

"To be honest, I am not really certain what the hell is going on." He leaned forward and whispered, "We got the call out twenty minutes ago, and we rolled in here. Now we are just cooling our heels while they decide if we are needed."

"No one has come out of the museum?" Shelly looked over at the massive doors.

"They are on lockdown," said the middle-aged woman as she walked over toward them, a scowl on her square face. "No one has even poked their heads out of that door since we came here."

"Lockdown." Shelly was suddenly curious. "What do you think that means, considering we were told shots had been fired?"

"Shots fired." The woman snorted a laugh. "Bloody hell. If you were told that, then you know more than we do."

Shelly walked away from the two EMTs and the ambulance. She wanted to laugh because once more her boss, Mr. Emmett White, had the pulse of the story even before there was a story. He knew more than the people on the scene, and no one had the faintest notion how he knew what he knew. Shelly walked past the door and peered at the iron facade. She knew there was no way in, but she had to look. Somewhere inside this massive building was the story of a lifetime, and she had to get to it before someone else beat her to it.

There was a sound on the other side of the door, and for a split second Shelly was convinced that it was about to open and give her access. Instead it remained firmly shut, and she was left outside, wondering what if anything she could do to change her fortunes. Other than the emergency personnel, there seemed to be only guards and police officers around, blocking the entrance to all but their own people. No one was talking, and no one was giving anything to the TV news crews that stood outside the ropes, poised to inform the world of what was happening. It was all so frustrating, and all the lack of information did was fuel wild speculation as the news reporters tried to fill empty air space.

Emmett White had told her that was one of the major problems with the twenty-four-hour news channels—they had a lot of time on their hands and very little with which to occupy that time. Stories that took time to develop and flesh out did not work well on an instant-pudding news show. So instead of really delving into the story, they made up shit to fill the minutes between when events of importance were happening. This gave the talking heads something to do, and it made them look important. The problem with making up stuff was that it caused a lot of disinformation to be disseminated, and that made life difficult for real reporters. Journalists now had to spend as much time clearing away the drivel as they did interviewing and investigating for the truth.

Shelly could see a leading news reporter from Channel 4 spouting out some useless information that in the end would mean nothing. He was being asked to speculate about the reason for all the EMTs and police around the museum that afternoon when the truth was he knew no more than the man in the pub sipping on a pint. She knew that some producer or director was shouting into his earpiece, begging for something that the network could use to be the ones to break the story wide open. They all wanted to be the darlings of the media. She had once thought that was what she wanted too, but now after spending one month in the shadow of Emmett White, she realized that TV journalism was a dying art, and if you wanted to report the real news, you still had to work for a newspaper.

She stood there for what seemed an eternity, her mind reeling from inactivity. No one seemed to have clue one about what had happened or why the museum was on lockdown, and no one was saying anything to the media or the people waiting outside. It made for a lot of tension and a lot of sour-looking people. So she headed back to her car—if waiting was all they were going to do, she might as well sit in her vehicle, listening to the radio. At some point the doors would open, and she would see the action from her car.

She was listening to the wild speculation coming from some on-site radio jockey when the door did finally open and a small timid-looking man walked out, flanked by two rather imposing figures in black suits. Shelly jumped from her vehicle and joined the crowd on the front steps. She pulled out her cell phone and pushed a button to record; that way, she would not have to rely on her memory for the details.

The little man introduced himself as the museum's director and nervously adjusted his tie as someone set up a microphone for him. As he twitched and shifted his weight from one foot to the other, Shelly could tell he rather would have been anywhere else than in front of this news-hungry mob.

"Ladies and gentlemen," he finally began, his voice hoarse, "I have some disturbing news to report, and I would request that you hold your questions for later."

There was a strained silence as the crowd waited for him to continue. He scanned the group, perhaps trying to find a friendly face, but when that did not seem to work, he grabbed hold of the microphone and gulped in some air. "This afternoon the president of the United States, his wife, and his children were having a private tour of this facility when some unknown assailant attacked the president. At this present time his condition is unknown, and the attacker is still at large."

The silence seemed to thicken as the crowd digested this tremendous turn of events. Shelly was shocked and could not believe what she was hearing. How could someone attack the most protected man in the world and be at large? The whole thing was chilling and oddly unbelievable. What shocked her even more than the information the director had given them was the unholy silence that followed. It was as if not one of these seasoned reporters knew what to ask.

"What is the condition of the president?" a voice finally squeaked.

"The American government will be releasing information on his condition as it becomes available," the director answered, his face white.

"What about his wife and children?" someone else screamed from the back.

"They were unharmed, but as you can imagine, they are in shock."

"How did the assailant get away?" A dozen voices seemed to scream this question, in one form or another, at once.

One of the men in suits leaned over the director to speak into the microphone. His accent indicated that he was from the American South. "We are reviewing the security tapes and are interviewing the witnesses at this time to ascertain how this tragedy happened. When we have more information, we will present it to the media."

A thousand voices seemed to ring out with a million more questions, but even Shelly, standing in the middle of the throng, could not make out the words of even one of those questions, so she was not surprised when the museum director and the Americans headed back into the building, slamming the door shut behind them. Yet she knew that if she returned to the office without some direct information or usable quote, Emmett White would kick her to the curb. Instead she raced for the door. She was not the only one seeking the attention of someone in authority. A dozen other reporters were standing there, some even banging on the door, demanding more than what had just been given to them in that short press conference.

Shelly knew it was useless to bang on that door or demand to speak to the men who had just left. They were not going to give out anything beyond the government line. Perry Lawson, Emmett's right-hand man, had told her that the most uncooperative people on the planet were members of the government and the military, and the more questions you asked of them, the less they seemed to know. He told her that she had to cultivate her own sources, people whom she could trust to provide little kernels of knowledge when all the doors had been slammed in her face. She was looking at a massive door right now and had no idea who to turn to for the information. She knew no one in the American Secret Service, the British government, or the museum.

She hated the idea of heading back to the office with the words of the director and nothing more, but what else could she do? No one seemed willing to talk, and the doors were never going to open while the investigation was ongoing. As she was turning to leave, she saw a rather nondescript man slowly appear from a side door and walk away from the building. He was in blue jeans, a scruffy jacket, and a cap. He walked with his head down, his eyes on his brown shoes. She watched him as he headed for the entrance to the tube and fell in step behind him. Shelly did not really know what made her follow the unassuming man afternoon other than the fact that he was the only one leaving the scene of the crime, and she wanted to be the one to grab him before the other vultures got their hooks into him.

"Sir." She reached him and patted him on his shoulder.

He turned around and smiled at her, which unnerved her. So few people smiled at anyone anymore. "What can I do for you, Miss?"

"Are you from the museum?" she whispered. She still wanted to make certain that this was her interview and hers alone.

"Yes," he whispered back, a mischievous grin on his round face. He was older than she was, perhaps in his early forties, and there was something kind in his large face that made her smile back at him.

"What do you do there?" She pressed on, hopeful that he would agree to an interview.

The man looked back over her shoulder at the melee outside the museum, and the smile left his face. She saw the indecision in his eyes and knew that he had already been given a warning about talking to the media. However, she could also see that he was a man who needed to talk to someone, anyone, who would listen to him, and at that moment she was the only one listening to him.

"I work at the front door as the security." His voice was so slow and methodical that she could barely hear him.

Shelly's small smile grew into a wide grin. This was even better than she had hoped for. One of the museum security guards was standing before her, and she had an exclusive. "Did you see the incident?"

"No." His voice was now so low that she had to lean forward to hear him. "I was in another room when it happened."

"Oh." Her smile dropped. "But did you see President Carlson and his family?"

"I did." He closed his eyes, and she had to wonder what he was thinking. He had just told her that he had not witnessed the attack, so why was he so upset by all of this? She had to find out.

"Can I have an interview about what you did see?" she asked, her fingers crossed. This was her chance to show Emmett White that she could get the hot story before anyone else.

"I don't know," he said, opening his eyes slowly. "I was told not to talk to the press about anything."

"I promise to leave your name out of it." Shelly knew that was a promise she might not be able to keep, and she hated lying to the man, but she had to say something to keep this conversation flowing. Emmett had made it clear to her that he had never used that unnamed-sources stuff and would never allow his reporters that sort of leeway with interviews. He wanted his paper to be a source that people could trust, and no one really trusted an interview that could not name its sources.

"Well," the guard said cautiously, "if you use that inside-source malarkey that they put in the paper, I don't see what harm it could do."

CHAPTER 3

George downed the rest of his drink and headed to the bar for another, leaving the pretty reporter alone. He knew the bartender and had for years, since this was the local place near his flat. He had always liked it since it was a dark, cozy tavern that was never busy. Other than him and the reporter, there were only four others seated around the bar, sipping pints and watching a test match on the television. He bought Shelly another round and set it down in front of her, though he noticed she had not even finished half of her first drink. He felt a little silly slurping down ale when something so horrible had just happened, but this was the one time in his life when he felt he deserved a drink.

He sat down and stared at the pretty young woman. He knew that she was far too beautiful to usually give a man like him the time of day, but today he had something she wanted. She was a reporter for a major paper, and he was a witness to a major historical event, so here they sat, sharing a pint or two. "You have to promise me that my name will not appear in the story, or I will have to deny that I ever saw you. I can't lose this job or end up in some dark cell simply to give you a juicy story."

"I understand that." Shelly sighed heavily.

He knew that he was making her life a little more difficult, but what else could he do? He had promised those stiff American Secret Service people that he would not talk to the media, and here he was, already breaking that vow.

"All right," George said, taking another long sip from his drink. "I guess I will have to trust you."

Shelly pulled out a pad and pen, forgoing the cell phone recorder. "Tell me about when the president's family first arrived at the museum."

"That is not really where I should begin with this tale." He scratched his head, and for the first time in a long time, George was very conscious of his thinning hair and rather fat face. He would never want to admit it, but maybe the real reason he was spilling this story to this girl was that he found her attractive and wanted to be seen with someone so lovely. "You have to understand what a visit like that one does to our regular routine."

"All right." Shelly wrote down some words and then waited for more information.

"When we know someone is coming that requires a shutdown of normal visitor hours, I make the announcement and then check the building to make certain none of the public is straggling behind."

"What announcement did you make to the general public?"

"Oh, just the usual nonsense about closing for maintenance." George smiled. "We never tell them that some VIP is coming to see the dead things."

"When you made that announcement today, did you know who was coming?"

"No," George said, shaking his head. "I am not worthy of such information. I think the only ones who were given the heads-up were the director, the governors, and the head curator. The rest of us just assumed it was the normal VIP tour."

"Those are normal then." Shelly nodded her head as she wrote.

"Sure, we have had dozens of them in the fifteen years I have been working there. I have met her majesty and most of the royal family, the prime minister, and most of the cabinet. They all want to have the private VIP treatment, and the governors of the museum agree to it if they are given enough notice."

"How much notice do you think they had that the president and his family wanted a tour?"

"Well, considering how long the G-20 meeting was set for London, I would guess months if not weeks in advance. But we were only told two days ago that we were closing the doors for a private showing."

"Is that normal?" Shelly bit the top of her pen for a moment. "To be given only two days' notice that the museum is closing for the afternoon?"

George scrunched up his forehead and thought for a moment. "Come to think of it, we are usually given a few days more, but it is not unheard of to have two days or even one to prepare for someone important. These things are sometimes a last-minute inclusion in their busy schedules."

"Well, the man has had a very busy schedule with the G-20 summit and the meetings he had in Paris and Berlin before coming here. Maybe including his wife and children and a tour of the museum was a last-minute decision—anything is possible."

"Makes a body wonder, then, how the assailant knew where they would be this afternoon." George ran his finger over the lip of his glass and wondered if it would be rude to down this second drink and get himself a third.

"I know the press knew nothing about it, and we usually have clues as to where he will be." Shelly drummed her pen on the table. "All right, so you made the announcement, cleared the building, and then what happened?"

"We waited," he said, grinning at the memory. "Actually, after I checked that the door was bolted, I damn near dropped off to sleep waiting for them to show up."

"What time did they show up?"

"Around one thirty or thereabout." He tapped the glass of his now empty mug. "I was then told that they were going to begin in the mummy wing because the wife and kids wanted to see those bloody things first."

"Is that normal?"

"Wanting to see those damn mummies?" George grimaced. "I suppose it is, but I do not see the fascination myself."

"What did you do while they were visiting their mummy?" Shelly giggled at her own joke.

George tried not to laugh, but he joined in. They both knew it was not exactly the time to be making jokes, but neither seemed able to stop the laughter. "I had a stupid job, Miss. I had to run ahead of them, clear each room before they entered, and then leave before they arrived."

"Wow." Shelly's eyes shot up in surprise, and George could tell that she was impressed.

The security guard knew that he had given her a major coup with this interview. She probably had originally assumed that George had sat at the front door throughout the tour. It had likely never occurred to her that he had been in the room where the president was attacked. Her eyes were glowing bright with a thousand questions.

"So you were in the room where he was shot?" she finally asked.

"Not when he was shot." George's face turned grim as he recalled that awful moment when he had run in to see the president on the floor and his children in the corner. He would have given anything to change that moment in time. "I told you I left moments before they came in."

"I know." Shelly was furiously writing in her notepad. "So you saw no one in the room before the president and his family entered?"

"No one," he said, shaking his head. "That is what no one can understand. There was no one in that damn room except a bunch of long-dead mummies wrapped up in their cases."

"So when you exited the room, it was clear."

George noticed that the young woman had written a question mark beside whatever she had just written.

She looked up at him and said, "I can understand why this is upsetting so many people."

George cleared his throat; this woman did not seem to understand the problem he was facing. He knew that the director and those American agents were looking at him sideways, placing the blame squarely on his round shoulders. Yet the only door available to the assailant had been locked when he did his run-through and when Harry went to deliver the computer cable to Mr. Meitson's office. He had run it through his head a thousand times since the shot rang out, but nothing made sense then or now.

"Miss ..." He suddenly remembered that earlier, she had insisted that he call her by her first name. "Shelly, I have gone over this with the American Secret Service, and it makes no sense. The door the assailant used was locked this morning, and a few moments after the perpetrator had escaped through the door, it was still locked. There are only a couple of people who hold the keys, and although it does lock automatically, there was no reason for anyone to open it this morning, so the killer must have already had the key."

"How did someone get the key then?"

"That is the question of the century, Miss." He looked around the room and lowered his voice. "Not one of us can answer it, and the Americans think we are somehow involved in all of this—and by we, I mean me. I would bet money that someone followed us here and is listening in on this conversation, trying to figure out who you are and if you are involved too."

"What?" Shelly spun around in her chair and looked around the room, apparently trying to determine whether any of the other patrons of the pub were Secret Service agents spying on them.

But there were only a handful of people in the pub: a young couple seated in a corner, making doe eyes at each other; a man at the bar discussing football scores with the barkeep; and a table full of rowdy young men arguing over an ongoing darts game. None of them seemed as if they were paying any attention to the dowdy man and his pretty companion, but if an agent was good at his or her job, the agent would blend into the scene. George knew these people, though; they were regulars. But that did not mean that there was not someone waiting outside for them.

"It was horrible, Miss," George continued. "One moment, the director and curator were explaining how the ancients made mummies, and the next, someone came through a locked door, shot the president, and escaped through a locked door. The building was on lockdown, and no one can find hide or hair of the individual."

"How is any of that even possible?"

"I have no idea, and it scares me." George glanced over at the group playing darts. "It makes me wonder where else this fiend could pop up."

Shelly's eyes narrowed, and she looked closely at George. "Are you worried that the killer will come after you?"

"No, Miss." He shook his head as he took another sip of the ale. "Actually, I think whatever this person had planned, it was accomplished. Whoever it was wanted the president dead, and that has happened."

"So the president is dead." Shelly tapped her pen on the pad in front of her.

"Oh yeah, I should think so." George placed the mug down on the table. "I would lay odds that they will announce his death within the hour. But the Americans will be hard pressed to explain any of it, and if they have to present me as a fall guy, they will."

"That is what really is worrying you, isn't it?" Shelly reached out her hand and patted his arm. "You are afraid they will accuse you of being a coconspirator just to shut up the cries for justice."

"I would if I was them." He gulped in some air. "I was in the next room, I was there just before the president arrived, and I do have the keys to the building, so it stands to reason that I must have helped this crazy nutter escape.

The problem with all of that is that I have no idea how any of it happened."

"And you have no idea who the shooter was?"

"Not a glimmer," he said, sighing heavily. "And if I did, I would have handed whoever it was over in a heartbeat. I am no hero, and I am not about to go after someone who can walk through locked doors on my own."

Shelly nodded her head in agreement. Whoever had committed this crime was some Houdini. If the door was locked and the building was locked down, only a real magician could have pulled this off without getting caught. She had a feeling that when she took this to Emmett White, he was not going to be overly thrilled that all she had was questions and that no one had any of the answers.

"I have to get going, George, and report to my boss." She rose stiffly to her feet.

"Remember what I said and leave me out of this." He remained in his seat, his eyes on the two pints in front of him. "I am in deep enough as it is."

"I remember." She extended a hand with a card in it. "This has my number on it. If you can give me anything more, please feel free to call me, day or night."

George reached out and took the card. He put it into his shirt pocket without even looking at it. "I doubt I will be of any use to you, Miss. Bloody hell, I am positive that by the end of the day tomorrow, they will have locked me up and thrown away the key."

"Try not to worry." Shelly smiled down at the man. She wanted to sound positive, but it did come out a little plastic. She was worried about George, and she had no idea why. She patted his shoulder and walked out of the pub, her eyes on the people around her. Considering that the man who had been shot was the president of the United States of America, it was conceivable that George was being followed and that the agencies that looked after these sorts of things would begin to tail anyone he met.

Outside, she stopped at her car and looked at the passersby on the sidewalk. None of them seemed to be giving her a second glance, but what did that really mean? A really well-trained agent would have been taught how to blend into the scene. She sighed heavily and slowly climbed into her car. As she drove off, she continued glancing in the rearview mirror.

CHAPTER 4

George downed the third pint and waited for what seemed an hour, but it was really only ten minutes. He then got up and walked to the flat where he lived alone except for a small tabby cat he had found wandering around the back alley months ago. It was really only a kitten, and he was enjoying having it for company. He knew that having a cat was a sure sign that he was getting too set in his ways as a bachelor and that at his age he needed to consider making some changes or no woman would ever want him. He had not thought about these things in a long time, but Shelly had made him wonder about his choices. She was such a lovely young thing, and sharing a pint with her had made him wonder if someone like her would ever find him worth a second glance. He glanced at the card with her number on it and wondered if in a day or two he could call and ask her to join him for lunch. She had told him to call if he had anything else to add to the story. He shook his head and placed the card back in his pocket. She would probably be angry if he called only to pass the time of day with her and had no information about the attack.

He was a man, and he was attracted to her; hell, what man in his right mind wouldn't be? But she was a beautiful girl, and she would never look at someone like him with those soft blue eyes. He knew that the only reason he'd gotten to sit with her in the pub was that she wanted something she could put in the paper about what he had seen in the museum. She was using him, and in truth he did not care; she could use him all she wanted, and he would welcome it.

He usually sat and watched the telly, but today he left it off. He knew that all the stations would be dissecting the goings-on at the museum, and he did not care to listen to their speculations. He had enough of that going on inside his own head without having their thoughts added to his own. He also worried that someone would ask the question that some of the agents had put to him over and over again: was he involved in the murder plot?

He could hear the TV playing in the flat next door, and he knew that Mrs. Whitney was watching the news. The old woman knew him and knew where he worked, so she probably thought that he had some tidbits to add that the telly could not, but she did not bother to knock on his door. Was that a good sign or a bad one? Did the elderly widow think he was involved, and was she afraid to ask, or did she think that he might not be at home yet? Perhaps she believed that the news had it right and that he had already been arrested for his involvement in the attack on the American president. Since he had not turned on his TV, she might not have heard him come into the building, so she might not think he was at home.

George wondered if he should bang a pot or stomp around the room so that she would know he was home. But what if that gave her the needed incentive to saunter over and bombard him with a million questions? He really was not in the mood to deal with Mrs. Whitney or her questions, mainly because he had no answers for her or anyone else. He had no answers for Shelly Jenkins either, but he wanted to talk to her even if he did not want to talk to Mrs. Whitney.

The large man sighed and turned off his lights, undressed in the dark, and climbed into bed. He knew that he would probably not sleep, but it was better than expecting the neighbors to beat at his door when they realized his lights were on and he was finally home. He had promised the Americans and the museum director that he would be back at the museum the next morning at nine o'clock to go over the entire incident again, as if that was going to get them anywhere. He could think of no new information that he could provide them or Shelly Jenkins.

His mind kept drifting back to the lovely reporter, which he knew was a useless endeavor—as useless as trying to come up with some explanation for the mysterious locked door and the invidual who had vanished through it. He giggled to himself when he realized that he was more likely to find an explanation for the attacker's escape than he was to get anywhere with the pixie who had taken him to the pub that evening. What was really sad was that none of his mates had seen him walk into their pub with that woman. Not one of them would believe that old George had spent more than ten minutes talking with her, let alone shared a drink with her. Still, he did have her card in his pocket, and that was some sort of proof that he had met the woman; it was something he could show Harry and the boys.

"I am more worried about her than the attack on that poor man," he whispered to himself and laughed again. "Doesn't say much for my character, does it?"

The kitten jumped up on the bed and curled up beside him. George patted the small little head and closed his eyes; maybe he would be able to sleep if he could guarantee his dreams would be about Shelly and not the attack. However, that was very unlikely; he was going to be dreaming about that damn attack for months, if not years, to come.

☙☙☙

The next morning, he crawled out of bed, his mind whirling with the memory of what he had seen the day before. He had slept but only very little, and he was exhausted. He did not want to go to the museum, and he did not want to be anywhere near that mummy room, but he had no say in the matter. He had promised the agents that he would be there, and they were not the sort of people you disappointed.

He showered in a haze, trying to wash away the images, but that did not work either. He knew that nothing would. He dressed and headed for the tube, desperate to not meet up with any of his neighbors or mates. George was an outgoing, extroverted soul who loved chatting with people, passing the time of day with everyone he met. However, on this particular morning he did not want to talk to anyone because he knew what the conversations would be about. They would all want to ask him what he knew about the attack, and what could he tell him? Nothing. He knew nothing more than had been reported in the news.

On the train he kept his head down and buried his face in the newspaper, which he did not want to read. All the stories were about the tragedy at the British Museum, a tragedy he knew too much about and yet knew nothing about. He could hear the others on the train discussing it at length, but he did not want to join in the conversation. He did scan the paper, looking for the name Shelly Jenkins, but he could not find it. This did not shock him all that much. She had told him that she was new at the paper and had yet to get her name on a byline. She had been hopeful that he could provide the intelligence that she would be able to parlay into a feature story. That was the real reason they had ended up seated around a pub table; she was using him.

He shook his head and rattled the paper. He was being such an idiot about this woman. She had affected him in a way no other woman ever had. Even in his school days, he had never allowed some skirt to turn his head, but in his weakest moment she had managed to muddle his every thought. Maybe that was the reason—he was weak from seeing a man lying on the floor, blood all around him. He had needed to talk to someone, and she had become that someone.

The tube rolled up to his stop, and he slowly got to his feet, meandering out into the sunlight as if he were in a daze. He headed to the back of the building, where he found Harry waiting for someone to open the security door. Neither man even said hello or good morning. There was nothing good about it, and considering neither man wanted to be there, talking would have made it worse.

They walked together up to the main floor and waited outside the director's office. The tension was so thick that you could physically see it, and George wondered why he had even bothered coming in today. Certainly, it had been an executive order, but what really was the point? There was nothing he could add to the story he had told them yesterday, and he was positive that there was not one thing that Harry could add either. This whole thing was a waste of time and energy. On the other hand, the Americans and the British agents had to look like they were doing something to catch the attacker, even if that meant going over the same material again and again.

"I sort of feel sorry for these poor sods," Harry finally sighed. "They want to be able to tell the American people something, and at the end of the day, what is there to tell them?"

"Houdini attacked the president." George thought about laughing at his own joke but decided it was not all that funny.

"It does seem to add up to that." Harry leaned closer to him. "How else can you explain the bloke disappearing like that from my screens?"

"There really was no sign of the shooter other than when entering the room?"

"Nothing." Harry shrugged his shoulders. "And honestly, George, that has me a little spooked. How can anyone get into this damn tomb of a building without being seen on my cameras? They are everywhere."

"I know." George glanced over his shoulder at the camera that was now peering at them. "I sometimes feel you watching me when I head to the loo."

"I never do any such thing." This time Harry did laugh. "But I know what you mean. They do watch these dead things twenty-four hours a day, which has often made me wonder what someone would pay to own a mummy."

"Yuck," George said, cringing at the idea. "Why in the world would anyone want one of those disgusting things in their home?"

"You would be surprised what some people spend money on when they have too much of the damn stuff and there is nothing left in the stores that interests them."

"Well, I do not have that problem."

Harry shrugged his shoulders again. "Most of us don't, mate. What do they call it—the more-money-than-brains club? Well, there are very few members."

"But to want a mummy?" George said, cringing again. "I can barely stand being in that room for more than five minutes."

"Life makes very little sense." Harry leaned back and closed his eyes. "Besides, it has nothing to do with this tale. This moment in time is a twisted edge of insanity all of its own."

George had to agree with him on that one. Whatever was going on, it had nothing to do with the mummy cases or the artifacts contained in the building. Nothing had been taken; all that had happened was that a man had been attacked. He was one of the most important men in the world, but in reality it was as simple as an attempted murder, if murder was ever simple. On the other hand, what made this moment a little piece of insanity was how the attack had been carried out, right under the noses of the American Secret Service and in a building with all its doors locked. George leaned back in his chair, and just like Harry, he closed his eyes and waited for the other shoe to drop.

Almost ten more minutes passed before the inner door to the office opened and a woman in a crisp blue suit poked her head out. "All right, you two, we want to see you now."

George poked Harry's arm, and the two rose in unison. They followed the woman into the office, and for a split second George thought that this must be what it felt like to be led down some hall to your own execution. For the next two hours he did feel like he was in an electric chair, as both American and British officials berated him with the same questions over and over about the attack on the president. The more he answered them, the more it seemed that they did not believe him. After all, someone had to have opened that door and allowed that individual access and then allowed the escape.

The problem with that theory was, how could it have been George or Harry? George had been on the move when the shot was fired, and when he came into the room, the door at issue was once more locked, and all the people in the room knew that he had not been the one to lock it. Besides, hadn't Harry told them he had George on camera the entire time and George had never gone near that stupid door? Harry, meanwhile, had been in the security room, watching the whole thing on camera, and the cameras proved that he had never left that location the entire time the president and his family were in the building. The two of them might have been in the museum at the time, but they were not the ones responsible, and something told George that these people already knew that.

"Can we go now?" Harry finally asked when the questions seemed to be going in circles. "I see no point to all of this."

"Really?" The American with the deep southern accent glared at him. "My president is dead in some damn British hospital, and you think there is no point to this."

"Look, I am sorry for all of that. It is horrible that such a great man has died so tragically." Harry rose to his feet and faced the man. "Really, I am, but I had nothing to do with his death, and I doubt George here did either. You can ask us the same questions a million times, but you will get the same answers, and what does that get any of us?"

There was a moment of stony silence that made George squirm. He was terrified that they were going to throw him into a cell and lose the key in some American bureaucratic swamp. He lowered his eyes and stared at his scruffy brown shoes. His mind drifted back to Shelly Jenkins, and he wondered if the young woman had noticed how worn his old shoes were last night. He had been thinking that he needed a new pair, and if he wanted to impress someone like her, he needed something more stylish than these old brown shoes. He knew it was totally inappropriate, but somewhere in the back of his mind, an old George Harrison song called "Old Brown Shoes" began to play. He knew that if he did not get out of that room soon, he might actually begin humming or, worse, singing it. He rose slowly to his feet and stared longingly at the door.

"There will be nothing else at the present time," said the woman in the blue suit, who remained unmoved. "You may think it gets us nowhere, but I will have more questions for you, so for now you will remain in the building."

"I have nowhere else to go," Harry commented as he walked toward the door.

George fell in step behind him, relieved that he was free for the time being. As they walked out into the main office, one of the Egyptian curators came running in, his face red and his eyes bulging out of his head.

"Carl, what the hell has you so steamed up?" Harry asked, reaching for the man's arm.

Carl turned and glared at him. "They told us to check and see if anything is missing, and one medallion is gone from the exhibit. It was there last week, and now it is gone." He pushed Harry's arm away and ran past them into the director's office.

George and Harry watched him for a moment and then left, heading to the cafeteria, where they assumed someone might have tea or coffee prepared. As they walked, Harry tapped his arm where Carl had pushed him. "I wonder if that medallion really does have something to do with all of this."

"Right." George shook his head. "Give me a break, Harry. Why the hell would anyone kill the American president only to steal a four-thousand-year-old necklace?"

"I know," Harry said, grinning. "And I bet money that the GI Joe Americans won't even bother looking for it, which will piss off my mate Carl. He really has a thing for those ancient bobbles, and if one is missing, it will cause his head to implode."

"Is he really a friend of yours?" George was a tad amused that Harry would even know one of the academic fellows who haunted the Egyptology department. Usually, the eggheads ignored the security staff and saw them as little more than walking, talking locks for their wonderful treasures.

"No," Harry laughed. "He is one of the more easily rattled types, so I like to pick at his edges to see him jump."

"I knew you had a mean streak in you." George entered the staff cafeteria and headed for a pot of coffee set up on a side table.

"You want to know something, George?" Harry said as he joined him. "I honestly believe that those academic types expect people like you and me to pick on them. More than likely, they've been used to it since their school days, and life without someone mocking them makes no sense to them."

"That is sad." George poured some cream into his coffee and reached for a spoon. "Makes me wonder how happy their lives really are."

"They seem content enough in their little ancient holes." Harry grabbed a cup. "And who are we to question their right to be content with dead things?"

George went to a table and sat down with his cup of coffee in hand. He normally did not drink much coffee, preferring tea during the day and a pint or two in the evening, but today was not normal, and he had to wonder if they would ever have another normal day at the museum. He took a long sip of the brown liquid and waited for Harry to join him. "I wonder what that medallion is about," he said as the technician sat down across from him. "It is strange that it went missing now."

"Now don't you feed into the paranoia," Harry said with a laugh. "The geeks do enough of that for all of us. It is just an old necklace, and nothing about it has anything to do with this murder."

"You don't believe it might be worth something then?" George glanced at the tray of pastries that sat across the hall from him. He could have eaten most of the tray all on his own, but yesterday he had met such a beautiful young woman, and now he was more conscious of the girth of his stomach, so he would forgo the doughnuts.

"Sure, it is worth something," Harry said as he spooned more sugar into his coffee. "It may be worth a small fortune, but the idea that someone would steal it and then kill the president is stupidity itself."

George nodded in agreement. The two events might be interesting, but they could not be connected, and the little Egyptologist who had raced past them to report the missing medallion was more than likely getting an earful about wasting the Americans' time. The director was probably yelling at poor Carl right now for disturbing everyone with the loss of a necklace when they had dozens just like it on display. It was just an enormous coincidence, but as George sipped on his coffee, he had to wonder if anyone today would believe in coincidences.

CHAPTER 5

George spent the rest of the morning sitting on his ass or answering the same questions over and over again. American and British government agents screamed at him more than once when frustration led to anger. They wanted answers, and no one seemed to have any that satisfied them. The necklace and poor Carl seemed to have been forgotten, just as Harry said they would, but the matter nagged at George, who could not seem to let it go. He wanted to ask someone about that medallion, but he had no idea who would know anything about it. So around two in the afternoon, he made his way to the Egyptian display. Most of the area was roped off as security agents poured over the scene, trying to determine how anyone could have gotten past them.

George made his way to the display cases and stared at the medallions and ornaments that blinked back at him. The case was one of the oldest in the museum, having been there forever. It was large and made of old, ornately carved wood, with a glass covering, and what was inside it made for interesting viewing. The medallions and necklaces were made of gold, precious metals, and jewels, featuring unique Egyptians designs. Images of cats, gods, and goddesses shone up at him. The hum of the agents circulating about the building seemed to be magnified in the quiet of the display room. He suddenly felt someone come up behind him, and he spun around, nearly knocking Carl over. "Sorry, old man. I was just looking at your pretty display."

"That is all right," Carl sputtered. "At least they are all back where they belong."

"What?" George stared at the display again. "The one you said was missing is in there?"

"Oh yes." The man giggled happily. "It was just mislaid. We found it this afternoon in the Roman exhibit."

"What was it doing in the Roman display?"

"I have no idea." He started walking away. "However, it wasn't actually in the display case."

George watched the man. "If it wasn't in the case, then where was it?" he called after him.

"In the trash bin," Carl sighed. "As if someone would throw away an ancient medallion."

George's mind reeled at the oddity of this news. Why would anyone throw something so obviously valuable into the garbage? He turned back to the display case and eyed the trove of treasures. He then ran after Carl. "Please, can you show me which one it was?"

"I really have no time for this." Carl kept walking. "Those agents are making a mess of our mummy cases, and we need to catalog everything before they destroy it."

"Just point it out to me," George pleaded. "I want to see it."

"Oh, very well." There was a gleam in the little man's eye that George found disarming. Carl was enjoying the security officer's interest in his baubles just a little too much.

They walked back to the display case, and Carl pointed to a round medallion with a cat engraved on it. George stared at the thing for a moment and realized he knew nothing about this pretty baubles or what it represented. He turned and looked at Carl, who seemed spellbound by the things before him. "Carl, what does that thing on it mean?"

"It is the goddess Bastet." He said the name with an air of mystery. "She was one of the protective goddesses."

"Protective goddess," George repeated, trying to understand what this meant. "Does it have any significance then?"

Carl smiled at him, and George smiled back. George knew that very few people ever asked about these special little artifacts, which would explain why the academic was beaming at the question.

"Each of the amulets and medallions had significance to the person who wore it," answered Carl, "especially something like this, which was made out of gold."

"Gold." George whistled under his breath. "Then it is worth something."

"More for its historical importance than monetary value." Carl frowned at the thought of someone selling his treasures. "Something like the Bastet necklace was worn by the high priest and protector of the tombs."

"Protector of the tombs," George said, again repeating the curator's words. "What was his job?"

Carl turned and headed back toward his office.

George fell in step beside the odd little man. "Please, Carl, I really am interested in this thing. Any information you can provide me would be really appreciated."

"Really, George," Carl said with a frown, "I do not have time for your questions today, but I can give you a book on the subject of the priests and their role in guarding the tombs."

"Will it have anything about the medallion?" George had no idea why he was so interested in all of this, but he really had to know.

"I suppose it will." Carl shrugged his slight shoulders. "The priests believed in magic, and something like the Bastet necklace would be considered powerful magic."

"Magic." George stopped and glanced back over his shoulder at the display case. "You are joking."

"I do not believe in those things myself," Carl mused, "but the ancients did, which is why they put so much effort into creating the mummies and the tombs."

"Of course." George smiled at the man as they walked. "Why would anyone believe in magic when just yesterday a killer mysteriously vanished through locked doors?"

Carl stopped walking and glared at him. "That is not the least bit funny, George. The American agents are not interested in ancient tales of magic, and neither am I. They are just stories used to terrify superstitious people, and they have nothing to do with the goings-on in this museum yesterday."

"Of course not, Carl," George said, grinning. "I just find it fascinating, that's all."

The little man stood staring at him, and for a moment George wondered if the curator was not going to provide him with the book he wanted to see so badly. The security guard was suddenly very interested in that medallion and its secrets, and the only person who could provide a link to that information stood glaring at him like he was a bug. Carl finally spun on his heel and walked briskly down the hall. George trailed behind him, careful not to say anything else to antagonize the man.

In the cold office cluttered with artifacts, Carl sifted through a stack of books, looking for the one George needed. The large guard felt oddly out of place in the dark little room. He realized that for most of his life he had been desperate to ignore these academics and their piles of books. He had been a mediocre student at best and had barely passed any of his classes. In his younger days he had worried more about football and cricket than about reading. History was not something he wanted to study, and it was almost on a dare that he had applied for the security job at the British Museum. His uncle Potter, his mother's brother, had been able to secure the post for him by pulling some strings, and for the most part George had been grateful. At least until yesterday he had been grateful; now he was not so certain that he wanted to remain at the museum.

Carl pulled out a small book from the pile, sending some of the dusty old tomes crashing to the floor. George bent over to help him pick them up and then helped to straighten them back onto the pile. Carl handed him the relevant book, a rather pensive look on his face. "This will tell you all about the magical tales of the amulets and medallions of ancient Egypt. They are just stories, though."

"I like stories," George lied. He had never been interested in those moth-eaten tales until now.

"Fine." Carl sat down into an old armchair behind the desk. "But make certain you return that book to me as quickly as possible. It is a rare edition."

George nodded, and holding the small brown book to his chest, he headed for the door. He did not bother with any formal words of thank you or farewell because he knew Carl would never hear him. The little man was already poring over some artifact that had been sitting on the desk. Men like him rarely acknowledged the rest of the world; their minds were on pieces of pottery and ancient baubles from four thousand years ago. Humanity simply got in the way of their study of humanity's past.

As George walked, he opened the book and began to peruse its first pages. The author was a doctor of Egyptology named Jasper Holds who had worked in Egypt for fifty years, from circa 1860 to 1910. His main field of study had been the tales of the priests and their use of magic to guard the tombs from the raiders who wanted to steal the many treasures the pharaohs included in their burial chambers. George could not believe that anyone would spend his entire life in a hot, dusty place like Egypt, tramping through the tombs and studying old stories of magical spells that probably were about as real as the legends of King Arthur.

The introduction was written by a member of the Royal Archeological Institute who believed that Holds had stumbled onto a secret of the ancient Egyptian priests. He honestly believed that those men had used spells, potions, and magical artifacts to protect the dead. George shook his head as he read, convinced that whoever had written this was a tad daft. Belief in ancient spells used to protect the dead! It was absurd.

George stopped and looked at the American Secret Service people who now stood outside the entrance to the Egyptian wing of the museum, and he shuddered. His mind drifted back to the images of President Carlson, a pool of blood spreading across the tiled floor. Wouldn't spells to protect the living make more sense than trying to protect the dead? He shook his head and continued on to the security office, but outside the room he stopped. He wanted to find a quiet corner where he could read a bit of this odd little book in peace, and with all the comings and goings, the office areas were anything but quiet. So he continued on to the main reading room in the center of the building.

He had never spent any time there in all the years he had worked at the museum, mainly because he had never had any reason to look at the old books that lined the walls of the oddly shaped room. He flopped down into a chair near the wall and opened the little book once more. He found some of the words difficult and the language beyond his meager education, but he forced himself to continue reading. He needed to find something about that medallion and its secrets.

Finally, after an hour or so, he stumbled upon a rather short, oddly worded paragraph in which Holds described some of the mummification process and the work of sealing up the tomb: "The priests would in an elaborate ceremony close up the tomb. It was believed that they used long, drawn-out incantations to seal the tombs with spells, which is why many believed opening the tombs would curse those who dared defile the sleep of the dead."

George shuddered at the thought of opening an ancient tomb. After all, it did seem to be little more than grave robbery, and yet in this building of archaeology, that was what they did in their pursuit of ancient knowledge. Were these academics cursed by the ancients? Were they doomed because they had opened those tombs? George looked around the room and smiled to himself.

He continued reading. "In some cases, the spells could take days or weeks to complete. The priests' long, powerful incantations were meant to connect their words to the gods of the underworld who held sway over the dead and the living. The use of powerful potions and artifacts allowed the priests to maintain this connection throughout the process."

George closed the book and rose stiffly to his feet. This whole thing was stupid. A long process meant to connect a priest to the underworld? What the hell was the point? He walked around the room and tried to imagine what it had been like four thousand years ago when the priests were chanting their drawn-out poems to close the tombs. That was what it amounted to if he understood what he had just read. He closed his eyes and attempted to picture these men in long white robes standing before some grand tomb, their arms raised to the sun, their voices ringing out, but he could not seem to conjure up the scene in his mind; he did not have the imagination.

He sat back down and reopened the book, hopeful that it might help connect him to the images the way the spells were supposed to have connected the ancient priests. The book continued, "The most common potions were made from honey and beer." George smacked his lips at the idea of a beer. Well, at least the ancients knew enough to have a beer when someone died; perhaps that was why even the Irish held wakes today. He looked at the next line and grimaced. "Some of the potions also contained ground-up beetles, scorpions, and the bones of the hippopotamus." Well, there went the theory of the ancients tossing back a few at someone's death—because who in their right mind would drink a beer laced with beetles and scorpions?

"The potions were only meant to help the priests reach a heightened state of awareness so that they could commune with the gods; the words spoken over many hours were what held the real power for the ancient priests. Those words were the key to opening the door to the other realm."

George sat for a moment staring at the words, his mind flooded with the idea that someone could actually open a door to other realms. *Open doors*, he thought. His heart suddenly seemed to stop, and he leaped to his feet. Was it even remotely possible that someone had used a magic spell to open a locked door? Even Carl, the man in charge of the ancient Egyptian relics, did not believe in the power this book speculated priests might have had four thousand years ago. George set the book down on a small desk near his chair and began to pace around the large room like a caged tiger, his eyes barely registering the room or the man who walked in.

"What the hell are you doing in here?" The man's voice echoed through the room, causing George to jump.

"Just trying to find somewhere to be alone." George raced over to the desk and grabbed the book. "Doesn't seem to be working very well."

"Well, excuse me for intruding into your meditation," Harry laughed. "I just thought you might want to know that the director said we can head on home. And we do not need to come in until called."

George held the book close to his chest. "Aren't they reopening the museum?"

"Not anytime soon," Harry said, shaking his head. "But they said we will be paid anyway, which sounds good to me. The only problem is that we are not supposed to leave London until cleared for travel, whatever that means."

"I can guess." George sighed as he headed for the door with the book tucked under his arm. "We are still suspects in the death of the president."

"Bloody hell!" Harry coughed as he fell in step behind George. "I don't like having these people think I am involved in any of this. They are too good at making a bloke disappear if they want to."

George had to agree with that sentiment. None of this made him feel very easy, and what he had read in the book made him feel even less at ease. He liked it even less that he was actually contemplating the idea of an ancient spell having anything to do with the death of a modern world leader. He was normally such a level-headed fellow, and such thoughts were for crazier people. He picked up his jacket and headed for the back door, his mind on the book he had secreted into his pocket.

CHAPTER 6

The main room of the newspaper building was a buzz of activity that made Shelly feel seasick. Some of those buzzing around were people she had never seen in the newsroom, and she wondered who they were. George's words about the Secret Service people tailing them echoed in her mind, making her feel even sicker inside. The journalists she did know were running all over the place, checking statements and calling for more information. Shelly had typed up a report of her meeting with the security guard, leaving out his name, and had presented it to Emmett earlier in the day. Now she was waiting for someone to tell her that it would be used or throw it back at her.

The staff had already been informed that the newspaper would be putting out a special edition along with the normal run, which meant more work for everyone, including the reporters. Emmett had screamed for a biography of the president, a historical breakdown of the museum, and a time line on yesterday's events. He had also sent people scurrying to the hotels to get quotes from all the world leaders who were assembled for the G-20 meetings. Shelly watched the organized chaos and marveled at how Emmett White seemed able to control all the people around him without losing the focus of the story.

"I want a meeting in ten," Emmett's voice bellowed over the din of noise. "All of you in the conference room."

No one questioned this; they all simply jumped to their feet and headed for the room like a pack of wild dogs following an alpha male. Perry, White's assistant editor, nodded at Shelly, who fell in step beside him.

"Did you look at my interview?" she whispered.

"Yes, and so did White," Perry whispered back, his voice hollow. "I think he may want to talk to you about it after this meeting, but do not hold out much hope since you did not provide a name. Emmett has never been one for covering sources."

Shelly shifted her eyes to the floor as they entered the conference room. She had known it was a long shot to get that past Emmett, but she had to try. She had promised George that she would keep his name out of the papers if at all possible. Why had she made a promise like that when she knew Emmett White might force her to name her source? Was she really that desperate for a front-page exclusive? She pulled out a chair and sat down, slumping forward over the long table. She wanted to crawl under it and hide. All day long, she had felt so useless, and now more than ever, she wondered if she had chosen the wrong career.

"All right, people, settle down," White bellowed again. "I want a rundown on the special edition. Keller, do we have the biography of the president ready along with pictures?"

James Keller leaped to his feet like a jack-in-the-box. "Yes, sir, most of it from the White House staff, but we were able to get some additional information from an unauthorized biographer."

"Don't let that stuff come back to bite us in the ass." White made a note on a pad in front of him. "Clear all of it with legal."

"Yes, sir." Keller sat back down, his eyes on the table. Shelly thought he looked like a beaten puppy.

"Now, have we gotten quotes from Buckingham Palace and Number 10?"

"All cleared," Perry chimed in. "We also have quotes from France, Germany, Belgium, Netherlands, Japan, and Canada. But Russia is still holding off on making a formal statement."

"Well, that is usual for them," Emmett sneered. "They are the last to say anything in these situations. But do not wait too long. If they have not said anything by the time we are ready to go to press, leave them out. I do not want even a hint that we think they are responsible for this mess." His eyes roamed around the room, looking for agreement from all those present. Heads nodded, and he pressed on. "Jillian, is the time line complete on this?"

A woman in a crisp blue suit with short blonde hair and deep brown eyes jumped to her feet. "I think so, Emmett. I was able to talk to my contact at MI6 this morning and cleared it with legal."

"Good," he said, smiling at her.

No one in the room had the guts to question Jillian Parker's right to call Mr. White Emmett or the way in which he smiled at her. The office rumor mill had wondered about the two of them for years, and although everyone snickered behind Jillian's well-tailored back, not one of them ever would have brought it up or placed an anonymous call to White's wife. It was not only none of their business but also a surefire way to lose a job and end a career.

"Now listen to me, people. This is a no-win situation for everyone involved." White sat down in his chair. "The White House is not making any announcements about who they suspect, and no known terrorist group is even dropping hints about responsibility."

There was a moment of guarded silence. Emmett glanced around the room before continuing. "I cannot emphasize this more: we cannot speculate about who we think it might have been because right now there is nothing to go on. We could say it was the man in the moon and be right, but we could also be dead wrong, and I will not have this paper called out on a lie or a rumor. We have to get this one right."

Once more, people nodded their heads.

"Now get back at it and make certain it is right. Perry and I have final editorial control on every word, so get it right the first time, people."

There was a stampede for the door as the team headed back to their desks and their assignments. "Miss Jenkins, hold it right there," Emmett called to her as Shelly neared the door.

She felt the weight of the world on her shoulders and slid into the nearest chair. Perry glanced back at her and offered a reassuring smile before he left the room, closing the door softly behind him. Emmett picked up his notepad and walked around the table. He stood over her and then stiffly sat down next to her. She squirmed at being so close to the great man.

"Miss Jenkins," he started slowly, "I read your account of that interview, and frankly, I was amazed."

"Yes, sir." She gulped hard. "But I did promise the man that I would keep his name out of the papers. He is worried about losing his job."

Emmett lowered his gaze to the table and the notepad before him. "Normally, I do not like that unnamed-source crap that other papers use."

She cringed at the tone in his voice. He was angry, and she had the feeling that a lot of that anger was directed squarely at her. "I know that, sir."

"There are too many times when using an unnamed source can hit you in the legal gray area, which is something I hate." He tapped the pad with his pen. "I want to make certain everything I print is on solid ground before I commit to it."

"I know that, sir," Shelly said, repeating herself.

"So I was a little more than shocked when you handed in this incredible account of the attack with no name to it, just an unnamed source." He looked up at her, and she froze.

She could feel his eyes boring into her head. "I did not know what else to do, sir."

"Can you give me a hint as to who this person might be?" He leaned closer to her, which made her blood run cold.

"No, sir," she said quietly, "not without hurting him and his position."

"I take it he works at the museum."

"Yes, sir."

"A member of the staff there," Emmett pressed.

"Yes, sir." Her voice was suddenly very low.

"All right then." He pulled away from her. "I am loath to print it, but the man's account is one of the best time lines we have for the event."

"Really?" Shelly suddenly felt her heart grow light. Was this happening? Was Emmett White really going to use her interview in the special edition?

"I want to run it by Perry. It still needs some work."

"Of course." She leaped to her feet and headed for the door.

"Miss Jenkins, even if it turns on us, it was a good piece of reporting." The editor smiled at her, and Shelly felt her heart skip a beat. "See if you can get some more from this source of yours. He may be our only leak from inside the museum."

Shelly felt a chill pass over her. She was not really certain that she wanted to press George for more information. He had been so reluctant to give her what he already had—not to mention that unless he called her, she really had no way to get in touch with him. He had her card, but she had no phone number for the man, and the only name she had from him so far was George. She shook her head as she walked toward Perry's desk. Why had she been so stupid as to not get a usable number for her only source in this story?

Perry smiled as she flopped down beside him. "So we are running your interview."

"I guess so," she sighed.

"Well, don't let your excitement overwhelm you." He laughed as he typed some information into his computer. "It is a good piece, and frankly, other than some tweaking, it is ready to go."

"Wow." She was thrilled, and for the first time she could feel some respect from the editors.

"There are a couple of small mistakes but nothing a little alteration in editing can't fix. Frankly, Shelly, it is the first time you have ever made me see you in a piece, which is what made the old man run it."

"He wants me to get more information from my source."

Perry looked up from his computer. "Is that going to be an issue?"

Shelly could feel his eyes on her, and she squirmed in the chair. "No, but it may take some time. I had a hard enough time getting him to open up about this story."

"Time is not always our friend on stories," Perry said with a grimace, "but see what you can do to pry a little more from this one."

"All right." She frowned as Perry helped her begin the editing process of her first major byline. She was thrilled that they were going to run her story, and she was also thrilled that someone like Perry was taking so much time to help her with it. But her heart was feeling more and more like a lead weight. How was she supposed to glean more information from George when she had no idea where to find him or what his last name was?

By the time they sent the final edits to legal, Shelly was exhausted. Perry had pushed her to make every word count, and when it was done, she was thrilled by the results. As she worked, her mind had drifted less and less to the man who had provided the information and more to the actual writing. She felt elated and ready to call everyone she knew to tell them that her name was going to be a part of the special edition.

"Make sure you get more from this source of yours," White called to her as she headed for the elevator.

"Oh." Her elation fell, and she suddenly felt sick. "I am not certain I can."

"We need to follow it up, or it is a dead duck." White closed his office door, leaving Shelly standing beside the elevator, her mind stuck on the word "dead." She suddenly did feel dead and buried.

She sat in her car for ten minutes, trying to remember anything and everything about George. Did she have anything that she could use to get his name or his location? She could not hit the museum because that would certainly cost him his job, and that was the one thing she had promised him she would not do. Finally, she decided to head to the pub where they had shared a pint. It seemed to her that people knew him there, and he had mentioned that it was his neighborhood bar. It was a place to start, and in truth it was all she had.

CHAPTER 7

Shelly pulled into the parking lot near the pub and sat there for a while, trying to figure out something she could say to the barkeep about the man she had sat drinking with the day before. How could she explain that she knew nothing about him except that his name was George and he worked at the British Museum? They would think she was stupid or something. She also hated the idea that George might think she was stalking him, looking for more information than he had already provided. She had promised to leave his name out of the papers, so he might wonder why she was back now.

Finally, she got out of the car and began the slow walk toward the door, wondering if she could tell Emmett and Perry that she could not find her source. It was ridiculous, and they would never buy it, or they would consider her idiotic for not having gotten a full name before committing to the story. She was just about to the door when someone bumped her arm.

"Excuse me, Miss." The man who bumped her was looking at a book rather than watching where he was going.

Shelly could not believe her good luck. "George," she exclaimed, almost squealing the name in delight. "I am so glad to see you again."

The guard looked up at her, his eyes suddenly round and full. He did not seem overly thrilled to see her, and he quickly tucked the book he was reading back into his jacket pocket. "I was coming in for a pint before heading home," he said.

"I understand." She stood smiling at him. "Actually, I came looking for you, so I am glad that I ran into you."

"Why are you looking for me?" he asked, his voice suddenly rough.

She realized that the kindly man she had met did not like the idea of her looking for him. Shelly's smile vanished as she realized her mistake. She should have not been so obvious about her reason for being there. She could have said that she liked the little pub and it was merely a coincidence that they had run into each other. Instead, she'd had to state outright that she was looking for him.

"I wanted to thank you for talking to me yesterday," she said. "It really helped us with the story."

"So you did manage to get a byline out of it." George opened the door and led the way into the pub.

"Yes, I did." Her smile returned. "My first one ever, and the boss agreed to keep your name out of it."

ℭℭℭ

George walked her over to the same table they had used the night before and held a chair out for Shelly before heading to the bar to order them some drafts. He held up two fingers to the barkeep, an old white-haired man named Joe whom George had known for over fifteen years. He looked back at the young woman and watched her shift uneasily in her seat. His eyes narrowed, and he wondered what she had to be so nervous about in a place like this with an old fool like him. She was so beautiful, and he was an old fat bore; he really believed that she held all the cards.

However, he also knew that she was there to pick his brain concerning the murder in the museum. That incident was the only thing that would bring a woman like Shelly Jenkins into his world. As he stood waiting for Joe to pour the pints, he fingered the book hidden in his pocket. Should he tell her about the lost medallion found in the trash or the idea he had concerning its magic? He did not want this woman to think he was a complete idiot, but it would be a way to keep the conversation going and maybe keep her talking to him.

ദദദ

George came back with the drinks and sat down, his mood seemingly very sour. Shelly could sense his reluctance to be there, and she wondered why he had come to the pub when a drink seemed to be the last thing he wanted. Maybe the pub was just a force of habit, a place that felt like home.

"How did it go today at the museum?" she finally asked.

"Not good," he whispered. "The police from both sides of the Atlantic spent most of the day pounding me with the same questions over and over again."

"And you had no answers for them."

"None that had changed since yesterday." He sipped at the beer.

"And they had no leads to explain how the killer got away?"

"You are still looking for a story, Miss Jenkins," he said, glancing up at her.

"Everyone is." She fidgeted under his intense gaze. "It is the story of the century."

"And I am your in to the juiciest parts of that story."

Shelly leaned forward, her eyes glowing in the pub's dim light. "George, I told you yesterday that I am a reporter and you are my lead."

"I know all of that," he said, nodding his head.

"And you can add nothing to what you told me yesterday?" She frowned, realizing that this lead might have dried up before it had even begun.

"Nothing about the murder of President Harold Carlson." He finally sighed and took another sip of his beer.

"Oh God than he really is dead." She was clearly disappointed.

"Twenty-four hours does not change a whole lot of things in my life, Miss Jenkins." He shook his head. "The entire world may change in a blink of an eye, but my life goes on exactly the same."

"How can you say that?" She slowly touched his arm. "Yesterday you were a key witness to the biggest assassination since John F. Kennedy."

"Was I?" He closed his eyes. "Whatever I saw was what I told you, and it amounted to very little. I am an ordinary man, Miss, and my words will not matter when they write the history books."

Shelly withdrew her hand and placed it in her lap. She stared at the pint of beer on the table before her and wondered if perhaps he was right. Did he matter, and did her story on his words matter? Certainly, this was a major historical event, but when the academics wrote their volumes on the subject, would any of them bother to quote her little article or her mystery source in the museum? She suddenly hated this feeling, and she almost hated the man seated across from her for making her doubt her place in the world. She had always imagined that a byline would assure her a place in the history books, and now he had made her doubt the veracity of that belief.

ᗰᗰᗰ

George cringed when she withdrew her hand from his arm. He once more traced a finger over the edges of the book in his pocket. This was a history book written almost a full century ago, and other than a few academic types, very few people had even read it, or at least that was what he suspected since he never would have bothered with it himself if it hadn't had something to do with that stupid medallion. He knew it was a ridiculous notion, but he was beginning to believe that the medallion was connected to the murder. He looked at his companion and wondered if he could make her understand the very thing he barely believed.

"Miss Jenkins," he said, speaking slowly and deliberately, "there was one odd thing that happened today, and if you think it means anything, go ahead and print it, but I doubt your publisher will agree with you."

"What happened?" She looked up, her eyes suddenly filled with expectation.

"A necklace from the Egyptian display case was missing this morning and was found near the Roman display cases." He stated the words flatly.

"Oh." Shelly's face fell into a frown. "Is that all?"

George suddenly felt a renewed wave of horror pass over him. "It never should have been moved, and considering that those cases are armed with alarms, we should have been alerted if someone even opened the cases, let alone removed one of the pieces."

"So an Egyptian medallion was moved from the Egyptian display not far from where the president died and was found in the trash in the Roman display." Shelly shook her head. "What does that even mean?"

George lowered his voice. "I have no idea, but no one seems concerned about it. The curator was simply pleased to have it back where it belonged."

Shelly leaned forward. "Did they tell the agents working the murder case about it?"

"Of course they did," he whispered. "We were told to report anything unusual, so the staff reported it missing this morning."

"When was it found in the trash bin?"

"This afternoon," he sighed, "which makes even less sense since those bins were searched yesterday after the attack for any evidence."

Shelly nodded in agreement. "Do you know what sort of medallion it was?"

"I asked Carl about it." George fingered the book again. "He said it depicted some goddess named Bastet."

"Who is Carl?"

"He runs the Egyptian artifact display."

"Oh, right." Shelly wrote down something in her book.

"I asked him a lot of questions about that goddess and the medallion."

Shelly's face froze. "What did he tell you?"

He looked up at her. "Just the usual ancient Egyptian nonsense about magic, mummies, and tombs."

"So it was connected to the mummy display?" Shelly wrote something more.

"That is what Carl told me, but he does not believe in the magical properties of his display. To him they are simply interesting baubles with amazing stories. Miss"—he leaned forward and touched her arm—"I am not saying that I believe in magic, but there is something odd about that medallion and its connection to this murder. I am certain of that even if I am not certain about anything else."

Shelly withdrew her arm. "George, it is just a necklace, and you have no evidence to suggest a connection between the two events. I have to deal in facts, and the fact is that your feelings are not cold, hard facts."

"I know that." He stared down at his hand. "I know you would think me crazy if I told you what I really think happened, but it is the one of the biggest oddities in a string of odd events."

"Why would I think you crazy?" She whispered the last word as if it might offend him.

"Because I think I am crazy for even considering it." He picked up the pint of beer and drank the rest in one gulp. He looked up to Joe at the bar and ordered another pint with a wave of his hand before looking back to Shelly and smiling uneasily. "Hell, it might be a pure fantasy, but it is the only thing that makes any sense to me."

Shelly rose slowly to her feet. "George, I am not here to listen to insane theories that my boss would never allow me to print. I am a newspaper woman, and I do not deal in fantasies."

George looked up at her and felt a wave of nausea wash over him. "Miss Jenkins, this is not about facts or fantasy. It is about something more like magical history, if it is possible to link those two things together."

"History is not magic." Shelly folded her arms as Joe set another beer in front of George and returned to the bar. "History is facts and has nothing to do with magic."

"I know all about history. I work at a museum," he growled. "I work at the largest damn repository of historical junk ever accumulated, and I see it every day."

"So deal with history." She sighed heavily. "Give me something the history books would believe, not some fairy tale."

George stared into her eyes and shook his head in deep remorse. "I am sorry, Miss, but all I have is a fairy tale of the ancient sort."

"Well then, I guess I should be going, Mr. ..."

"Marsh," he said, sighing again. "George Marsh."

"Mr. Marsh." She extended her hand, and he shook it. "If you come up with something more historical and factual, let me know," she said. "You have my card."

"Yes, I do." He picked up the second pint of beer and took a long sip.

ଓଓଓ

Shelly walked out the door angry with George Marsh and with herself. She had allowed the insanity of the day before to cloud her better judgment. George was a guard at the museum, so she had assumed he would have the inside track on how the investigation was going. Instead, the man had gone off the deep end and was sputtering about medallions, magic, and ancient history. She slammed her hand down on the door of her car before unlocking it. She now had to explain to Perry and Emmett that this major source she had touted as the best in to the museum was a complete nut who was talking about believing in some ancient amulet and its ties to mummies and magic.

CHAPTER 8

The next morning found George standing outside the local library, where he knew he could gain access to the computers and where maybe, just maybe, they might have some books on ancient Egyptian gods. He knew that Clancy would have laughed to see his old mate at a library because the old fool probably thought George could barely read. Actually, Clancy's assessment of George was closer to the truth than the guard wanted to admit. He knew enough to read the sports page and could get by with most things, but the fancy words in the little book Carl had given him were far beyond his basic understanding, and that worried him. Was he missing some vital clue that could help unravel a mystery simply because he had been a failure at school?

ʚɞʚɞʚɞ

The head librarian, a woman named Miriam Longsworth, glanced at the shabby man who lumbered up to her desk, his eyes darting about. "Can I be of some help, sir?" She kept her voice even, but she could not keep the contempt out of her voice. She had little use for these working stiffs who seemed to think that her library was a lounge of some sort where they could check out the latest football statistics.

"Can you show me some books on ancient Egyptian gods and goddess?" His eyes were suddenly glued to the floor.

"Ancient Egypt?" She could not keep the shock out of her voice.

"Yes, ma'am." He nodded solemnly.

Miriam shook her head and slowly rose to her feet. "Follow me, and I will show you what we have on the shelves."

He shuffled behind her, and Miriam's only image of the man was of some working grunt watching the Premiere League on Friday night in a pub with his mates. She showed him where some very simple books could be found that retold the ancient tales, and then she made her way back to the main desk. But the fussy middle-aged woman could not help herself; she continued to glance over at him, her pale gray eyes peering at him over horn-rimmed glasses.

When she could no longer contain her curiosity, she walked back to where he sat at a table, reading through a book that was geared toward schoolchildren interested in history. "Are those books helpful, sir?" she finally asked him.

"Not really." He shook his head. "I learned all of this at the museum."

"Well, if it is important, you could try the computers." She hated recommending the machines since the computers were there for academic types doing research.

"It is vital, ma'am." The man offered a slight smile.

"As long as it is not frivolous." Miriam adjusted her old gray sweater and led him to the computers, where she logged in to one of the machines. "I detest when people come in here and look for silly things like sports scores or the latest gossip on the actors."

"I swear to you, ma'am, I am only interested in information on an ancient Egyptian goddess." The man pulled up a chair and sat down beside her.

"Really?" Miriam's brow crinkled in disbelief. "That is an interesting topic. Are you looking for one in particular?"

"Bastet." He whispered the word, as if it was not something he wanted everyone in the library to hear.

"She is one of the lesser gods." Miriam pulled up a search engine and typed in the name Bastet. "This should give you some of the things that you will need. And if you need any more help, let me know." She rose to her feet and walked toward the main desk.

Every few minutes, she looked up at the man as he studied the words on the screen and the images of the goddess that had popped up. He made notes on a piece of paper every once in a while and seemed to be drawing some of the images. She watched as he surfed between different sites as if he was trying desperately to discover as much as he could about a goddess who was rather obscure; this made Miriam wonder what was so important to the man, who was obviously just a working stiff.

Finally, her curiosity got the better of her again, and she strolled back over to the computer, where he still peered at the screen. "Have you found everything that you need, sir?"

"I am not really certain." He frowned at the images before him. "What does it mean that she was a protector of the pharaoh?"

"I am not an expert." She sat down beside him. "But I can only assume that people would pray to the goddess to protect the pharaoh."

"When he was alive or when he was dead?"

She was shocked at the seemingly simple but actually complex question. This was a topic a scholar would debate. "I have no earthly idea. The Egyptians were known to believe that the world of the dead was just as vital as the world of the living."

"So it may have been both," the man said, smiling uneasily. "The priests may have been asking her to protect him in his tomb."

The more he stared at the screen, the more his interest bothered Miriam. In all her years in the library, she had never seen a scruff so determined to learn about the world of the ancients. She had to know why he had come here to learn about this topic. "Can I ask why you are so interested in this particular goddess?"

"Just something I saw at the museum the other day."

"Before the attack on the president," she said with a sense of wonder in her voice. The only place anyone in London called "the museum" was the British Museum.

"Of course," he stated flatly. "The place has been locked up tighter than an old pharaoh's tomb since that terrible day."

Miriam nodded in agreement. "It was terrible, wasn't it? Hard to believe someone so protected could be so savagely attacked right before the eyes of his bodyguards."

The man seemed to cringe at the mention of guards. "They may have seen things that they can't tell us about."

"There are always things they can't tell us about," she said, nodding. "But the newspapers are full of some wild story that the shooter came through a locked door and killed the president and then vanished through that same locked door. How is that even possible?"

"How indeed?" He shuddered and rose stiffly to his feet. He headed for the front door, leaving Miriam at the computer. At the door, he turned back and said, "Thank you for your help. I think I have all the information that I need."

"You're welcome." She smiled at him and turned back to the machine to prepare it for the next visitor. As she cleared the search engine, her thoughts remained on the man whose outward appearance certainly did not match his thoughts and curiosity.

ଓଓଓ

George watched the librarian for a moment before heading out the door into the murky gray fog that had blanketed the city all morning long. He liked the fog and had since he was a small boy. He used to tell his mother that it gave the world an edge of mystery. However, today it made him feel small and frightened, as if it hid some truth that was just beyond his grasp. He pulled his jacket zipper up to his collar and headed for the tube. He had no idea where he was going and actually had nowhere *to* go. The agents had told him not to leave London, and although he had many friends and mates he could have popped in on for a nosh or a pint, he had no desire to be with any of them. For the first time in his life, George Marsh wanted to be alone.

He spent the rest of the day riding the tube and getting off at different locations to stroll aimlessly around the city. He went to Trafalgar Square and walked right up to the large column statue of Lord Admiral Nelson. He had never given much thought to the life of the man, and now he wondered what Nelson had done to earn such a tremendous tribute in the middle of the city. The square was bustling with the usual crowd, but he ignored everyone as he walked to Number 10 and stood outside the entrance of the prime minister's residence, watching the guards as they passively held their posts. His mind drifted to the image of another world leader dying in a pool of blood, and he shuddered. Considering all that had occurred over the last few days, he wondered what was happening behind the gate and the massive doors at Number 10. He continued toward the Houses of Parliament and Westminster Abbey. Both were rather impressive buildings, one rather tall and stately with the large clock ringing out the time and the other ornate and rather Gothic. He stood and stared at each one, his mind whirling.

He had often called these places the haunts of tourists and said that real Londoners would never bother to come here. He himself had not walked these streets in the last ten years because he honestly believed one time was enough for anyone. He headed back to the tube and actually thought about going to the Tower of London, which was another favorite of the tours. It was so bizarre, but he was actually playing tourist in his own city.

He closed his eyes as he rode the tube, but he could still see an image of the medallion and the cat goddess Bastet. She had become his talisman and his only companion. He thought about what Carl had said about finding the stupid thing in the trash bin the day after the attack. He opened his eyes again and stared at the elderly gentleman seated across the aisle. He then thought about watching the curator and his assistants handle the artifacts over the years; he knew exactly how they would have moved the necklace once it was discovered. They would have brushed it off, and wearing those silly kid gloves, they would have gingerly placed it back in its case in the Egyptian room.

It would sit there for all of eternity, people passing it without knowing exactly what it was or what role it had played in the president's death because no one thought it did have anything to do with murder. He smiled at the thought that perhaps he was the only one who believed it was magical and had opened a door as it had done thousands of years ago. The smile on his face turned to a scowl. "How did it open the door, and how would that help those stupid priests protect their musty old pharaoh?"

George had never been one to talk to himself, but on that night as he rode home, he tried to answer some questions in his head, which seemed to be the only way to make sense of the world around him. *After he died and was in the tomb, they sealed it.* He considered this a fact because that was what he had heard the tour guides say when they led people around the museum. *It was closed until someone robbed it or until the archaeologists pried it open.*

He placed his hands behind his head and closed his eyes again. *Maybe that was the point—maybe that was why they needed a special spell to get through those closed doors. If they wanted to check on the old man after he was dead and mummified, they would have to be able to get through a sealed door.* George smiled to himself at the realization that he finally understood what the little book was trying to tell him. The priests had wanted to make certain that the king was doing fine in the land of the dead, and the only way to do that was to walk through a sealed door, a door no one was supposed to be able to open except some ridiculous dead god.

The problem was that in order to use the medallion and its spell in the present, the person holding it would have to know the incantation, which according to the book had been lost to the sands of time. His smile left his face. *Bloody hell, how would anyone learn a spell that no one has known for thousands of years?* He bolted up and slammed his fist on the seat beside him, causing the old man across from him to jump.

He smiled sheepishly at the old man and shook his head before standing up to head for the doors. It was a couple of stops before the one near his flat, but he wanted off the train and away from the people who were glaring at him. He left the tube and walked home, his mind in a fog thicker than the fog of London itself. He had to find a way to discover the spell used all those eons ago, and he did not have clue one about where to begin.

Upon arriving home, he shook his head at the kitten curled up at the foot of his bed and wondered if it might have some of the answers. After all, Bastet did have the head of a cat. But he had to admit that idea was a little too far-fetched even for him. So he climbed into bed and turned off the light. The cat meowed softly and then inched closer to George's head; George listened to the soft ruffling noise and settled under the covers. He sighed and closed his eyes, wondering one more time whether there might be some way to get the answers he sought, someone out there with the knowledge he needed.

As he drifted off to sleep, he thought back over the last couple of days—thoughts of murder, necklaces, and a beautiful reporter were jumbled in his mind, and none of it made any real sense. Did anyone know anything about any of it? Suddenly, he bolted up in bed, making the little cat beside him jump. "Damn it!" He did know someone, and he would have to seek that person out. "First thing in the morning," he said.

The cat glared at him, and he smiled at the little orange ball of fur. "Sorry, little one, but I finally have an answer."

CHAPTER 9

The next morning he headed for the tube and a long trip across the city. He carried the little book in his pocket, and during the long ride he periodically pulled it out and thumbed his way through its pages, trying to come up with a way to ask the relevant questions that were running through his mind without coming off as too much of an idiot. The library had given him some of the information, but there was so much more that he needed to know, and today he was praying that he would be able to find some of the answers.

As he walked from the station through the streets of London, he had an odd sinking feeling in the pit of his stomach that this was all a waste of time. He already knew the name of the goddess whose face appeared on the medallion and that she was a protector of the pharaoh both in death and in life. He had gotten that much from the book and the computers at the library. What else did he need to know? He stopped on the steps of an apartment building and stared at the windows and doors. He hesitated because in reality he had nothing to ask except where he could find the spell that worked the medallion. The problem was that this was a question that possibly no one knew the answer to.

George stood there for ten minutes, consumed with indecision. He was almost ready to turn on his heel and head back to the tube station when the door opened and Carl, the little Egyptologist, stepped into the sunlight. The little man glared at him, his eyes round with shock. "George, what are you doing here?"

"I wanted to return your book." George held out the book. It did seem to be a logical reason to be in the area. "There is no telling when the museum will open again, and I did not want to lose it."

"Oh." Carl gingerly took the book and put it into a satchel he was carrying. "That is very decent of you." He then turned and walked off down the street, but he stopped when he realized George was walking beside him. "Is there anything else I can do for you?"

"Well, I did have one question about the book." George grinned foolishly at the little man. "If it isn't too much trouble."

"I am heading to the butcher's, so if you care to walk, we can talk."

George nodded and fell in step with the man. "That will be fine. I do not want to be a bother."

"It isn't a bother." Carl stared straight ahead. "It is nice to find someone who is interested in those ancient stories."

"Oh, I am interested," George said, "very interested."

They walked in silence for a few minutes, and then Carl finally asked, "So what is your question?"

"The book said that the spells and mystical incantations were lost," George said, speaking slowly. "Is there nowhere that they can be found?"

"Why would you want to find them?" Carl turned and stared at him. "They are of no real use to anyone."

"I just thought it would be interesting to hear what they were and how they sounded." George lowered his gaze. "After all, the book said that the priests thought the words were very powerful."

"Words are powerful," Carl said, nodding his head, "but we are not talking about abracadabra or some such nonsense."

"I know that." George lowered his voice. "Dr. Holds, the man who wrote the book, said that some of the spells could take days or even weeks to recite."

"Which may explain how they became lost," said Carl. They turned a corner and headed toward some small businesses. "We are talking about things written in hieroglyphics, George, which means some people may not have known what the incantations were even if they found them. The Rosetta stone was not cracked until 1824, so before that, something as long and cumbersome as the full text of an incantation might have been tossed away or broken up since it would have been on papyrus or on stone."

"I see." George frowned at the thought of something that took a week to recite written on stone tablets. "But someone might have found it?"

"I have heard nothing about such a discovery." Carl placed his hand on the door of a small butcher shop. "If they had, it would have been in all the journals."

"All right," George said, disappointed. "Thanks for your time anyway. I will see you again when they reopen the museum."

"Of course." Carl entered the shop and closed the door behind him.

As George slowly made his way back to the train, he wondered if the odd little academic was beginning to think George had lost his mind. He smiled and shook his head as he sat down on a bench to wait for the train. Considering the wild thoughts running through his head, maybe Carl would be right to think he had lost his mind; George was beginning to wonder that himself.

ଓଓଓ

Shelly was happily reading her own name in the byline for her article in the special edition that had come out that morning. It was macabre to be so thrilled when the edition's stories were about the death of a world leader, but she could not seem to wipe the smile off her face. Emmett had even told her that he was pleased with the results of her edits; she knew that was more Perry's doing than hers, but she took the compliment with a smile.

She had been so depressed by the fact that George Marsh could provide her with no more information except some daft idea about a missing necklace. She had told Perry about the conversation, and he'd advised her to forget about it, which was what she was already planning to do. She would have liked her source—her private source—to be the one to lead to some breakthrough in the story, but it was not to be. That river had dried up, and she had to come to terms with that sooner rather than later.

"Don't worry about it," Perry had said, grinning that father-knows-best smile. "A lot of sources are only good for one kick of the can, and we do with it what we can."

"I just thought that since he worked at the museum, he might be able to get me something more." She had sat at her desk, chewing on the end of a pencil.

"He can't give you what he might not know." Perry had pulled the pencil out of her mouth and playfully tapped her on the head with it. "Now you have to go after something else, or the old man will think you are a one-trick pony."

"I know," she had said, smiling at him as he walked back to his desk.

Shelly knew that Perry was right. George was a dead end, and now it was her job to find a new road to travel, which she was trying to do as she read her own name over and over again.

She was a little scared that this might be the only time she would see her name in print, but she also knew that if she could do it once, she could do it again. "Perry," she said, walking over to where he sat sipping tea at his desk. "Could I do a piece on the average people and their reactions to this story?"

"Well, that is being covered in other papers and on TV." He frowned at her. "What new angle could you bring to it?"

"Well ..." She rubbed her chin, thinking it over. "I could talk to political students at the colleges. They do not have as much to lose or gain as the professors or the commentators, so they may have a fresh perspective."

"The future politicians." Perry closed one eye and winked at her. "That is not bad. You will need to jump on it right away while they are still debating it over their coffee cups. People are easily distracted, and they will move on to new topics of conversation before you have even asked them about the last one."

"I know," she laughed as she turned and ran for her purse. "I will head to the college coffee hangouts right now."

Perry was laughing as she hit the elevator button, her mind reeling with ideas of how she could get the political majors to open up without coming off as a know-it-all herself. She had only graduated a couple of years ago, so she knew how these people worked; they wanted to be seen as having all the answers. Hell, she had been one of them, but the real world of a big-city paper had quickly taught her that she knew nothing about anything. Emmett White had been the one to teach her that college taught you basics but the real world was the groundwork of higher learning.

She headed for the bistros and coffee shops where she had sat expounding on the day's events when she was in school. She prayed that in the few years since she graduated, things had not changed and the elites were still there. She walked into a little shop twenty minutes later, sensing the buzz of the academic brain trust even before she saw the little tables surrounded by twenty-something-year-olds discussing the world as they saw it. She could sense the arrogance and blustering from every corner, and it sickened her because she knew it was all show. As much as they thought they knew, every last one of them was terrified that she or he would never be able to make it past the walls of the college into the real world.

She bought a coffee, and just as she had done in years past, she sat down near one of the larger groups and listened for her opening. She was young enough and pretty enough that they accepted her presence, which meant she was able to listen without altering the flow of intellectual drivel that spouted out of every orifice. If they had for one moment seen her as an interloper, they would have shut down and the conversations would have dried up. These students never discussed the rambling thoughts in their heads with anyone they viewed as an outsider. It was a form of paranoia that made little sense, but it was all very real to them. Shelly placed her phone on her table as so many of them already had, as if the world was about to call them and they could never afford to miss the call. What they did not need to know was that her phone was recording everything they said.

"I am telling you, the Americans are too afraid to tell us the truth about this attack," one dark-haired youth said, banging his hand on the table. "It would mean admitting that their foreign policies are garbage."

"The American policy has been garbage for years," said a young woman with horn-rimmed glasses and long mousy-brown hair. She shook her head. "What I want to know is, what made this president any different from the ones who came before him?"

"Was he any different?" Shelly leaned forward, placing a law textbook on the table. It was an old cue that a person could use in a college crowd in her day to indicate that the person was one of the group. She was not certain that it would still work, but it was her only way into this conversation.

"That is the problem," said the dark-haired boy. "He really isn't all that different. He has followed the same line of idiot maneuvers that the rest have been doing since the 1990s."

"So what the hell does killing him get anyone?" A tall, gangling man with short blond hair joined them, his coffee perched in his left hand and a stack of books in his right.

"Nothing." The woman sipped at her coffee. "The vice president won't change any of his policies, and since he is the puppet of the Senate, they are going to play along. Killing Carlson was a waste of a good bullet if you ask me."

"Has this president changed anything?" Shelly leaned closer to the dark-haired man who seemed to be carrying the conversation. "I mean, has he brought forth any new policy that was not there in the old administration?"

There was a moment of silence as the group considered her question. She could hear the gears grinding as they puzzled it out for themselves, and she waited, knowing she could not lead them where they did not want to go. Finally, the blond man put his stack of books down on the table and leaned forward. "He is the one who started the multinational assessment bill."

"That's right, Lawrence," the woman giggled. "As if Congress will ever pass that thing. It is viewed as the death of companies that move manufacturing to other countries but still claim America as home base."

"They would have to toe the line or be penalized," the dark-haired man said, nodding. "So they have been fighting it."

"Didn't it get through a first reading, though?" Shelly asked, pressing them.

"Oh sure, all bills get through that first reading, but that does not mean it will make it past the second or third, and it sure as hell won't get past the Senate subcommittees."

The woman grabbed for a muffin in front of her and took a large bite.

"I wonder if it will die with his death." Shelly scratched her chin, deep in thought.

"Now that is the billion-dollar question." The blond man sipped at his coffee. "And if it does die, a lot of companies, including some British multinational corporations, will breathe a lot easier."

"You don't think that could be the reason for his death, do you?" A petite girl in a short black skirt sat down beside the woman in the glasses. "That some company ordered a hit on him?"

"Now, Helena, you know that would be an American thing to do," Lawrence said with a laugh. "And it would be something right out of a movie."

"But why do it on British soil?" Helena mused. "Wouldn't killing him in America have been easier?"

"She has a point," the other woman said, nodding her head. "It makes Britain look bad and points the finger at our government as a coconspirator."

"God, you can't believe that our government ordered a hit on the American president?" Shelly was shocked at the turn this conversation had suddenly taken.

"No," said the dark-haired man, smiling knowingly, "not our government, but someone working deep within the bowels of those damn spy agencies like MI6 might have."

"Oh, brother." Lawrence was suddenly giggling. "Here we go again with the paranoid spy agenda. Percy here thinks every slice of the political pie is being orchestrated by MI6."

"Don't you?" Percy frowned at the way his companion was belittling him. "It explains why they did not catch the target."

The woman in the glasses scratched her head. "You must admit it was odd. And that piece in the paper about the locked door makes it sound very much like a spy caper."

"Mary, that piece was probably written by the government to throw so much confusion into the mix that no one will ever figure out what really happened." Percy leaned back in his chair. "It was too fantastical to be true."

Shelly felt her heart skip a beat since she was the one who had written the article. She wanted to defend her story, but how could she if she wanted to use this conversation in another piece? But she knew that sooner or later she was going to have to come clean with this little group and tell them she was a reporter, or she would never get the signed releases that legal demanded for every interview.

"I mean, did anyone believe that unnamed-source crap they used?" Percy took another sip of coffee. "They only use that when they can't prove anything that they are writing."

Helena shifted in her seat, her movements suddenly uncomfortable. "I am not so certain about that. I mean, if it was me, I would not want my name used. The people in charge might take offense at whoever told the story, and he or she could have ended up in real trouble."

The group nodded their heads, and Shelly breathed a sigh of relief. "It is possible that the source was afraid of losing his job," she said.

"The article did make it sound like he was a museum employee, and if he was telling the truth, it might explain a great deal about the murder." Lawrence ran his fingers around the rim of his cup.

"What do you mean?" Shelly leaned forward again.

"If it was a locked-door caper, then it could only have been a conspiracy." The blond man continued to run his fingers over his mug. "The question then becomes who was actually involved."

Percy slowly rose to his feet, grabbing his empty cup. "Makes me wonder who is protecting that unnamed source from the conspirators. If he knew enough to tell that story, someone might see him as a danger to the whole thing."

Shelly gulped hard and felt her mouth go dry. Had she placed George in danger even without naming him in the story? Spy types with deep pockets might be able to determine whom she had been meeting with, and if he was being followed, they would know he talked to a reporter. God, what had she done to the poor man?

An hour later she was running back to the paper with the recording and the signed releases, which actually shocked her. The four students who'd said the most had signed without a second thought, as if being quoted in the paper would be the highlight of their lives, even if it was the paper they had earlier called out for using an unnamed source. Shelly did not want to ask them about that inconsistency since it might have led to some embarrassing doubts and a withdrawal of the signed consent. She wanted to get back to the paper and get a first draft ready for Perry, not to mention check with legal about their obligation to protect George if it came to that.

CHAPTER 10

Shelly felt on edge for the rest of the evening, her mind reeling. Even though Perry had given her college interview the green light, she still worried about the question Percy had raised: was she willing and able to protect her source? The next morning she made her way to George's flat after looking his address up on the computer, her heart racing. She walked up to the door and knocked softly. When there was no immediate answer, she pounded. Her imagination was running away with her, and she was far too scared that some government figures from either America or the United Kingdom had spirited away her only link to the story—her story.

She stopped with her hand on the cool hard surface of the wooden door and stood there glaring at her own hand. Was she worried about the man, or was she more worried about losing the only lead she had ever gotten as a reporter? She suddenly felt a wave of nausea creep over her, and she thought she might throw up. She had never wanted to be one of those narcissistic reporters who cared more about page one than about the people who might get hurt along the way. That was not who she was. She began to pound again, fear and terror driving her.

George finally opened the door, his voice rumbling. "God, Clancy, it is still early." He closed his mouth when he saw Shelly standing on his landing.

"No Clancy." She smiled weakly, her voice shaking. "Just me."

"Y-you," he stammered and rubbed a hand through his mussed hair. "What are you doing here at this hour of the morning?"

"I wanted to check up on you."

George stared at her. "Well, as long as you came all this way, you may as well come in." He opened the door further and allowed her to walk past him.

Shelly tried not to look around at the bachelor apartment and its meager furniture. There were no pictures anywhere, not even a sporting poster on the wall, and the place smelled of unwashed socks and dirty dishes. She wrinkled her nose and pulled out one of the kitchen chairs, her hand still shaking. She managed to sit down.

"I read your piece in the paper yesterday," he said, sitting down opposite her.

"What did you think of it?" She clasped her hands together.

"It was okay." He pointed to the kitchen counter, where a pot of coffee sat brewing. "Would you like a cup?" When she feebly nodded, George stiffly got to his feet and poured two cups. He put the cups on the table and then sat down again. "Are they going to let you do any more stories?" he finally asked.

"I have a personal piece tomorrow on the viewpoints of college students." Picking up a carton from the table, she poured some milk into the coffee and absently stirred it with a spoon. "It is about how they see the murder."

"Interesting." He took a sip from his cup and glanced at the biscuits on the table. "Would you like something to eat?"

When she shook her head no, George picked up a biscuit and began to take large bites. Shelly watched him eat, wondering what she could say to him. "It doesn't seem to matter very much in the grand scheme of things," she said. She took a sip of coffee, her heart a little less full. "After all, the viewpoints of students pale when compared to the death of a world leader."

"No one cares about that or the medallion," George grumbled under his breath.

Shelly could see in the sudden dark cloud that came over him that there was something bothering him about the medallion. However, a part of her was terrified that if she pressed him too far, she might lose him. "Why are you so fixated on that necklace?" she finally whispered. "I know that you think it has some bearing on the assassination, but honestly, George, how can it?"

"I am not really certain." He stared at the cup in his hand. He seemed to have an idea but apparently was not yet ready to share it with her. "All I know is that it does, and no one else seems willing to buy into that scenario just yet."

"All right." She calmly reached across and placed her hand over his. "I will accept the fact that you believe it is important, but George, for now can we talk about something else?"

"Fine." He leaned back and looked up at the ceiling. "What do you want to discuss?"

"I was wondering if anyone has talked to you about my story." She gulped hard. "What I mean to say is, has anyone figured out that you were my source?"

George shifted his eyes to look at her directly. "Isn't it a little late to worry about that now?"

She flushed a deep scarlet. "I know."

"So now you are worried that whoever was so desperate to kill a president in front of witnesses might be after me because they think I know something." He smiled at her.

"I was worried more about getting the story to press." She closed her eyes. "It never occurred to me that my enthusiasm might place you in danger."

"It is all right, Miss Jenkins," he said, sighing heavily. "I doubt anyone thinks I am so key a witness that they will come gunning for me."

"Are you sure about that?" Her voice rose in concern. "I need to be sure."

"Why?"

"Well," she said, shrugging her slender shoulders, "there are people who think that a locked-door mystery might make it a conspiracy, and if there was a conspiracy, then the people involved might not be happy that you exposed their means of committing the murder."

"Really." George let out a low chuckle. "A locked door makes someone think it was a conspiracy. I guess that would make sense if there was more than one shooter, but we do not have a grassy knoll. All we have is a locked door and a medallion that turned up in the trash."

"So you don't buy the scenario of a conspiracy?"

"Not in the way you mean it," he said, shaking his head. "It is much more complex."

Shelly stared at him for a moment, her mind racing. "Why do you think the medallion is important when no one else does?"

"The medallion is just another inconsistency in a long line of inconsistencies."

"Don't you think that the death of a world leader is the biggest inconsistency of them all?"

"Of course it is." He chuckled again. "Presidents are targets all the time, which is why they have the Secret Service types all around them. What does not make sense is how a locked door was magically opened and then locked again when the only person to go near it was the killer. The shooter had to have had the key."

"The medallion is not a key." Shelly slammed her fist on the table. She was suddenly very angry with this man. She wanted to help him, and he was making no sense.

"It might be if it does what Carl says it used to do."

"Who is Carl again?" Shelly sighed with exasperation.

George told her about the curator and the story of the priests who had guarded the tomb and goddess they had prayed to. Shelly sat listening to him, her head nodding periodically, but inside she was wondering if her only source was a few biscuits short. Her frustration was mounting with each passing moment.

"What does any of this have to do with the locked door in the museum?" Shelly took a biscuit and bit into it.

"Well, that is the question, but I think the priests realized that after the tombs were sealed, people were breaking in to steal from the mummies." He took another biscuit from the table.

Shelly held a biscuit halfway to her mouth, her eyes full and round. "Let me get this straight. The priests used the medallion to unlock a sealed tomb and then lock it again?"

"That is what I think." George smiled as he chewed on the stale cookie. "Of course, it is all just speculation and could just be a silly story."

Shelly took another bite. "But it would explain so much about what you told me."

George smiled at her, his blue eyes dancing. "The only problem," he said, closing his eyes, "is that no one seems to know the incantation that the ancient priests used to activate the medallion."

Shelly stared at him. "So there is some trick to using it, but no one knows the trick—is that what you are telling me?"

George kept his eyes closed. "That is what Carl told me. He said it was a long-ass poem that had been lost to the sands of time."

"But if someone did know it"—Shelly's voice suddenly rose in excitement; this was a new twist on the tale and one that could earn her a whole new story—"they could use it to open any door they wanted."

George opened his eyes and stared at her excited smile. "I am not really clear how it works."

"So is there anyone you can ask other than that Carl fellow?" Shelly felt her excitement deflating. It was odd, but the more complex the story seemed to become, the less she liked it.

George seemed to sense her trepidation, and his smile faded too. "If you think about it, this is an Egyptian medallion, and outside of Egypt itself, the museum has the largest collection of mummies and ancient artifacts ever collected."

"So maybe for the medallion to open a door, that door had to open on to mummies." Shelly's smile returned. "You know, in a twisted way that makes sense."

George looked at her for a moment and then suddenly roared with laughter. "I am glad that I am not the only one who is twisted by this thing."

Shelly reached across and patted his hand. "Twisted has been the only logical way to feel the last few days."

They both sat laughing for a few minutes as they drank coffee. They no longer seemed shocked by the oddity of the medallion or the story of its ability. However, now they both were concerned with how to discover a poem that had been lost for thousands of years.

"I will lay money that whoever found the poem traveled abroad." Shelly walked over and put her cup in the sink. "How else could he find the poem?"

"Not necessarily." George took the wrapper from the biscuits and headed to his kitchenette. He placed the wrapper in a rubbish bin and returned to where she sat waiting for him. "The medallion was here in the museum, so the poem could be a part of any collection that holds ancient junk."

Shelly leaned back. "So Egypt and Britain are not the only places with mummies?"

"Heavens no." George ran a hand through his hair, trying to straighten it. "During the tours I have heard the guides tell people that there are mummies in France and America. The Nazis even had some in Germany, but I have no idea where those ended up after the war."

"Probably right under your nose in the museum," Shelly sighed.

Tracking a mummy would be almost impossible, but it was not the mummy they needed, just the poem.

"Was that Carl person certain that the poem would be so long it would take weeks to recite? That seems a tad inconvenient if you ask me."

"Actually, it was a guy named Holds who made that suggestion in some silly book." George leaned across the table. "But Carl seemed to back him up."

"What if they are wrong?" Shelly smiled uneasily. "What if it was simpler and only a couple of words?"

George stared at her for a moment. "It would be only a few glyphs long then."

Shelly frowned at him. "Glyphs?"

"You know, those picture things they used for writing—hieroglyphs."

The young reporter looked embarrassed. "All right, a couple of glyphs. But where do we look for them?"

There was silence as they considered that question. George rose to his feet and slowly began to pace around the room. Suddenly, he stopped in the middle of the room and spun around to face Shelly. "Miss Jenkins, I think we need to have a closer look at that medallion. It might be not only the key to the door but also the key to finding the incantation."

ᏣᏣᏣ

As George looked at her excitedly, Shelly felt her heart go into her throat. The medallion was in the museum, which was on lockdown for the rest of the investigation. Perry had made it clear to the entire staff that he did not want anyone from the paper breaking the police barricade around the building. He had always worked Scotland Yard and MI6 with a delicate hand, cultivating pure sources, and there was no way he was going to tolerate a rookie reporter alienating his buddies at the Yard for some publicity stunt to get the edge on a story. So she knew it was a risk, but as she watched George pace around the small flat, there was some part of her that knew the risk would be worth it when she had the goods on the story of a lifetime.

CHAPTER 11

"We may be pissing into the wind on this one," he sighed as they neared the museum. "We can ask, but I doubt they will let us in, or if they do, they are never going to let me near that floor again."

"We won't know unless we try." Shelly walked arm in arm with George. "What could they do even if they do stop us?"

"Throw us into some cell somewhere and toss the key into the Thames." George tried to laugh, but the sound came out hollow.

"I have never been in a cell," Shelly chuckled. "It might be worth a story."

George looked down at the woman walking beside him, "I really hope you are joking with me, Miss Jenkins. I would rather not be locked in some cell."

"I was joking, George," she said, patting his hand. "If we get into the building, I will take the lead and say it was all my idea. The press is often scolded for pushing things too far, and sometimes they let us cool our heels in a cell, but the paper would never allow them to keep me for long."

George stopped and felt his body go rigid. "Would you really be willing to risk jail time for a story?"

Shelly smiled knowingly at him. "Most reporters would. It is all part and parcel of the journalistic code."

George stood still for a moment, his mind racing through the newspapers he had read since he was a lad. Was Shelly telling him the truth? Were reporters willing to risk incarceration just to tell a story? She was such a tiny little thing, all sweet and goodness. He hated the idea of her doing time to protect him, but on the other hand, she had the press and the power of some paper's owners to back her play. What did he have on his side? He sighed and headed for the museum's side entrance. This was not going to be easy, no matter what Shelly thought.

As they neared the door and the man in uniform who stood there, George fumbled for words. "Hello, mate. I work at the front, or I used to, and I need to get some stuff out of my locker."

"Who is she?" The man pointed a long finger at Shelly.

"My niece," George mumbled under his breath. "She is visiting me from Oxford."

"You have museum identification?" The officer pulled out a long pad from behind the door.

"Of course." George pulled the card from his billfold and waited while the man checked his name against the list. "So have they found out anything new?"

The uniformed officer grunted, "Wait here." He then headed into the massive building, closing the door behind him.

Shelly cocked her head to one side and glared at the closed door. "Have you ever had trouble getting in before?"

"Course not," George said, frowning. "I have a set of the master keys, so I can come and go as I please."

"Why don't we just walk in then?"

George let out a laugh. "Are you daft, girl? That will get us arrested!"

While they waited for the officer's return, George leaned against the door, and Shelly bounced from one foot to the other. "Why did you tell him that I was your niece?" she finally asked him.

"I was going to tell him you were my steady girl." He chuckled under his breath. "But I doubt he would have bought that tale."

"Oh, I don't know." She reached over and squeezed his arm. "Anything is possible."

"Possible is unlikely," he whispered under his breath and shifted his arm.

ᏣᏣᏣ

Shelly removed her hand from George's arm and wondered why he was so determined to maintain some distance between them. It really was like George was afraid of her. She could tell from the little time they had spent together that he was not a shy man; actually, he was rather outgoing. She shook her head and looked down at the skinny jeans and form-fitting blouse she had thrown on that morning. Was she making him uncomfortable by coming on so strong? She had gotten so used to trying to make an impression on men that she had never once considered that it might cause some of them to back away.

"What do you think the officer is going to do?" she asked. "Will he let us in or tell us to piss off?"

"Anything is possible," George said, repeating her earlier remark, "but if I were to guess, I'd say he will let us in, but only to the basement area where my locker is."

"What do we do then?" she said, lowering her voice. She really was scared by all this intrigue.

"We get lost in this massive building, which is possible," George laughed. "Hell, my first weeks here, I got lost in the corridors all the time. We can then tell whoever comes across us that we were trying to find a shortcut out when we accidentally ended up in the mummy wing."

"All right," Shelly said, nodding. It did sound like a believable story, albeit a little too easy. She could not help but feel that soon she would have to call Perry and explain why she was under arrest in the museum. What would she tell him, and would he believe any of it?

The door opened, and the same officer came out. He stared at them with seeming contempt. "They said you can head down to the basement."

Shelly wondered who this magical "they" was, but she decided not to ask. Instead she fell in step behind her uncle George, who led the way into the building. She tried not to giggle and to keep a firm, resolute frown on her face; after all, a man had been murdered in this very building just two days ago. They walked down a set of stairs and then marched down a long corridor to what appeared to be staff quarters. She was amazed at how long the hallway was and how blindly George seemed to follow it. But she knew from their earlier conversations that he had worked at the museum for fifteen years, so it was possible that he knew every inch of the place.

"Wait here," he whispered to her and then headed into a room marked "Private."

Shelly fidgeted uneasily, her hands clasped behind her back. She felt very exposed in the hallway and prayed that whatever George needed in that room would not take too long to find because she did not want anyone to come along and ask her any pointed questions. She seriously doubted her ability to give a coherent answer. It was less than a minute, though, before George came out carrying a brown canvas bag.

"What is in the bag?" she asked, unclasping her hands.

"Nothing really. Just some old socks someone left behind. But it will give me an excuse if we are stopped."

"All right," she sighed. "Now where do we go?"

"Up this hall. Then we take a left into the back staircase." He pointed with his left hand. "We then follow it to the second floor, where there is a side entrance into the mummy display. Keep to the left though because Harry once told me that area of the hallway is a blind spot for his cameras."

"Cameras," she really did not like the sound of that but her mind was on something else. "Are we going to see where the president was shot?" She asked the question with so much enthusiasm that George turned and stared at her.

"God no," he finally answered. "We can bypass that room and head for the display of artifacts down the hall from there."

Shelly averted her eyes. Was she really excited to see where a man had died? She had never thought of herself as the morbid type, so why had she sounded so thrilled at the idea of being near a room associated with death? Her entire body shuddered, and she shook her head. "I did not mean that the way it sounded, George."

"I know you didn't," he said, smiling at her. "No one really knows how to react to death; we simply do."

He turned and headed toward the far end of the hall. Shelly waited a moment and then joined him. They walked in silence as they quickly entered a stairwell and headed up toward the second floor. With each step Shelly could feel her heart pounding faster and faster. She knew it was not from the exercise of climbing flights of stairs; it was from a mixture of excitement and fear.

When they reached the door to the second floor, George stopped. "This is where it gets tricky, Miss Jenkins. There will more than likely be a lot of security people on this floor since it is near the place where he was killed. So let me do the talking. I can explain how I thought this was the way to the main entrance."

"All right, Uncle George," she said.

He looked back at her and winked. "You do not look anything like anyone in my family." He took a step and then laughed. "Which, trust me, is a good thing."

Shelly let out a low giggle and followed him into the hallway.

They did not initially see anyone, and for a moment she thought they might get away with this thing, but suddenly a man in a crisp uniform came out of a room and stopped to stare at them. "You two, where did you come from?" he screamed at them in a decidedly American accent.

George smiled at him. "We were in the basement. They said I could go to my locker and get my laundry, and then we were heading for the main entrance."

"Does this look like the main entrance?" The American snarled.

"Well, no." George glanced around nervously. "See, girl, I told you we had not gone far enough to find the entrance. I have worked here for years and still get turned around in this place."

The man pushed George in the direction of the staircase down the hallway. "Get going and do not linger here. We are sweeping for bugs."

"You're kidding." Shelly's eyes suddenly widened. "Do you really think there might be listening devices around here?"

As the American glared at her, George grabbed Shelly by the arm and pulled her along the hallway. "Come on, girl. We have no time for your questions today."

Shelly allowed herself to be pulled along but could not help but glance back over her shoulder. This was information that Emmett would be thrilled to hear, and she was the one who had gotten it first. She could not help but give out another laugh as they turned the corner.

George let out a short breath and stopped near the entrance to the staircase. "Come on." He opened another door marked "Egyptian Ornamental Displays" and walked slowly into the room.

Shelly stood behind him, surveying the room, her eyes darting back and forth. She was so filled with excitement that her body was vibrating, and she knew that if she did not calm down, she might give away the whole operation. She tapped her foot and wondered how spies managed to remain so composed when dealing with dangerous situations. She was becoming unglued just following this man into an empty room.

George walked over to the display cases and looked at the array of artifacts twinkling in the room's bright light. Shelly walked over and stood beside him; she followed his line of sight down into the case and studied the medallions, necklaces, and amulets that were arranged under the glass. She had no idea what she was looking at; George was in charge here. She watched with trepidation as the large man took a deep breath, reached out his hand, and touched the case as if it was on fire. They both held their breath and waited, but nothing happened.

George finally let out his breath. "They must have turned off the alarms on these cases to sweep for their listening devices," he said, "which is good, or we would have been thrown to the floor by some large American GIs."

"Now you tell me." Shelly hit his shoulder.

He grinned at her and shrugged. "Well, shall we take a closer look at Carl's little treasures?" He lifted the cover and took out the round medallion with the depiction of a cat on it. He held it out to the young woman and laughed. "This is the goddess Bastet, so let's see what she can tell us."

Shelly sighed heavily and motioned to the door. "Why don't we slip that thing into your pocket and get the hell out of here before GI Joe finds us and we end up riding a slow boat to some American prison?"

"Good idea." He knew he should be worried about fingerprints but he also knew that overall it did not matter. If they were caught with this treasure they were going to prison so, he simply slid the necklace into his pocket. He had not originally been intent on stealing the thing, but it would be easier to study it somewhere else, away from the eyes of the police. He patted his pocket, and the two headed for the door and the stairs. They tried to look calm and nonchalant, but they could feel their hearts pounding as they walked out of the building.

George looked at his companion and sighed once more as they made their way to her car. "So where do we go to study our trinket?"

"We can go back to your place," she said, straightening her slender frame. "It would be best to get off the street anyway."

CHAPTER 12

Shelly could sense the tension in the large man, who reacted every time she touched him. It was sweet but did nothing to help the situation they now found themselves in. They returned to the very chairs where they had begun their wild odyssey. Shelly kept looking at George's top pocket, wondering when he was going to bring out the very thing that had sent them to the museum, but he seemed content to sit and stare through the small window at the afternoon sun.

She finally leaned across the table and looked intently at him. "Can I take a look at what will get me sent to jail if the police find it on us?"

"Oh." George let out a low grunt, stuffed his hand into his pocket, and pulled out the medallion. He wiped the thing across his shirt before he handed it to her.

Shelly ran her fingers over the smooth surface of the back and then turned it over to study the relief picture of the cat on the front of it. She sighed and placed it gingerly back on the table. "It really is a rather unremarkable thing."

"Sometimes the most amazing things in the world do not seem worth our time at first," George whispered under his breath. "The damn Rosetta stone is really just a hunk of rock with some writing on it, but when they finally figured out what the writing meant, it became one of the most important archaeological finds of all time."

"You sound like one of the guides at the museum," she said, laughing.

"I have heard it all enough times," he said with a smile. "I could probably give the tour just as well as one of the guides."

She nodded. "I am certain that you could. So what did they tell you about Bastet and her necklace?"

George leaned closer to the medallion. He picked it up and peered at it. He then repeated the information he had learned about the goddess and her role in the ancient world.

"So she offered protection to the dead." Shelly cringed at the thought. "What does this medallion have to do with protection of the dead?"

"That is what we have to figure out."

ꟹꟹꟹ

Hours later, the two of them still sat peering at the necklace and poring over the material George had printed out at the library, but they were no closer to figuring out its secrets than when they'd stolen it from the museum. George ran a hand through his hair, frustrated that this whole day might have been a waste of time. What was worse was that he had included this beautiful woman in his wild crime spree. If the agents knew he and Shelly had been in the museum, he would be easily identified. Hell, he was half-expecting some storm trooper to come banging on his door, demanding this little treasure back.

"I am so sorry, Miss Jenkins," George said slowly. "I made a mess of everything, and now you could end up getting in real trouble because of me."

"George," she said with her eyes closed, "I knew what I was getting into when we headed for the museum, so do not chastise yourself because of me."

"Still does not make me feel any better." He picked up the medallion for what seemed the millionth time that day. "And this thing is becoming a millstone around my neck." George turned it over. "Maybe that is our problem. We are looking at it all wrong."

Shelly opened her eyes and sat up straight. "What are you talking about? We have looked at that thing every which way and are no closer to figuring it out."

"But neither one of us has put it on." He held it out to her.

"You want me to wear that ancient thing?" She shuddered at the very idea.

"Well, if you think about it"—George lowered his gaze, suddenly feeling very shy—"it is a necklace, and the men who used it four thousand years ago would have worn it around their necks."

"All right." She grabbed it and slipped it over her head. "I wonder who the last person to wear it was."

George frowned at the question. What if the last person to wear it was a presidential assassin? Would that do something bad to the next wearer? If so, had Miss Jenkins just sealed her own fate by putting the stupid thing around her neck? He wanted to grab it and rip it off her, but he also knew that whatever the magical qualities of the piece, it was too late to change their impact on the lovely woman. He held his breath and waited.

CHAPTER 13

The medallion began to glow against Shelly's skin, and although the sensation was rather strange, she liked the feeling. "It seems to be radiating some sort of energy."

"Is it hurting you?"

She could hear the urgency in his voice and reached out to take his hand. "No, actually, it feels wonderful."

George held her hand. "Miss, can you feel anything? Is it saying anything?"

"Wait," she whispered into his ear. "I think it is about to reveal its secret to us." Never in her life had Shelly felt so alive and so scared. She was practically vibrating in time to the energy of the medallion, and she knew that was part of its power—the energy it projected into the wearer.

A white light seemed to emanate from the medallion and filled the little space of the flat with an intense glow that made George take a step back, but Shelly held fast to his hand. She was too scared to let him go, but she also wanted him to share this moment with her. In the white light eight hieroglyphic symbols suddenly flashed onto the wall across from where they sat and then just as quickly disappeared. The light dimmed, and the two of them were left in the room alone, both of them shivering from a cold that did not really exist.

"Did you see that?" Shelly finally whispered.

"Yes, I did." George let her hand go and walked over to where the symbols had appeared. He traced his finger over the wall and let out a low moan. "I guess we now have the answer to the question about the incantation and why it was lost to the sands of time. No one has put on the necklace until now. Grab a pencil and draw it quickly, before we forget what it was like."

"And it was not as long as that book said it was." Shelly pulled a pencil and notepad out of her bag and began to draw. She then pulled off the necklace, placing it back on the table. "Now we just have to figure out what the symbols mean."

"I have an idea about that. We can get some books from the library to figure out what they mean." George's growing excitement and renewed energy were apparent.

"Fine." Shelly kept one eye on the necklace as they spoke. "And who will know how to pronounce the words even if the books tell us what they mean?"

"I think Carl knows, and he will help without needing too much prodding."

"Will we have to tell him why we want to know?" She looked up at George. She did not want to share their discovery with an academic who would want to write it up in some historical tome.

"I doubt it." George flopped down into the chair opposite her. "I can just tell him that I found the symbols in a library book and was curious what they meant and how to pronounce them."

"He would buy that?"

"You would be surprised how uncurious a man he is." George let out a low breath. "All he really cares about is keeping his little treasures safe."

Shelly grinned. "Won't he be a little pissed when he discovers that one missing from the display case?"

"Of course he will," George said, drumming the table with his huge fingers. "Hell, he will go scurrying through the halls right to the director. But he is locked out right now just like I am, and since he would be the only one to notice its absence, we have some time on our side."

"All right." Shelly turned the paper around and showed George what she had drawn.

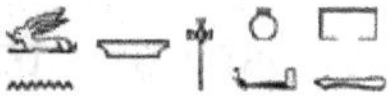

The two studied the pictures for a moment, and then both began to laugh at the absurd little lines on the paper.

"That first one looks like a bleeding rabbit." George doubled over with laughter. "Maybe some bunny will be the clue we need."

"Very funny," Shelly said, sharing his mirth, "but from what I know about these things, they are not a simple direct translation, so that thing may not mean 'rabbit.'"

"I know that." George stood up and went to his refrigerator, where he pulled out two bottles of beer. He walked back and handed her one. "I have been around the museum long enough to have learned that the hieroglyphics are not so easy to read as people think, which is why they needed the Rosetta stone to get the first translation."

"So we have our pictures." Shelly took a long sip of the cold beer. "Now we need Carl to translate them and pronounce them for us."

"We could go now since I know where he lives, but he might get real suspicious if we show up there late in the evening. So it might be best if we go see him tomorrow." George sat back down.

Shelly sat and wondered what she was supposed to do for the rest of the evening. She could not fully explain even to herself why she did not want to leave George alone for that length of time. "So we have an evening free. Why don't we go to a movie or something?"

CHAPTER 14

George stared at Shelly, shocked by her suggestion. This wondrous creature was actually asking him to join her on a date. It was too fantastical to be true.

"They are showing a Monty Python retrospective across town," he said. The moment the words left his mouth, George wanted to take them back. What if Shelly didn't like the Python troupe or their silly antics? He loved them and always had, but not everyone did.

"Wink, wink, nudge, nudge." Shelly laughed at her own crude attempt to recite one of the famous bits.

"Say no more." George laughed at her and took another sip of his beer. "That is one of my favorite bits."

"Well, there you go." She smiled over the rim of her beer. "I knew we had something in common besides ancient Egypt."

George gulped down some more beer, almost choking on it. He could not imagine having anything in common with this woman. In his heart he knew that she never would have considered going to the movies with him if not for the story he was so much a part of. She was with him simply to keep the piece flowing and her name on the byline. He had to keep that truth in his head, or he would lose his heart.

An hour later, they arrived at the theater where *And Now for Something Completely Different* was playing. They had argued about what to do with the medallion since neither wanted to leave it in the flat. George had finally placed it back in his pocket, but it made watching the movie a tad difficult. He could feel it weighing him down all evening long. The stupid thing did seem to radiate its own heat, and he worried that the other patrons at the theater could sense its presence. He did not have to worry, though, since no one appeared to take any notice of the odd couple or the necklace in his pocket. People simply milled about and watched the movie from their seats, laughing at the odd antics of the comedy playing out before them.

When the scene came up with Eric Idol and Terry Jones playing out the "wink, wink" sketch, Shelly poked George in the ribs, and they both began to laugh. George blushed at the end when Idol asked Jones to explain sex to him; he could not help but feel the pressure of Shelly sitting so close to him. He hated himself for feeling so old and ugly with this woman, and he wondered if she realized the effect she was having on him. When he glanced at her, he saw that her focus was totally on the big screen, so he turned his attention back to the movie, willing himself to remain a little more calm.

ଓଓଓ

When the movie let out, a tall woman with long brown hair tied up in a severe bun at the nape of her neck milled about with the rest of the audience, along with her companion, a younger man whose long coat did not seem to fit him. They barely spoke as they kept their eyes on George and his companion. The man slipped his phone out of his jacket pocket and quickly took a picture of the girl.

"Tonight find out who she is and how she knows this man Marsh," the woman whispered in a decidedly American accent.

"Yes, sir," the young man said in a deep Texas drawl. He grimaced immediately. "I mean Mama."

The woman did not acknowledge his gaffe but headed for the dark sedan that they had parked illegally in the bus lane. She got into the driver's seat and waited for the young man to jump in next to her. He barely had time to close the door, let alone fasten his seat belt, before she pulled out, following George Marsh and his friend as they weaved through traffic.

ଓଓଓ

Shelly drove George back to his flat and then headed home. She was pleased with the entire day's events and had to wonder why it had been so easy—perhaps a little too easy—to grab the necklace out of the museum. Maybe George had been right on the day of the assassination; maybe he was being followed and someone had followed them today. Gary had often suggested that she was not as observant as she could be and that she often missed important elements of an event.

So it was possible that someone had been tailing them, as the Americans would say, and she would not even have noticed. She cringed at the thought as she showered and prepared for bed. "Tomorrow I will keep my eyes open," she said out loud as she turned off the light. "Tomorrow I will check to see if we are being followed." The problem with that idea was that she did not even know what actually being followed would look like. She was far too exhausted to even think clearly, so she slipped into an uneasy sleep, terrified of what tomorrow would bring.

CHAPTER 15

The next morning, George was up early, waiting for Shelly to return. He even managed to run the broom through his flat and dust some of the cobwebs away. He looked at his living arrangements and realized that he was a slob of a bachelor. He was embarrassed that Shelly had seen the way he lived, and he vowed that if they managed to make it through this adventure, he would try a little harder to keep his home clean. Hell, he might even go out and buy some new furniture and hang up some pictures to make the place a little more like a home, just so it would be a little more presentable for some woman to visit.

As the morning stretched before him, George began to worry that something might have happened to the young reporter. He did have the medallion, but he did not even consider heading to see Carl on his own. He and Shelly were in this together, so he waited, pacing around the flat like a wounded bear. He had not wanted to frighten her, but he'd had the uneasy feeling the night before that someone was tailing them after they left the movie theater. A dark sedan that turned every corner with them, keeping up with them all the way home, had left him worrying less about the necklace in his pocket and more about the agencies crawling over the museum.

Shelly arrived around ten o'clock, a little later than they had arranged, and knocked on George's door. She actually half-expected him to still be asleep, but he quickly opened the door as if he had been standing on the other side, waiting for her. She smiled at the crisp, clean white shirt he wore over black jeans and wondered if the clothes were new. Maybe he was trying to impress her, or maybe he was just tired of looking like an unkempt slob.

"Sorry I'm late. I thought it would be a good idea to check in with the office to see if there were any developments." She walked in and stood tapping her foot impatiently on the kitchen floor. "Do you still have it?"

He touched his top pocket to indicate that he had the medallion with him, and they got into the car for the trip to Carl's place. Neither spoke, and after the animated conversations of yesterday regarding the necklace and Monty Python, the silence seemed oddly out of place. Shelly glanced over at him as they rolled to a stop at an intersection. He seemed so sullen and gloomy as he stared at the buildings across the street. The only time he had spoken all morning was to give her the address of the curator's home; after that he had fallen into a deep silence that made her nervous.

"Are you all right, George?" she asked, giving in to her own need for conversation.

"I think so," he said as he continued to stare out the passenger window. "I just wonder if keeping this stupid thing on me all the time is such a good idea."

"Do you want me to hold it?"

He spun his head around and looked at her. "God no. I don't want either one of us holding it for very long. It reminds me of the Lord of the Rings ring. It might turn us into some crazed creature who calls it 'my precious.'"

Shelly smiled at his concern for her safety. "Maybe we can put it in my safety deposit box at the bank after we visit with this Carl person."

George gave her a quizzical frown. "What on earth do you put in a safety deposit box?"

Shelly smiled at the question even if it did fill her with a touch of sadness. "My passport, an old watch of my grandfather's, and a copy of my dad's will. Actually, the box belonged to my dad, and I just kept it after he passed."

"Oh." George turned to look out the window again.

They continued the trip in silence, and Shelly wondered whether the idea of putting the medallion in the box at the bank had been agreed upon or thrown out. She thought about asking but decided to wait until after they had spoken to the academic. His words might send them in a different direction and change everything that they would do from now on. She was becoming more and more nervous about this whole adventure, but how could she even consider backing out now? This was all too important and might be the story that would make her career. On the other hand, she had begun to worry that something so fanciful might never make it to press; after all, Emmet was never one for printing anything people would label fantastical, and this fit into that category.

They reached the street Carl lived on, and Shelly waited in the car; they had decided that both of them descending on the little man might be a tad overwhelming. Besides, he would be more than curious about someone like Shelly Jenkins knowing George, and the ruse about her being his niece might not work with someone George worked with at the museum. She hated waiting because she wanted to hear what the symbols meant and how to pronounce them firsthand from the source. Emmet had always told her to never accept any information secondhand, and that was what this felt like. She did trust George, which was odd since she had only known the man for a few days. She had never been someone who trusted people that quickly, but he was an easy fellow to trust. She smiled at the thought; he really was like a big teddy bear. She leaned back against the seat and wondered why this teddy bear was still single. Her mother had often told her that there was someone for everyone, so there had to be some woman in the world who would appreciate a gentle man like George Marsh.

ଔଔଔ

While Shelly mused over his love life, George sat in the tidy little kitchenette belonging to the curator. He marveled at how clean this place was in comparison to his tiny little flat. Hell, Carl's place was smaller, but it seemed homey and more lived-in than his own home, and this made George feel very self-conscious. He shifted uneasily in the small chair and wondered if he would break it since he was such a large lad. He had refused the tea Carl offered since he did not want to extend his stay too long; after all, he had someone waiting for him. That in itself was a new experience for George; he had never left anyone waiting in the car, let alone a lovely lass like Shelly.

"So you have more questions about the goddess Bastet." Carl sat down across from him, a cup of tea in his hand. "I am surprised that this has grabbed your interest so thoroughly."

"Me too." George nervously rubbed his hand through his dark hair. "But with the museum closed, I have a lot of free time on my hands."

"Don't we all." Carl sighed heavily. "I am trying to keep busy by working on my own study of the ancient references to Ra, but I would rather be back in the museum."

"Always work to do at the museum." George smiled as he thought about the staff scurrying through the exhibits like any of it meant something. They always seemed so busy and stressed. However, he had never seemed able to figure out what made them all so tense about a bunch of dead things.

Carl nodded his head solemnly. "And you can just bet those agents are making a mess of the exhibits."

"They have no idea what they are doing or how important it all is," George said. He thought agreeing with the academic was the best way to get him to talk, although he had no idea how anyone could make a mess of dead people.

"So what do you want to know about the goddess?" Carl put down his tea and leaned forward.

"Well, it really isn't about her, or at least I think it isn't." George pulled a piece of paper out of his jacket. "I found this in a book, and I wondered if it had a meaning." He laid out the drawing of the symbols that he and Shelly had seen flash on the wall.

Carl studied it for a moment, his eyes pinched as they focused on each symbol. "You found this in a book? That is odd."

"Why?" George felt his heart skip a beat. "What does it mean?"

"Roughly, it means 'open to protect the pharaoh,' which is silly for anyone to put in a book unless they were trying to be funny." Carl traced his fingers over the symbols.

George felt his hands become warm as he considered the implications. If it did mean "open to protect the pharaoh," then the medallion may have been used in a ceremony to open the tomb, but how was it used? He wanted to ask, but he knew that if he did, Carl would realize that he had taken the medallion. George lowered his gaze and tried to think of some way to broach the subject without giving away the entire game. He sat there for what seemed an eternity but was only a few seconds before he suggested, "Maybe it was a special spell like 'open sesame'—you know, like in the tales of Aladdin."

Carl stared at him for a moment before he burst out laughing. "Don't be silly, George. Things like that did not really exist. They are tales told for amusement. The tales of Aladdin were created to keep the sheik entertained and were never meant to be taken literally."

"Of course." George lowered his gaze. He felt rather silly and sheepish for even suggesting such a thing. "Do you know how they would have pronounced these words in ancient times?"

Carl's smile vanished. "Sort of but not really." This was a man who hated to admit that he did not have all the answers. "A lot of the pronunciation is only a guess because most of the language was lost along with the writing. We guess using modern and old Arabic languages that are now spoken in Egypt."

"Okay," George said with a smile. He would take what he could get, even if it was only a guess.

Carl closed his eyes and then said the words in a brash voice, which George found hard to follow. He knew that he would never be able to repeat it for Shelly, and she would want to hear it exactly. He pulled out the cell phone she had given him and pushed the record button. "Can you repeat that for me? I want to make certain I get it right."

Carl obliged him, and George suppressed a giggle at how the man kept his eyes closed the entire time, as if that was the only way to speak ancient languages. George was even able to pocket the phone before Carl reopened his eyes.

"I hope that was some help to you." The curator picked up his tea and took a sip. "Although I still don't understand your interest in ancient stories of the goddesses."

"To be perfectly honest, neither do I." George slowly rose to his feet. "It is just a way to kill time until they reopen the museum."

"Have you heard anything about when they might be opening it, at least to the staff?" The man's eyes were suddenly filled with an eagerness that George found endearing. Carl did so miss hanging out with dead mummies.

"Nope, not one word." George shook his head and headed for the door. "But I can't imagine it will be too much longer."

Carl leaped to his feet and followed him. "If you hear anything, please let me know. I do so want to get back to work."

"Me too." George offered his hand, which Carl stared at before shaking.

George left the flat and headed out into the foggy London morning, pleased with the information he had been able to glean from the curator, even it only added to his sense of confusion.

Shelly pressed a button to open the car door and sat quietly as he settled down in the passenger seat. When she could take it no longer, she exclaimed, "All right, let me hear it—what does this damn thing mean?"

"Open to protect the pharaoh."

"That is a little vague."

"I know." He lowered his eyes. He hated not being able to give her a more precise answer. "But that is what it means. Perhaps it will explain how someone used the medallion to open a locked door."

"How do we open it?" She banged her head on the steering wheel. "And how does that protect the pharaoh?"

"I couldn't ask that. Carl would have known something was up. But perhaps if you wear the medallion and speak those words, something else might happen."

"Maybe another line in the incantation might come up."

"It is worth a try." He smiled at her.

Shelly shook her head in exasperation. The more information they received about this thing, the less they actually seemed to know.

George sat dejected, with his hands on the dashboard in front of him. He went over the conversation with Carl again, trying to ascertain whether he had anything else to add, but other than the supposed pronunciation, there was very little that Carl had been able to tell him. He leaned back and closed his eyes, wishing he were somewhere else.

"Good God, George, didn't he give you anything we can use?" Shelly was clearly becoming excited at the prospects of what this thing might mean.

"Only what he thought it might sound like in the ancient language, and he wasn't exactly 100 percent certain about that. He said it was only a guess since most of those languages were as lost to the sands of time as the medallion's code was."

"Let me hear that then."

George opened his eyes, held out her phone, and pressed the play button. Carl's voice filled the little car with the phrase that still sounded like so much gibberish to George. He focused his gaze on the young woman's face and hoped she heard something he did not. Instead she took the phone and replayed the recording over and over again. He could tell by the look in her eyes that she was just as confused as he was. She put the phone back into her purse and leaned against the car seat.

George waited for a while, wondering if he could say anything to make this day better for both of them, but he knew there was nothing. He had hoped that the hieroglyphics would give them more than a stupid message that was about as useful as the sign over the men's room in the train station.

Shelly patted George's hand. "One step at a time, my friend." She put the key into the ignition and pointed to his seat belt. "We'll see where this one takes us and go from there."

The security guard finally smiled and straightened himself into the seat before clicking the belt into place. He knew that she was right; they had only one way to go, and that was forward. Whatever happened next, and whatever opened with the medallion, they had to keep going.

CHAPTER 16

George was conscious of the fact that the young woman did not suggest her place, but perhaps she had a flatmate or maybe a live-in boyfriend to whom she did not want to have to explain this old man. He had spent so much time fantasizing about Miss Jenkins that he had not even bothered to ask if she had a boyfriend or someone special in her life—hell, she could be a lesbian for all he knew. As she drove through the streets of London back to his place, he closed his eyes and realized that he did not want to know any of these things. He wanted to keep the fantasy alive as long as he possibly could.

When they reached his apartment and were seated once more at the table, neither reached for the medallion. They sat with it between them and stared at it for a moment. The thing did seem alive, and although they knew it was all in their imagination, both of them would later swear that it was already glowing with its own life force. Shelly finally picked it up and slowly put it around her neck. Her hands were shaking, and George could see the beads of sweat on her forehead even though his flat was decidedly cold that afternoon.

The medallion began glowing the moment she put it on, and the symbols flashed once more on the wall.

George pushed play on the phone, and Carl's squeaky voice recited the words in the ancient language. Neither of them trusted their own pronunciation, so they hoped the recording of Carl saying it would work just as well. If it didn't work, Shelly would try it. They waited, both holding their breath.

Suddenly, the symbols faded from the wall, and an image of a door appeared before them. George sighed, grateful that they were not faced with another set of symbols that they would have to take over to Carl to figure out, but a door was almost as ridiculous. What did it mean, and what did it expect them to do?

"Open to protect the pharaoh," Shelly said, repeating the translation.

George nodded his head and then lowered his eyes in frustration. As much as he did understand, he was also completely confused. "What door where?"

"There is only one door that matters," Shelly said, smiling at him. "The one to the exhibit, the one the killer came through on Friday."

"You know, this thing looks real," George said, pointing at the door. "I could almost reach out and touch it."

"What if we can?" Shelly rose to her feet. "What if we open this door? Could it take us to the museum?"

"Well, are we going to try it?" He took a step toward the door and extended his hand to Shelly. If he was going to travel through the looking glass, he wanted his Alice to join him in Wonderland.

"All right." Shelly gulped hard and took his hand in hers. With the other hand, she reached for the doorknob and turned it, opening the door slowly.

Beyond the doorway, they could see the mummy cases of the museum. Milling around, looking at the dead pharaohs, were three of the American agents George had met only a few days earlier. Shelly let out a slight gasp, and the agents raised their heads at the sound. George grabbed the handle and pulled the door shut before they could turn toward that infamous door.

Shelly reeled back in surprise and steadied herself against the wall. "Did you see that? We were really at the museum."

"I know." George walked back to the table and fell into one of the chairs.

"This is unbelievable." Shelly joined him, taking off the necklace and setting it down on the table. "At least we know how the assassin got into the museum and through a locked door."

"Do we?" George closed his eyes and lowered his head to the table. "Do we know anything?"

"What do you mean?" Shelly stared at him as she flopped into the other chair. "It is obvious to me that the killer used the medallion to open the door and then escaped the same way."

"Miss Jenkins"—George opened his eyes and stared at her—"explain how it was managed to place the silly thing in the trash in the Roman display room. And why even bother returning it? Why not simply keep it?"

Shelly's smile faded, and she lowered her eyes to the floor. "You are right. We do have more questions than answers, but it is a beginning."

"There has to be a reason why the killer did this thing." George gingerly picked up the necklace. "We just need to figure out how this thing really works and what it has to do with the death in the museum."

They sat there for over ten minutes staring at the medallion and the cat carved onto the round surface. George turned it over and ran his fingers over the smooth back of the medallion, his mind racing over the last few days. Had he really just stepped through a magical door? Was any of that real? His senses told him the experience had been real, but his mind did not quite want to believe any of it. He had always been such a practical individual, never believing in anything he could not see or touch. Yet this was a very solid little object, and although the door had appeared out of thin air, he had been able to touch it and open it. How could he explain that to the more logical side of his mind?

"Have you ever believed in magic?" she finally whispered.

"Not until today," he whispered back.

CHAPTER 17

George handed the necklace to Shelly, who asked, "What are we going to do tomorrow?"

"I am not really sure yet." He held the door for her as she walked out of his building. "But I will think of something."

He had no idea what that something would be, but he had the entire evening to come up with something. There was an issue with the idea that the assassin had used the door. How had the assassin known when to come through the door? No one had been given a great deal of warning about the president's visit to the museum. George worked there, and even he had not been told until that morning, and from the reaction of the director, George was certain that the office had not been told either. So how could the killer have known where to find the man he wanted to kill at the exact right moment? The timing would have been critical to the plan.

George sat up most of the night musing over the timing issue, but he could come up with very little that made sense. As he considered the problem, the only thing that he could think of was something Shelly had dismissed out of hand when he first proposed it: "What if the medallion could allow the wearer to travel through time and place to whenever the mummy needed protection?" When he had first said it, he had not really believed it was possible, but then again, he had not really believed in a magic door either. Now he was beginning to wonder if perhaps anything was possible, including time travel.

The next morning as he waited for Miss Jenkins, he busied himself by once more cleaning his apartment and stopping by the corner store for some tea and cakes. He wanted to please his guest and prove that he was more than just some crusty old bachelor. As he set up the tea, he hummed Beatles tunes and caught himself singing "Yesterday" more than once. He had never cared for that song, but today it seemed to have caught his imagination. What if he could travel back in time through the door and stop the assassination? Would he? Doing so would mean never getting to know Shelly, and that thought terrified him.

The knock on the door at a quarter after ten startled him, which was silly since he was expecting her. Yet there was something unnerving about these recent intrusions into his life. She was the biggest intrusion but also the only one he really appreciated. "Hi," he said as he opened the door and allowed her to come in. "Did you bring it?"

"Hi to you too, and yes, I did." Her voice was almost a song to his soul. "I still don't understand what you want with it; we already know what it is capable of doing." She set a box down on the table and took a seat.

George handed her a cup of tea and smiled down at her. "I thought about that all night, and the only thing I can come up with is the one thing you dismissed too eagerly yesterday."

She frowned at him. "What was that, sir?"

He chuckled at her intonation. "Time travel."

Her eyes grew to the size of saucers, and she shook her head. "You have to be joking. George, you have nothing to base that theory on."

He flopped down in the chair across from her and rubbed his hand over the box. "I think I am on solid footing with this one, my dear. You just have to think about it and suspend a little bit of logic to get there."

"Try suspending a lot of logic if you are trying to prove time travel."

"Shelly." George looked into her eyes and slowly elaborated on his theory: the only way anyone would have known where the president would be was through the use of magic and time travel.

Shelly froze, her mind seemingly reeling with the implications of what George was saying. "You are telling me that the timing had to be perfect, and there was no way to time it that accurately."

"How could there be?"

The young woman rose to her feet and began to pace around the room. She finally stopped beside George and placed a hand on his shoulder. "Let's say for a moment I agree with you, which I am not saying that I do, but let's say that I do—how does that help us now?"

"Well," George said, gulping at the touch of her hand, "we need to test the theory."

Shelly moved back to her seat and fell heavily into the chair. "I was scared that was going to be your next suggestion."

"You have never thought about time travel?" His smile was suddenly more like that of a schoolboy suggesting something naughty.

Shelly laughed at his enthusiasm. "No, I have never thought about it."

"Well, I have." He leaned back in his chair and closed his eyes. "Maybe that comes from working in the museum around all that history for the last fifteen years. I have often wondered what it would be like to go back to ancient Egypt, Rome, or Greece—to see when they built the pyramids, the Parthenon, or the Colosseum."

"I am a modern journalist, Mr. Marsh, not a historian, so I have never thought about things like that, not even for one moment."

He opened his eyes, and a touch of sadness filled them. "You have never thought about going back to be there when the *Titanic* went down or when the bombs were falling on this city during the blitz?"

"All right, let's say for argument's sake that I have thought about it. But science says time travel is impossible. Einstein, Hawking, and all those eggheads say it is impossible, and there is nothing to prove them wrong."

George let a smile curve his lower lip. "You are thinking of science, and I am talking magic. You are the one who asked if I believed in magic, and until yesterday, I would have said no." He reached out and ran a hand over the box. "This thing changes all of those beliefs."

"Fine." She shook her head solemnly. "How do we test your theory?"

"We open the door again, and this time we say a time and see if it takes us there instead of simply to the mummy room."

Shelly stared at him in wide-eyed wonder. "And how do you intend on proving that we have reached our desired time when all we can see is the stupid mummy room?"

George had to admit, that one had him a little stumped. "Well, we will have to leave the room and perhaps go to the museum gift shop."

"Leave the mummy room!" Shelly was shocked by the suggestion. "And what if we were to meet a particular guard at the front desk—namely, you?"

George laughed at the absurdity of the situation and wondered what he would do if he saw himself walking through the halls of the museum with this lovely young woman on his arm. "Well, if we go back, I can pick a date and time when I wasn't working. I can then easily tell the other staff that I am taking my niece for a tour."

"Really?" Shelly shook her head. "And later when someone on staff asks the you from that time about your so-called niece, and you tell them you have no niece, what then?"

"Why are you trying to poke holes in this plan?"

"I am trying to be realistic about this." Shelly gripped the sides of her chair and leaned forward. "I wish you were."

"Shelly," he said, leaning over and taking her hand in his, "if someone had asked me about my so-called niece, I would today recall such an event. Well, no one did, so we should be good to go."

"But we haven't gone back in time yet, so why should they have asked you about me?"

George squeezed her hand. "You are thinking too literally about all of this. But if we do return and I suddenly have a new memory of someone asking about my niece, then we will know it was a successful experiment."

"God." Shelly slowly extracted her hand from his grasp. "This whole thing makes me sick inside."

"Yesterday when that door opened, you were excited."

"I was." She cringed at the memory. "But to be honest, it did not seem real. It seemed more like a dream, and today you want to step through the looking glass and make it real, and I am not ready to do that."

"Why not?"

"I don't really know." She sighed heavily. "Perhaps I am not as much a dreamer as you seem to be."

"Me, a dreamer?" George was stunned at the idea that he might be considered a dreamer; this was one thing he had never called himself. "Shelly, I have never thought one fantastical thought until these last few days."

"You were the one who said you thought about traveling through time. I have never given that a passing thought, so to my way of thinking, that makes you much more of a dreamer than I have ever thought about being."

"All right." He slid back into the chair and allowed his body to relax. "What else do you suggest we do with this magical thing?"

"I am not certain we need to do anything." She rose to her feet and began to pace around the room. "Maybe we should take it to someone in authority and show him or her what it can do—let him or her decide what to do next."

George normally would have agreed with her, but something deep inside him told him that if they took the medallion to anyone in authority, that person would simply place it back it inside the case. No one would dare to believe that medallions could open secret passages. The authorities would call the two of them fools, and the entire thing would be forgotten. He hated that thought more than he hated the idea of allowing someone else to know about their findings. The idea that someone would call him a fool or, worse, put him away for believing in magical amulets made him sick inside; he could not allow that to happen. Even if it meant going against Shelly's wishes or traveling through the door without her, he had to find out, and he knew only one way to do that; he had to try. He closed his eyes and filled her in on his concerns.

Shelly stared at him. "You think no one will actually listen to us."

He opened his eyes and looked up at her. "Would you?"

Shelly flopped back into the chair, looking defeated. "No, I would not. Why the hell would anyone believe such nonsense?"

"It is nonsense." The guard smiled, his eyes twinkling merrily. "Hell, it is absolute nonsense. But at this moment, I am willing to believe in nonsense, if you are."

"I wish I could say I did not. I wish I could tell you to go jump into the Thames and sink." She drummed her fingers on the table. "But yesterday I saw a magical door open when some ancient words were spoken, and that makes me wonder what other magical abilities this thing has in store for us."

"In for a penny, in for a pound." George picked up the box and opened it. "Do you want to put it on, or should I do the honors?"

"Give it here." She reached for the necklace. "If we are going to do this, I want to be the one wearing it."

"If we are able to get into the museum, put it under your blouse so no one sees it." George rose to his feet and helped her adjust the medallion around her neck. "I do not want to have to explain to someone like Carl why you are wearing one of his trinkets."

"Right, if we get into the museum." Shelly giggled, her voice suddenly rising in nervous tension.

They waited, and when the symbols appeared, Shelly pressed the button on her phone to replay the translation that Carl had given them. The door appeared before them, and both stood still before it, spellbound, even though they had known this would happen. George took one hesitant step, and Shelly grabbed hold of his arm. "What if we find out that it does work? How the hell do we get back here?"

The large man grimaced, both at the question and at her touch.

The two held hands, and as George turned the knob of the door, they both held their breath. When the door jerked open, they saw the mummy cases and a man standing guard at the far end of the room. George was not surprised to see someone in uniform because it was the site of a homicide, but Shelly let out a gasp when she saw the gun at the man's side. The guard spun around at the sound, and George said softly, "June 7, 2020, 0900 hours."

There was a flash of light, and the room seemed to melt before them. It shimmered and spun in a graceful circle before coming to a stop. The mummy room then stood before them completely empty. Shelly froze at the sight, her mind reeling. "There was someone in there."

"Yes, there was, but if it is 0900 on June 7, there is not anyone in the room yet because we have yet to officially open the doors to the public." He squeezed her hand and led her into the unknown.

CHAPTER 18

Holding Shelly's hand, George took a step into the room. She remained frozen in the doorway, almost too terrified to move. "Come on, girl. We have to check this thing out."

"Yes." She quietly allowed him to drag her through the room and toward the exit. "We should." She did not want to be a part of this. She did not want to be in this place. But how could she tell that to George? He seemed to be so excited by the whole thing. He held her hand, pulling her along behind him like someone walking a reluctant puppy who did not want to learn to walk on the leash.

The corridors were quiet, but around them they could hear the movements of the staff as they prepared for the day. Shelly clasped tight to George's hand, digging her fingernails into his palm. George did not pull his hand away, and she had to wonder if he was just as scared as she was; maybe the pain of her nails digging into his hand helped reassure him that he was not alone in this insane endeavor. They headed for the main staircase and stiffly walked down to the floor below, where the gift shop sat off by itself.

As they walked into the space, a voice called out in greeting, "Hey, mate. What are you doing here on your day off?" The man strolled over and slapped George on the back.

Shelly saw George cringe at the touch of the man's hand on his shoulder. "I promised my niece a little private tour, Harry."

"Niece?" Harry stared at Shelly for a moment. "I didn't think you even had any siblings to give you a niece."

"Well," George said, gulping in some air, "actually, she is my cousin's kid, but I call her my niece."

"Sure." Harry held out his hand to Shelly. "My name is Harry. I work in the secret little world of cameras, which I use to watch the dead."

She eyed his hand suspiciously. "I am Shelly." She did not give a last name.

"Are you into history?" Harry fell in step with them as they walked the aisles of the shop.

"Not really." Shelly kept her eyes on the displays. "I prefer modern stories."

"Don't we all?" the man said with a laugh. "But then your old uncle here drags you to this dusty old place to look at dead people and their junk."

"Only for a few minutes, and then I promised her mom I would take her to Harrods," George said.

"Now that sounds much more entertaining than this old tomb." Harry scratched his head and then headed toward the door. "See you tomorrow, George. And Miss, don't let this old fossil talk you into spending the whole day in the pub either." Harry laughed at his own joke as he walked out of the gift shop and scanned the hallway for someone else to talk to.

George shook his head in exasperation. "You have to forgive Harry. He means well, but sitting in that dark little room, staring at the computer monitors all day, has made him a tad squirrelly."

Shelly watched the man as he headed for the staircase. "Will he ask you about me the day after this?"

"Maybe." George picked up a paper and headed for the cashier. "But more than likely, he will forget he ever met you. Harry has a great memory for computers but very little else."

George paid for the newspaper without looking at the date, and then the two of them headed back toward the main staircase, where George suddenly stopped.

Shelly bumped into him. "What is it?"

"Bloody hell," the guard said, slapping his thigh. "Harry will be watching that stupid screen, and he will see us go through that damn door—a door that is supposed to be locked all the time."

Shelly was suddenly filled with horror. How could they explain walking through a locked door? "Couldn't you just tell him that it was unlocked and you decided to see what was on the other side?"

"Sure I could, and then when the president is assassinated, Harry will suddenly recall me opening that door, and I will be deep in the soup."

"He did not say anything just now about you opening that door five minutes ago."

"That is because he was here on the main floor and not in his cubbyhole watching the screens." George spun around and looked toward the office area. "We are going to have to run for it and hope that we get through the door before that fool makes it back to his hole." He grabbed her hand, and they sprinted up the stairs, heading for the mummy room and the secret door. Shelly's heart was pounding.

As they neared the mummy room, George glanced inside to make certain it was still empty. The room was clear, and they headed for the door at the end of the room. Shelly pulled the medallion out from under her blouse and pushed the play button on the phone stuck in her pocket. The door shimmered and glowed with a white light and silently opened. George then whispered the date and time, and they walked through, back into his apartment.

ଓଓଓ

The door shut behind them, and George let out a deep sigh of relief. He could only pray that Harry had not seen them walking through a locked door.

Shelly fell into the chair, slipped the medallion over her head, and placed it back inside the box on the table. "Well, what date is on that paper we went to get?" She looked up at George, who stood with the paper in his hand.

"Right." He slid into the chair and placed the paper on the table. "Time to see if time travel is possible."

They sat for a moment, both of them almost too terrified to actually look at the date on the top of the paper. Shelly finally reached over and pulled it toward her. She closed her eyes and then opened them, focusing on the date. "June 7," she said slowly, her head suddenly aching.

"It is, isn't it?" George sighed again. He had known it was true, but a part of him had been praying that he was somehow wrong.

"June 7," Shelly repeated. She leaned forward and pushed the paper away from her. "God, now what the hell do we do?"

George looked at her and saw the fear radiating from her. It was supposed to be so easy. They were going to prove that someone had used the medallion to gain entrance to the museum, but now that they had the proof, he had no idea what to do with it. "Who do we tell?"

"No one will believe this!" Shelly was suddenly screaming. "I was there, and I don't believe it myself."

George reached out and grabbed for her hand, but she slapped him away. "Shelly," he said softly, "please try to calm down."

The young woman vibrated with terror. "I can't be calm about this, George. I said time travel is impossible, and now we have found some way to do the impossible. How can I write about this without my boss throwing it into the rubbish heap? I am not H. G. Wells, and I do not write fiction."

"This is not fiction." His voice was very low. "However, I am not certain that you can write about it."

"What the hell do you mean by that?"

He looked over at her and smiled uneasily. "Shelly, you and I both know that no one can know about this just yet. No one would believe it even if you did write it up. Besides, we may have the proof that time travel is possible, but we still do not know who used it to kill the president."

Shelly slumped forward. "All right, we don't know who used it. How do you propose that we find that out?"

George rubbed his hand through his hair. "That will be harder to figure out, but I still think that the medallion itself holds the answer."

The young woman nodded her head. He heard her curse in a soft whisper. She was a writer, and he had just informed her that she could not write about the greatest story of her young life.

"I wonder if we could ask the medallion itself about its past owners." George scratched his head thoughtfully. "It might even have a rewind button or something like that."

"It is not a movie on your telly." Shelly snorted a small laugh. "But I know what you mean—it may actually maintain some type of record that we can access if we can figure out how to ask the right questions."

"Did you also notice that when I said the date I wanted the medallion to take us to, I didn't say the words June 7 in ancient Egyptian?"

Shelly leaned forward and studied the necklace. "I did notice that. Perhaps even when we say the words to open the door, we don't necessarily have to use that recording Carl made for you. Maybe it is about intent more than the actual words themselves."

"You mean this thing can read our minds and knows what we want or where we want to go?"

"It is a disturbing idea, but it makes some sense."

The two of them gazed down at the medallion, suddenly aware of how frightening an object it really was. If it could read minds, then it might be able to take them anywhere they wanted to go, and that widened the possibilities even further. George let out a deep breath, suddenly conscious of the fact that he had been holding his breath for the last few moments. He sighed and then leaned back in his chair. "So what do we ask?"

"Why."

"That is rather philosophical, don't you think?" He chuckled hoarsely.

"Not in the broad sense of the question." Shelly giggled. "I mean, we ask why someone would want this particular lame-duck president dead."

"I have often heard that expression in the media." George crossed his hands behind his head and closed his eyes again. He was suddenly very weary of this whole thing. "And to be honest, I never actually understood what it meant."

"Really?" Shelly said. "It means that he cannot run for a third term; the Americans allow their presidents to be in office for only two terms or eight years."

"Oh." George kept his eyes closed. "So he can start something, but he can't see it to its conclusion."

"Sort of," she said, nodding. "So if someone wanted him dead badly enough to hop onto a magic amulet, why wait until he had only a few months left in his term?"

George bolted upright and looked intently at the woman sitting across from him. "Now that is an intriguing question. There had to be something that he was about to do that would be a problem for someone, or why take such a huge risk?"

Shelly smiled at his sudden enthusiasm. "So how do we find that out?"

He pointed a long finger at her and smiled. "You, my dear, are going to find that out at the paper. Someone in the political realm must know what was about to happen in America."

"All right." She got slowly to her feet. "This afternoon I will run down to the paper and ask around. Maybe I can even make some contacts at the American networks. They must be reporting on his career and what he accomplished."

"Or more than likely would have if he had lived another few months."

Shelly stared down at George for a moment. "You really believe that whoever killed him came from the future and wanted to stop something that messed up their lives?"

"We have to consider the possibility."

Shelly headed toward the door. "I will go for some lunch and then down to the paper." She glanced back at him. "What are you going to do this afternoon, George?"

"I think I will go back to the library and do some more research on this goddess Bastet. There was a lot of information on the Internet about her, so maybe someone out there knows something we can use."

"All right," Shelly said, opening the door. "But be careful. I am beginning to believe that too much information about this thing could be dangerous."

"Are you telling me that a newspaper woman believes knowledge is a dangerous thing?" George wanted to laugh, but something made him stop.

"No." She turned back and gave him a smile. "But the person who committed this murder is dangerous. We have to keep that in mind."

ଔଔଔ

George watched her leave his flat without any further comment. He knew she was right. They were walking through some dangerous territory, and neither of them was prepared for where it might take them. When it started, George had simply been curious about the medallion and the role it might have played in the murder; now he was traveling through time and sailing into uncharted water. He had no idea where the next step might take them, and if he was not very careful, he might place himself and Miss Jenkins in real jeopardy. He sat there looking at his door, the one Shelly had just left through, and he felt sick inside.

This was no longer just about him and his curious nature; he had included that lovely woman in his escapades.

He knew that if he were a more responsible man, he would pull the plug on the entire adventure. He would keep her out of the line of fire and perhaps himself as well. The problem was that he no longer wanted to stop looking for the truth. It was no longer simply a question of curiosity; he honestly believed that if he could figure out how the necklace worked, he could save the man who had died Friday afternoon. He could change history, and that was a thrilling prospect.

CHAPTER 19

Shelly had said that she was going for lunch before she headed to the paper, but the truth was that she was not very hungry, so she headed to the office. She still had no idea whom she could approach about the president's agenda for the remaining months of his term. There were a great many writers delving into his work and his career, but who knew where those accomplishments might have led in the future? That was the real problem; no one had a crystal ball.

That image made her laugh because she did have a crystal ball in the shape of a little round necklace resting in her safety deposit box at that moment. She had gone to the bank and deposited it safely into the vault before heading to the paper. She wasn't sure why, but she felt better knowing where it was and that no one would be able to get to it except for her. Also, there was something unsettling about the thing, and she did not want to carry it around on her person, so it was better off where it was.

She sat at her desk and pretended to edit her piece on the college students and their perspectives. It was actually already done and had been sent to the editors. She was done with it, but she had to give herself something to do, or she would go insane. So she rewrote the thing that Perry had said was fine. Emmett had actually complimented her on the way she handled those kids, but the more she read the piece again, the less she liked it. Yet what if the very thing she was looking for had come up in that conversation among the students—the new bill on international companies? Could that be the thing someone wanted to kill along with the man?

Shelly leaped to her feet and headed for the editors' desks at the far end of the room. She needed answers, and the only person she knew with enough juice to give her some of those answers was Perry. She hated the idea of pumping him for information, but she could think of no one else to approach. He was pounding away on his laptop when she walked over to his desk, her heart beating so loud that she was certain he must have heard it across the room.

"Perry, can I ask you a question about my piece on the college students?"

"I told you it was fine." He did not even bother to look up. "Emmett said it was good to go."

"I know," she sighed. It was so odd that a few days ago she would have been thrilled to hear those words, but now she was feeling empty. "I was just wondering if those students were right about that bill the president had before Congress on international companies. Was it going to pass?"

"Unlikely." Perry shook his head. "Even if he had lived, it wouldn't have made it past the Senate."

"Oh." Her heart suddenly grew heavy. "So no one would have gone after him to stop that particular bill from going through?"

Perry looked up at her. "You have to be kidding. Shelly, that bill was never going to pass. Everyone knew that. Hell, I would bet that even he knew it was not going to pass, but it made the American public think he was doing something other than sitting on his lame-duck ass, waiting for the end of his term."

"So why do you think he was killed?"

Perry stared off into space. Shelly knew he had been considering that very question since Friday, just like the rest of them. Everyone around the world was asking the same thing and really getting no answers.

"Well?" she said, pressing him.

He shrugged his shoulders. "I seriously have no idea why anyone would go after him. He was done with his presidency, so killing him gets them nothing."

"Maybe it was a symbolic thing." Shelly cringed at the thought. She had thought the reign of terrorists was a thing of the past.

"Hardly likely." Perry drummed his fingers on his desk. "Besides, even if some terrorist group was reasserting itself, it would have already claimed responsibility, and not one of them as done that yet."

"Oh." She suddenly felt defeated. She worried that she would have nothing to bring back to George and their investigation. "There has to be someone who wanted him dead."

"You know, Emmett had a theory yesterday that fascinated the hell out of me." Perry was smiling, his face lit up. "Although it boggles the imagination to even consider it."

"What?" Shelly was very interested in anything that boggled the imagination because magic amulets certainly fit that bill.

"He wondered if it might have to do with the speculation that the president was going to be heading the newly created Polar Expeditions Oversight Committee for the UN after he stepped down from the White House."

Shelly gulped hard. She had been hearing about the Polar Expeditions Oversight Committee for years, but this was the first time she had heard anything concrete. "What would that committee do anyway?"

"Well, no one knows for certain except that they would be the ones to determine who would be allowed access to some of the international polar waters."

"That is interesting." Shelly leaped to her feet, her heart racing.

"Where are you going now?" Perry chuckled at her obvious enthusiasm.

"It might be worth talking to some eggheads at the university," she said as she headed for her desk. "You know, what do they think this might change in terms of who gets access to the north?"

"That is all speculation," Perry called after her. "But it may be worth a line or two, so go for it."

She was already heading for the door when it opened and two people in crisp uniforms appeared. She stopped, and her mind froze. They were clearly American military types, and the way they looked at her made her blood run ice-cold.

CHAPTER 20

The woman was older and had an air of authority that was unmistakable; she was in charge. She glared at Shelly with a look of pure contempt, and it made the young woman cringe.

"Miss Jenkins."

Shelly jumped at the sound of her name.

"We need a word with you."

"Who the bloody hell are you?" Perry exclaimed as he came running over to her rescue.

"I am Lieutenant Major Catherine Charter, and this is Sergeant Bell." The woman nodded at her companion, who seemed to be holding up the wall. "We need to ask this young woman some questions about the attack at the museum."

"If it is about her source," Perry said, his face rigid, "she is protected under the Privacy Act. Our journalists are protected just like yours are."

"We already know that she has been spending time with a security guard from the museum." Lieutenant Major Charter pulled out a notebook from her pocket. "A Mr. George Marsh to be precise. And if my guess is right, that is where she got her information."

Shelly gulped hard and nodded her head. She'd known it was possible that they were being followed, but this was a little too close for comfort. Did these people know she and George had been to the museum? Did they already know about the amulet? Were they here to take it away from her and end her investigation before it had really begun?

"So what if she has seen this man Marsh?" Perry was standing toe-to-toe with the uniformed woman. "That does not give you the right to barge in here like you're storming the beachhead at Normandy all over again. She is a journalist, and she has the right to interview a guard from the museum."

"Perhaps she does." Charter smiled knowingly. "But that does not explain why she attended a movie with this man and why the two of them used some pretext to enter the museum yesterday."

Shelly felt her heart drop into her shoes. "I wanted to see the crime scene," she finally whispered.

Perry turned and glared at her. "That was truly an idiotic thing to do."

"I know." Her voice was so low that he probably could barely hear her.

Perry then turned back to the woman who stood before him. "I am not saying she did the right thing, but it was understandable given the circumstances."

"Maybe it is." Charter smiled, which only gave her face a harder look. "However, what we do not understand is their interest in the display cases. It appears that they took one of the pieces and left with it."

Shelly thought she might throw up. George had been right about those stupid cameras being everywhere. God, was she about to be led off to a cell somewhere, never to be heard from again? She could feel the sweat building on her forehead as her mind raced. She had to come up with something fast to explain the damn missing amulet. "Well ... it is pretty," she finally stammered. "We could not get near the room where the president died, so Mr. Marsh took me into the room where the artifacts are displayed. He showed me the one that they found in the rubbish the day of the murder."

"Is that the one you took?" the young man in the corner asked, finally speaking for the first time.

Shelly jumped at the sound of Sergeant Bell's voice. "No, I saw another that was even nicer, and I asked if I could borrow it for a couple of days. George—I mean Mr. Marsh—argued about it, but I slipped it into his pocket anyway. I wanted to wear it just once to see what it felt like. I intend to give it back next week after my date."

Charter stared at her for a moment and then shook her head. "You have to be kidding me. You stole a four-thousand-year-old artifact to wear on a date?"

"Well, when you put it like that, it does sound stupid." Shelly laughed nervously.

"Where is the necklace now?" Bell asked flatly.

Shelly's laugh was cut short. She did not like where this was going. Were they going to ask for it back? "I actually put it in my safety deposit box this morning."

"So that explains your trip to the bank." Charter nodded her head in understanding.

"Do you want me to go get it?" Shelly fumbled with her keys for a moment. "I could, and you could return it to the museum. I know that I should not have borrowed it, and I am willing to face the consequences of my actions."

"Bloody hell," Perry snorted.

"No, that is all right." Charter shook her head. "We do not have time for fools' errands. I do have one more question, though: what else have you and Mr. Marsh discussed besides stolen necklaces?"

"His life at the museum." Shelly gulped hard. She knew instinctively that this woman was not buying any of this story. "I thought it would be a nice follow-up piece later on when the dust settles on the case."

"Has he given you anything interesting?"

"Not really." Shelly fumbled with her keys again. "He is actually a rather boring man."

"Too bad." Charter turned and pointed to the elevator, and Bell fell in step beside her. "Just get that stupid necklace back to the museum after we allow it to reopen. I do not want you using it as an excuse to come down there while we are still investigating the crime scene."

"Is there anything you can add regarding the investigation?" Perry quickly asked, his reporter's instincts kicking in as the pair stepped into the elevator.

"Not at this time." Charter smiled coldly as the elevator door closed.

As Shelly stood staring at the elevator door, she could feel Perry's anger growing with each passing moment.

He finally spun around and glared at her. "What the hell were you thinking, going to the museum when it's locked and stealing a necklace like that? Have you gone completely mad?"

"Perry, it is not how it sounds."

"It bloody well better not be," he said, slamming his fist against his thigh. "I was ready to smack you when you said you wanted to wear it on a date. You have to know that those people did not buy any of that idiotic tale and that they will be on you from now on." As he stared at her, his eyes suddenly glimmered with knowledge. "You did take the one that was found in the rubbish bin, didn't you?"

"Well ... yes," she stammered.

Perry's eyes softened, and a knowing smile crossed his lips. "I had a feeling you were not as stupid as you pretended to be."

"George—Mr. Marsh—he thought it really did mean something even though the investigators dismissed it, so we wanted to study it up close," she whispered. She hated giving up this much information, but she had to say something to appease Perry.

The editor cocked his head to one side and suddenly smiled from ear to ear. "Smart girl. When you do have something, let me know. And keep one eye on your back because those people are nobody's fools—they know something is up." He turned and headed back to his desk.

"Yes, sir," she giggled as she grabbed her purse and headed for the elevator that the Americans had just used.

☙☙☙

Perry watched her leave, and for a brief moment, he felt a wave of fear wash over him. He had no idea what had suddenly made him so afraid. After all, she was doing exactly what she was paid to do: digging for the truth. He leaned back in his chair and glanced over at Emmett's door. He was the best newsman in the business, and that was the only thing Emmett ever got right. Perry sat back up and began to type again on the computer. He needed to work. He needed to feel a story pulsing through his fingers. He did not want to think about Shelly Jenkins or that confrontation with the Americans, and for the first time in his long relationship with the chief editor, Perry was not going to fill Emmett in on a major breaking story. It might be a mistake, but it was one he would have to live with. Besides, if the medallion turned out to be just an old piece of junk, he did not want Emmett getting on Shelly's case about stealing the bloody thing.

CHAPTER 21

George sat at a computer in the library, perplexed by the material in front of him. Bastet was the protector of the pharaoh and was one of the many deities that the ancient priests prayed to each day. The whole thing seemed rather silly to him, but then he had never been a praying sort of man. Hell, he had not been inside a church since his mother's funeral five years ago, and he had found that to be an exercise in futility. She was gone, and nothing the minister could say would make him feel any better about it.

He had never been close to his father, who had left when he was eight, and when his mother had gotten cancer, George felt as if the God the old lady prayed to daily was letting her down. Maybe that was the real problem with his life—he really did not believe in very much, and now here he believed in the most outlandish thing imaginable. He headed outside and sat down on a bench outside the entrance to the subway.

"Mr. Marsh."

Startled, George looked up and saw a woman in a military uniform standing before him.

"We need a word with you," she said with an American accent.

"All right," he said, faking a smile. He knew that showing fear would only add to their suspicions. He thought he recognized the woman from the museum and the security teams that had been crawling over the building for the last few days. "Anything I can do to help."

"Really?" the younger man standing behind her growled. "You want to help, yet you were told not to talk to the press."

George walked into the bright sunlight and squinted. "I know I was."

"Yet you did talk to them." The woman sat down beside him. "We just met with her at the newspaper."

George frowned, and for a moment he wondered what he could say to protect Shelly. He decided a little bit of the truth would not do any harm and might in the long run help them discover who had killed the president. "I know it was foolish of me, but she is such a pretty thing."

"So she flattered you," the woman sighed, "and you folded like a bad poker hand."

George laughed at the image. "Yes, I did. I am not that strong when it comes to lovely young lasses, and she is the best-looking bird I have seen in a long time. I know it was stupid, but when she flashed that smile, I had to say something to keep her talking to me."

"Oh brother," the young man said, rolling his eyes. "This is the dumbest thing I have ever heard."

"Sergeant, be nice." The woman shook her head, and a smile began to form on her tight face. "Mr. Marsh is a typical male, and when a lovely woman like Miss Jenkins flashes a smile, many do react. I will not criticize him for that, but I do take exception to his bringing her into the museum when we are investigating."

George felt the smile leave his face. What had he pulled Shelly into? "You know about that?"

"We are not stupid, Mr. Marsh," the sergeant growled. "We have it on tape, and we have evidence that you allowed her to take a necklace from a display case."

"She told us that she wanted to wear it on a date. Is that why you allowed her to steal a four-thousand-year-old piece of jewelry?"

George wanted to laugh but could think of nothing funny about any of this. Had they gone too far in taking that thing out of the museum, and would Shelly face criminal charges because of it? Was she really willing to go that far for a story? He also had to wonder how far he was willing to go and why he was bothering with any of this. "I thought when she said she wanted it for a date, she meant with me. However, I know now that she meant with someone else."

The young officer shook his head in frustration. "You have got to be kidding."

"I realize I am being an old fool, but she is so pretty."

"Mr. Marsh," the woman sighed again, "Miss Jenkins said she would return the necklace after we reopen the museum, and we are willing to leave it at that, but the two of you must stay away from the museum during this investigation. Is that understood?"

"Yes, it is understood." George sighed. Shelly seemed to have gotten them out of this mess, but it still terrified him that the American military was watching him.

"Good." The woman smiled at him and started to leave but quickly turned back. "One more thing: did you notice anything odd going on the morning of the day before the attack?"

"Before the attack?" George asked. "Why?"

"The cameras were off for two minutes, and the techs can't seem to explain it."

"I never heard anything about that." He cringed at the thought that two minutes of footage was missing from the logs, but this might explain when the necklace was originally taken. "But then the techs don't seem to consult me about a hell of a lot."

"They just discovered it yesterday." She tapped a finger against the back of her hand. "The problem is that two minutes is a very small window of opportunity to do anything, especially when nothing was tampered with."

"What do you mean?"

"She means that the security system remained intact, and no alarms were set off." The young man seemed to go rigid, his eyes dark and menacing.

"That doesn't make much sense," George said, shaking his head. "They couldn't have even deactivated the alarms to the mummy cases in two minutes when there were so many people in the area."

"That is what I said." The woman started off down the sidewalk, with her colleague following her. "But if you think of anything that might explain it, let me know. You can contact us at the museum."

"Yes, ma'am," he called after her, his mind reeling.

George stood outside the library for another ten minutes, the events replaying in his mind. He tried to come up with something that could explain those missing two minutes, but the Thursday before the attack had been like any other day; nothing had happened that warranted special attention from the guards. No alarms had been set off, and no one had said anything about missing footage from the camera logs. He certainly would have remembered that. He shook his head and headed for the tube.

The Americans had been right about one thing: two minutes was not a lot of time to get to the mummy cases, let alone tamper with the alarms. There had to be something about that time period that had allowed someone to access the cases and take the medallion without arousing suspicion, but how could that be done? He had walked the floors of the building many times, and even at a dead run, a person couldn't make it from the security offices where the cameras were controlled to the artifact display in two minutes. So there had to be some other explanation for the lost moments in the log, but what could they be?

He entered the subway and headed down the stairs, his mind on the museum and its long staircase. The goal the morning before the attack had to have been the retrieval of the necklace; it was the only explanation that made any sense. In order to use it to kill the president, the murderer needed to steal it. So the assassin must have cut the camera feed to cover up the theft. Yet two minutes seemed a rather short period of time to accomplish such a monumental task as entering the display area, deactivating the alarms, and taking the medallion. George played it over and over in his mind as he waited for the train, but he could come up with nothing to explain it.

In the dark outside his flat, he saw Shelly's car and held his breath. There were corners, alleys, and bins where the American agents or others could be hidden to watch his every move, and that worried him. They had to know where he lived and even now could see Shelly parked in front of his building. He did not even bother to smile as he walked up and knocked on the window of the vehicle. She was staring off into space, her mind obviously elsewhere. She unlocked the door and gestured for him to get in.

"Did the Yanks come calling on you today?" she asked as he slid into the passenger's seat.

"They found me outside the library just after I left, and they had a lot of questions about you and some medallion you stole to wear on a date." He closed the door and waited for her to start the car.

"I couldn't think of anything else to tell them." She kept her eyes glued to something that only she seemed able to see outside the window. "I told them we took a different medallion, not the one that was found in the rubbish bin. But Perry knows it really was that medallion. I wasn't able to fool him ... And now that I think about it, they probably know it was the one in the trash. It would be easy enough for them to figure that out."

"All right." George fidgeted uneasily in his seat. "But the Americans know we were in the museum. We have to be careful that they do not pull us in and question us about the medallion because, girl, I do not foresee myself lasting in prison."

She spun around and stared at him. "Do you think it will come to that?"

"I don't know," he said, shrugging his shoulders, "but the hard truth is that we have to be a little more wary, or we will both be called to the mat and have a lot of explaining to do."

"Explaining," she said with a nervous chuckle. "I doubt I could explain it even if I wanted to."

"I know," he said, nodding in agreement. "But they did give me a piece of information that intrigued me and adds another layer of mystery to the whole adventure."

Shelly smiled for a moment and then shook her head. "Like we need more layers to this mystery."

"I know. It is beginning to hurt my head too." The guard laughed uneasily, and he told her about the missing minutes.

"Two minutes." Shelly was shocked. "What the hell could anyone have done in two minutes?"

"I have no idea, but that is what they told me. Now we have to piece it together with what we have learned about the medallion's powers."

Shelly stared out the window of the car at the gathering twilight. She leaned forward and put her head on the steering wheel.

"What are we going to do, Miss Jenkins?" he whispered.

"George," she said as she finally sat up and sighed heavily, "if I could, I would run and hide, but I doubt if that is even an option now."

He wanted to reach over and pat her back, soothing away all her fears, but what was the point? He had no way to take away the horror of this moment. They were stuck in a mystery, and the only way out was to move forward and pray that in doing so they did not end up in prison or, worse, dead. He shuddered at the thought, but he had been thinking it since they stepped through the door into June 7. Someone was playing for keeps and had already killed once, so if that person discovered that the two of them were on the trail, it was altogether possible that George and Shelly might end up just as dead as the mummies in the display cases.

"Shelly," he finally said, "let's take this one step at a time. We need to figure out why this is happening. Why did someone want this man dead, and why did he or she go to such extreme lengths to make it happen?"

Shelly sighed again and turned the motor back on. "I think I might have an answer for that one. I will explain it over some curry and chips."

ঙঙঙ

They headed to Shelly's favorite Indian takeaway restaurant and ordered some curry to go. George paid for the meal, and as they drove back to his flat, they listened to some Beatles tracks. They did not discuss the ongoing mystery that seemed to be pulling them toward disaster. Back at the flat, as they ate, the silence deepened and grew to an unease that threatened to engulf both of them.

Shelly finally decided it was time to end the stalemate, and as she took a long drink from her bottle of ale, she shook her head in anticipation. "Perry thinks that President Carlson may have been killed because he was going to take over some Polar Expeditions Oversight Committee for the UN after he was finished with the White House."

"You have to be joking." George popped the last chip into his mouth. "What would that get anyone?"

"Well," she said, leaning back in her chair, "from what I have been able to piece together, there is a lot of unexplored territory at both ends of the globe. And since some of that region is deemed international, whoever can claim it can be the one to develop the territory if he or she can get the UN to agree."

George chewed thoughtfully on the chip. "So ... you think that someone thought the president was not going to approve some development among the penguins, and because of that they stole a four-thousand-year-old necklace and risked time travel in order to ice the man."

Shelly smirked. "Sounds rather ridiculous when you put it like that."

"But don't you see? It isn't ridiculous at all." George leaned across the table. "It makes perfect sense."

"How do you come up with that?"

"The person who had the most to gain by killing him now would be someone who had invested a lot of money in Arctic or Antarctic funds. Risking time travel to change that makes a whole lot of sense."

Shelly hated to admit it, but she had been thinking the same thing since talking to Perry and the academics she had been able to waylay at the university coffee shop earlier in the afternoon. "All right, say I agree with you—and to be perfectly honest, I do. How do we figure out who had the most to gain from his death? There are a great many developers who hate his stance against polar development."

"There is a way we can really narrow this down."

The smile on his face made her very uneasy. "Please tell me you are not thinking about doing something stupid like using the medallion to jump forward to see who made the most from his death."

"Why not?" he said with a smirk. "It would help us narrow our search and give us access to the key players."

CHAPTER 22

"Oh my God." She jumped to her feet and began to pace around the room. "I can't believe you are even considering this."

"Shelly," he said, trying to keep his voice even and calm, "I know it is a rather bizarre thing to do, but I do not see how else we can make certain we go after the right one."

She stopped directly in front of him. "Say you do narrow it down to one killer—the right one. What then?"

He looked up at her, and for the first time since the idea of traveling to the future had crossed his mind, he had to admit he had no earthly idea what he would do with the information once he had it. Would they then be able to go back in time and stop the murder, perhaps talk to the individual's younger self to stop the assassination before it even occurred? Or maybe they could use the medallion to interfere with the plot in the future to stop this murderer from traveling back to kill the president. There were a lot of theoretical courses of action, and none of them actually sounded remotely possible. Yet they did have a magical amulet, so perhaps the actions were possible if they were willing to take the risk.

"Again, we will have to cross that bridge when we come to it." He rose to his feet to face Shelly. "But we are the only ones who can cross it."

Shelly flopped into a chair and glared up at him. "What if I do not want to cross that bridge or go through that damn door with you? I am tired of the unbelievable being suddenly real. I have always been a realist, George, and you are asking me to believe in a fantasy. I can't do it."

George tried smiling at her, wishing he could find some way to ease her fears, but he knew that in reality there was no way to do that. "Shelly, I can think of no other way to find out what we need to know. Today there are a lot of people putting in bids to the Polar Expeditions Oversight Committee—hell, even I know that from what your paper has reported about the dumb thing. We need to narrow that list down to one name or a group, and in order to do that, we need to discover who had the most to gain."

"One name," she repeated, her voice small and meek.

"One name or a group, like I said," he said, nodding in agreement. "And in order to get it down to that, we need to jump forward in time."

"How far are you suggesting we jump?" She seemed to be staring straight ahead into space now.

"Well," he said, smiling uneasily, "that is an interesting question. We would have to go far enough that the museum would be open and that the person in question would no longer see an investigation as a threat. Plus, it would also help if I was no longer working there, so we would no longer risk running into me."

She sighed heavily. "You are talking a lot of years ahead then."

"Well, in some ways it would help if it was a lot of years, so that it would appear that we are studying the crime from a historical perspective. Fifty or a hundred might be right."

"A hundred years." She sounded like a child crying over a lost toy.

He reached out and patted her back. "Shelly, we have no choice in this thing. We have to go far enough ahead to make it look like a historical study rather than a police investigation."

"Historical." She looked up at him, a thin smile on her frightened face. "I never liked history."

He smiled back at her. "Today the future is historical for us."

"And that is supposed to sound logical?" She shook her head. "All right, when do we make this leap forward?"

He rose to his feet and held out his hand to help her up. "Tomorrow morning should be fine. You pick up the medallion at the bank and meet me here, and then we can open the door."

"You will have to pick the date."

At the door, he could tell that she was a feeling a little wobbly, and the two held hands for a moment. She seemed terrified to let go, and George did not like the idea of letting her go either, even for one evening. He knew it was stupid to think about, but he was falling in love with her.

Shelly leaned forward and put her head on his chest. "Please tell me again what we will do if we find out who killed the president."

He pulled her close and hugged her tight. "I actually have no idea, but it is the only option that we have right now."

After a few minutes he let her go rather reluctantly and held the door for her. After she walked away, George leaned against the door, breathing heavily. Had he just had that beautiful young woman in his arms? Had he really held her? Just a few days ago, he would have considered that to be out of the realm of possibility, and now she was here, a part of his life. He knew it was wrong, but he actually wanted to meet the assassin in order to thank him for bringing Shelly Jenkins into his life. He finally walked back to the table and sat down. Leaning forward, he placed his head in his hands. He had a lot to think about. Shelly had left the details of their journey up to him, and the truth was he had no idea as to where or when they should travel. Tomorrow was about to be a hundred years away, and he needed to be exact, or the door might not comply with their request.

The kitten padded over to him and wound around his legs, purring. George reached down and patted its tiny head. "I wonder if you can give me some hints, little one. After all, the goddess Bastet is shaped like a cat."

The cat looked up at him and gave out a little meow. George laughed and rose to his feet. "No answer, but I will feed you anyway." He headed to the cupboard and pulled out a can of food for the animal. "But if you do have any contributions to make to this expedition, now would be a great time to do that."

The animal waited patiently for the food to be placed on the floor and then began to eat. George watched the cat for a moment and then headed into his bedroom. He knew that he would not get much sleep, but what else was he going to do? He undressed, lay down on the bed, and waited for morning to bring Shelly back to him.

CHAPTER 23

George got out of bed at eight in the morning, but the truth was that he had not slept. He spent the morning watching television, but nothing seemed to hold his interest for long. Besides, too much of it was about the assassination, which made him comfortable, so after an hour or so he turned it off. He wandered around his flat for a while, and by ten thirty, he was beginning to wonder if she was ever going to show up.

"Did I scare her off?" he finally asked the animal sleeping on the chair. "Asking her to travel that far into the future may have been too much for her."

The cat did not even wake up at the sound of his voice. George shrugged his shoulders and laughed at his own behavior. He had never been one to talk to pets, even though he'd had them around most of his life, but now he was asking for a kitten's input into his sudden interest in Egyptology and the woman who had been visiting them the last few days. It had slowly occurred to George that Shelly was the only woman who had ever really stepped foot into his life, and that made him feel rather sad and pathetic.

"I wonder what she must think of me," he said as the cat stretched in the morning sunlight streaming into the room. "Especially after that hug last night and the way I have reacted when she has taken my hand. God, I am such an old fool!"

The cat purred and curled into a ball before closing its eyes again. George shook his head, a slight smile on his face. "You really are no help. Do you know that?"

He was beginning to believe that he had seen the last of Shelly Jenkins and the medallion. He also worried that perhaps those American agents had picked her up and were now grilling her over the medallion and her and George's interest in it. He was ready to leave and look for his companion when there was a timid knock on his door at 11:05 a.m. When he opened the door, the young reporter walked into the room and flopped into a chair at the table. Things were beginning to seemed strained between them. Or maybe they were both beginning to realize that they did not really know each other at all.

Shelly pulled the box containing the medallion out of her bag and placed it on the table. "So have you determined where this damn thing is going to take us?" Her voice was filled with sarcasm and venom, and it made George shudder.

George sighed and sat down across from his visitor. "Shelly, if you are so afraid of this, then I can go alone."

"What?" Her eyes shot daggers at him. "After all of this, do you really think I would let you go alone? I may be afraid—hell, I am terrified beyond belief—but I am going to go through with it."

"Only if you are certain." He smiled at her.

"Of course I am not certain." Her eyes fell to the box that lay between them. "We are discussing jumping one hundred years into the future. But if it is the only way to discover the truth, then I am willing to try it."

"All right." He reached out and opened the box. "Let us begin with some decisions. First, I have given it some thought, and fifty years makes more sense than one hundred. We don't want to go so far into the future that we will look completely out of place and attract undue attention."

"God, you are right." Her eyes were suddenly the size of saucers. "Who knows what they will be wearing in 2120? Look at the changes between 1900 and 2000."

George nodded in agreement. "Exactly. Not to mention the changes in technology. Your cell phone may look like a dodo in 2120. The leaps forward in the last twenty years have scared me half to death, so it is terrifying to even think about what they will come up with in the next fifty years." George was a bit of a dinosaur when it came to technology. He had no cell phone, did not carry a tablet, and did not have a computer in his flat. He had forgone that part of the twenty-first century.

"Yeah, they may even have perfected the flying car by then."

"Yikes." He cringed at the thought. "We will need to dress very plainly and be as nondescript as possible. I do not want to be tossed into a jail, trying to explain who I am to a bobby from 2070."

"All right." She was suddenly smiling. "So maybe it will be easier if we do not carry any identification of any kind. I don't know about you, but even my driver's license has an expiration date on it."

"Not to mention your birth date."

"Oh my God, I never thought about that." She pulled her wallet out of her bag. "I doubt I could pass for seventy-five."

George stared at her for a moment. Was he really falling in love with some twenty-five-year-old beauty? He shook his head and placed his own wallet on the table. "We will also have to leave all our money behind. The old girl may seem immortal, but I doubt the queen will be around in 2070."

Shelly roared with laughter. "I am glad you are in charge of this little expedition because I never would have thought of any of these things." She put all her change and paper currency on the table beside her identification. "I wonder who will be on the throne in 2070."

"Maybe William," George said, sighing at the thought. "He is still young enough that he should be alive then, but it could also be George by then. So check your bag and pockets for anything that indicates a date."

"Right, boss." Shelly saluted him and then began to rummage through her purse. "Do you think I should take my cell phone then? I mean, it does have a date indicator on it."

"God no. Leave it." He put his own money beside hers. "The problem is that we may need money, and without cash what will we be able to use?"

Shelly's face fell. "How long do we plan on being in 2070?"

George froze, his hands on the table. He had not really thought too much about that. How long would they need to be there to determine who was responsible for the murder? He finally shrugged his shoulders and sighed. "I am not certain, but it could be only a few hours or a couple of days at the most."

"Days!" Shelly's voice rose an octave. "You are kidding."

"Did you really think the information we need would be so easy to come across that we could get it within a few minutes of landing there?"

"No, I guess not." Her eyes fell back to her bag. "I was just hopeful that we would not have to be there too long."

"Shelly," he said, reaching out and taking her hand in his, "I am not thrilled by the idea of spending too much time there either, but we have to be realistic about this thing. No one is going to hand us exactly what we need the moment we walk into the museum."

"Realistic." She shook her head at the word. "What the hell is realistic about spending multiple days fifty years in the future?"

"Realistic or not, we may still need some form of currency."

Shelly looked down at the money on the table and gingerly picked up a twenty-note. "You know, it might not be a bad idea to take some of it with us. If it's not useful as currency, we could take it to an antique coin dealer or something like that, and it may get us the cash we need to make it around 2070."

George picked up another note and turned it around in his hand. "Now who is thinking clearly? I never would have thought about that."

Shelly smiled at him and placed her money in her pocket. "Who knows? They may even give us more than face value for it."

George put his own cash back into his pocket. "Now we need to consider the exact date in 2070. It should be when the museum is open, which is six days a week. I do not know about you, but my knowledge about the days of the week in 2070 is a little rusty."

"That is easy to determine." Shelly pulled her tablet from her bag and turned it on. She typed away on the keypad, and it gave her access to a perpetual calendar. "So what day of the week do you want?"

George chuckled uneasily. He wished he was a little more at ease with computers and technology, but he had never seen any real use for computers until now. "Well, if the present day is anything to go by, Monday is the slowest day of the week at the museum, so it would be the best day for us to show up. And if we do the same thing as before and show up just after the museum opens, there should not be too many people in the mummy room."

"All right, a Monday." Shelly stared at the tablet. "Any month strike your fancy?"

"September," he said, nodding solemnly. "If we keep it close to the actual month we are in and maybe close to this date, it will be easier to remember."

"Trust me, I am not going to forget this day anytime soon." Shelly continued to type away on her tablet. "So September 17, 2070, would be our best bet."

"Sounds good to me." He sighed and rose stiffly to his feet. "Are we ready to go then?"

"Now?" She glared up at him.

"Do you have any objections?" He offered his hand, and she took it.

"I just wish I was not so damn scared, George." She took a step toward the large man.

"Me too." The problem was he was just as scared about having her near him as he was about the prospect of traveling through time. "So we need the necklace, some paper for notes, and some old money to exchange for the local, and we are good to go."

"Right." She grabbed her bag and checked for paper and a pen. "I wonder if they will know what a pen is in 2070."

"Let us not overthink this thing, my girl," he said, laughing at her. "But do try to use it very little."

She laughed and then opened the box. She stared at the necklace for what seemed an eternity before slipping it around her neck. "We will need my phone, George, because it has the recording of Carl saying the words."

"No, we won't." He took her hand in his. "Remember, it can read our intent, so we do not need the ancient language. It will know what we mean once the door appears. We have to trust it, and if it opens with English, we will not need your cell phone."

The two held hands, and Shelly whispered the words: "Open to protect the pharaoh." A moment passed, and they both began to wonder whether the door might not open with the English translation. Maybe they would need Carl's recording to make it work after all. Then suddenly, the door opened, and they saw the mummy room. No one was in the room, but Shelly did not want to risk the security guards seeing them. Quickly, she whispered, "September 17, 2070, 0900 hours."

CHAPTER 24

As it had before, the room before them swirled and shimmered into a graceful circle before coming to a stop. The two of them stared into the mummy room, and then hand in hand, they stepped through the door, which closed softly behind them. As it closed, Shelly realized she had been holding her breath and slowly let it out. She released George's hand and walked over to the mummy case. "These things are so creepy."

"Yes, they are." The voice behind them made both of them jump. A young man in a bright blue uniform came up to them. "Considering how long ago these people were entombed, it would be hard not to be a little creepy."

George walked to where Shelly was standing. "How long have you worked here, sir?"

"Three years now." The young man smiled, but he looked at them as if they were as out of date as the mummy in the case. "The mummies are really rather interesting, but not too many people agree with me about that."

Shelly noticed George studying the man, who had short brown hair and soft brown eyes to match.

"Do many people visit the museum?" George asked.

The young man's smile faded. "Not as many as they say used to," he answered sadly, "but history does lose its charm after a while."

"Someone told me that a man was murdered in this room." Shelly grabbed for George's hand. "But that might just be a story."

The young man brightened again. "Oh, it is no story. An American president was assassinated here in 2020; actually, it was almost exactly fifty years ago."

"Oh." Shelly cringed. "George, can we get out of here? This place is really beginning to give me the creeps."

"Certainly, my dear." George headed for the door and did not glance back at the employee, who was staring at the mummy cases. "We can't spend all day in the museum."

It was odd, but Shelly really did not want to be in a room where a man had died, even if it had been fifty years ago. It had been only a day or two since she had wanted to be shown the death room, and now she had no desire to be anywhere near it. Perhaps the truth was that she did not have the stomach for crime scenes. She had recently asked Perry and Emmett for the crime desk, which she now realized was a stupid request. When they got back, she would withdraw that and ask for something a little less gruesome.

"Nothing has changed much around here," George whispered as they walked down the hall. He looked around, seemingly fascinated. "Then again, in all the years between when this place opened and our real time, what the hell has changed? There are a few different cases and displays here, but otherwise, it all looks the same."

Yet both of them knew that the museum was not the real world, and outside of its hallowed halls, the world might look vastly different.

They headed for the main staircase and for the large main doors. Shelly held her breath and wondered if it would be appropriate for her to take some pictures of the world around them. She then remembered that George had made her leave her cell phone behind. Besides, what difference would it make if she did record the images she saw? No one would ever believe they were real.

"Look, girl. Even that silly door looks the same—huge, ornate, and oddly important," George laughed, "just like it does every morning that I unlock it."

Out on the street, the world changed, and the two stopped to stare at the scene playing out before them. The first thing Shelly noticed was the lack of traffic. It was London, but the congestion seemed to have disappeared. The cars were basically unchanged in design, although they did seem a tad smaller and a little more streamlined. Shelly stared in complete awe at the little motorcars as they zoomed past her at a pace she had never witnessed on the streets of London. She wondered where all the cars had gone in the last fifty years.

Although there were people on the street moving along at a brisk pace, as they always had, there seemed to be less chaos than in the London they knew. The street seemed cleaner and filled with a calm that Shelly Jenkins had never witnessed in her life. The sun reflected off the grass and the stonework on the massive building behind them. The passersby stared at them as if they were part of the exhibit in the main hall of the museum, and for the first time in her life, she knew what the saying "a fishbowl existence" really meant.

She realized that it was not just the calm or sun that created an atmosphere of color in this new London; it was also the people moving briskly past them. They were wearing a rainbow of colors and patterns she had never seen in fashion. The only word she could think of to describe the clothes and the looks on people's faces was "happy." Everyone seemed happy, and that was not something she was used to in her city.

"Where do we go?" she finally whispered.

"I have no idea." George laughed as the pair realized that he had no real plan as to how they could get the information that they needed.

"There is a library not far from here," Shelly suggested, "or at least there used to be."

"All right." George took her hand, and they began to walk toward the library. As they walked, both were visibly shaken by the feeling of being stuck in a place they did not belong.

"Why are they wearing all these colors?" George whispered uneasily.

"No kidding," Shelly giggled. Everyone she knew wore dark blues, greens, and browns. They certainly did not go around in purples, bright yellows, and pastels, but here even the men wore bright yellow suits. "Maybe the world is a happier place today, and that is reflected in the clothing."

"Now that sounds nice." George smiled as someone stared at his tailored white shirt and blue jeans. "But it makes the two of us stand out like a crow among a flock of peacocks."

"We need to find an antique dealer and exchange our money fast so that we can buy some clothes and blend in." Shelly was suddenly vibrating with excitement. She had not wanted to come on this trip, but now that she was here, she could not imagine anywhere else on earth she wanted to be.

"Well, there used to be some down this way." George grabbed her hand and pulled her toward a side street.

It took some time, but they finally found a dealer of rare coins and bills who eyed the crisp 2020 notes with a skeptical eye. "I have not seen ones this good or in this fine shape in many years."

"I came across them in my grandmother's attic," George said, nervously glancing around the very clean shop, "and I thought they might be worth something."

"Did you find those clothes in her attic too?" The man shook his head at their odd attire. "I have never seen clothes like those outside some display cases."

"Yeah, he did," Shelly said, "and when he showed them to me, I thought it might be a hoot to wear them for at least one day." Shelly smiled coyly at the dealer. "Don't you find them interesting?"

"Interesting maybe," the man said, scratching his thick head of hair, "but also rather boring in terms of the color."

"They are rather drab colors," George said, laughing uneasily. "I told you, girl, that we look ridiculous in these togs."

"Oh, loosen up, will you?" She poked him in the ribs and then glanced at the dealer. "He never wants to try anything new or different."

The dealer shook his head, and although he was still frowning, Shelly could see the tiniest glint of humor in his steel-gray eyes. She had won him over with the crazy teenager act, at least for the time being. "So what will you give this stiff for that old money?"

They negotiated for fifteen minutes before settling on a price for the coins and bills. The travelers briefly stared at the money the dealer gave them in exchange, almost terrified to look at the picture on the bills or at the dates on the coins. They left the antique shop and walked to a clothing store down the street that Shelly had noticed earlier. The girl in the shop wanted to buy their blue jeans, but they thought it would be better to keep their clothes for the return journey to their own time. Thirty minutes later, the two of them were walking down the street, George in a bright orange suit and Shelly in pastel-purple pants and shirt featuring a lively pattern. Each time they looked at each other, they could not help but laugh.

"I hope no one I know sees me looking like this," George giggled. "I look like some Las Vegas pimp."

"No one you know would still be alive in this time," Shelly said, patting his hand. "Hell, there may be very few of my age around and if we are lucky the ones still alive won't bump into us."

"All right." He cringed at the idea that everyone he knew was more than likely dead. "We look the part. Now can we head to the library and find out why someone fifty years ago wanted the president dead?"

"I was thinking we could also find something to eat. I am starving."

He stopped and looked at the smiling young woman on his arm. "You know, for someone who fought me tooth and nail about this trip, you certainly seem excited to be here."

"I know it is stupid," Shelly giggled. "I should be shaking in my go-go boots, but George, this is exciting even if a little terrifying."

He looked down at her feet. "They do sort of look like those 1960s go-go boots I have seen in old movies." George began walking again.

"Styles are cyclical, you know." Shelly smiled knowingly. "My aunt used to say she kept everything because sooner or later it would come back into fashion."

"When did men ever wear bright orange suits?"

"Well, that does not always apply to all fashion." She laughed again. "But I must admit, that color rather suits you."

George stopped again and pulled her to him. "No one looks good dressed as an overripe piece of fruit."

She saw the hardness in his deep blue eyes, and she realized that he was very serious. "George, come on. I was just teasing you. I know that you are uncomfortable, and quite frankly, so am I, but we are stuck with these bizarre clothes until we can go back through the door."

He loosed his grip on her arm and relaxed his gaze. "I am so sorry. I just feel so stupid in this outfit."

Shelly patted his hand and pulled him back down the street. Twenty minutes later, they found the library and realized that they had no idea what constituted a library in 2070. The sign for the redbrick building before them read "Depository," and both of them stared at it in utter amazement.

"Depository of what?" George whispered.

"Only one way to find out." She grabbed his arm and dragged him through the open door.

Inside, the room was brightly illuminated with yellow light. Across the back of the main room stood banks of computer terminals, with a number hanging over each bank. The sign for the group of computers at the far end read 2000, and beside it was 2010; the terminals seemed to be in increments of tens. Shelly walked over to the computer at the end of the row and stared at it, uncertain about what she was supposed to do.

"Can I help you, Miss?" asked a young man in a rather outlandish purple uniform as he walked over to her. "Are you interested in early twenty-first-century history?"

"What?" She was suddenly quite flustered.

"Yes, we are," George said, joining her. "But I am more interested in the 2020 years myself."

"Oh, that is an interesting time period." The man pointed to the terminal marked 2020. "So much upheaval, and of course, there were the Mars rovers debates in 2029, which led to the immigration to the colonies in 2042."

"Mars rovers," Shelly repeated. She suddenly felt sick. Was that where all the people and traffic had gone? Was most of the human population now living on the red planet?

"I thought about going myself," the young man said, tapping the terminal in front of Shelly, "but my mother was dead set against it, not to mention I had already applied to the history society to work here."

"Hard to turn down a good job," George said, smiling at the young man.

"Yes, it is." The young man turned to leave them to their studies. "Besides, it is hard to find work in my field on a brand-new colony like Mars."

"What is your field?" George called after him.

"History, of course," he answered before heading to the far side of the room.

George smiled, and Shelly could see he was amused. Even in 2070, there were still people who were fascinated by the past. Every era had its historians.

"So what can this stupid machine tell us about the years following the death of the president?" asked George.

Shelly flexed her fingers and tapped the screen, which brought up a list of dates and names. They both stared at the information, unsure of what to do with it. "We could start with the days following the assassination and go from there. Besides, someone may have already solved the crime," said Shelly.

George shook his head. "I doubt it, but it is worth a shot. And then we can look into exploration of the polar regions in the years following that moment in time. Why don't we try something later and work backward?"

"How much later?" Shelly tapped the screen again.

"Try 2025," George said with a grimace.

Shelly tapped the screen and brought up a file on 2025. She scanned the files but quickly realized that they needed to narrow their search. She typed in the words "polar committee" to see what that might get them. A long list of results popped up that seemed related to the ongoing debates surrounding polar development. She tapped one result, which brought up a holographic video that began to play, showing ice and snow in the background. Shelly had heard that some high-tech firm was working on this technology, but the effect still took her breath away.

They listened as the narration began. "The UN subcommittee was still holding evaluation meetings in 2025 concerning the oil fields that many considered unnecessary, considering the newer technologies being developed. No one could foresee the fields making anyone a profit when the oil was really no longer needed for commercial usage. Considering the environmental impact such developments would have on the northern and southern poles, the reasons for the development were unclear. By 2027, when biodegradable fuels replaced oil in all commercial enterprises, the oil fields were abandoned."

"That is good to hear," George whispered in her ear. "I never did like the idea of drilling in the ice fields."

"Me neither," Shelly agreed. "But if the development was called off, why go after the president? There has to be some reason for his death."

The video continued. "The polar committee then was reconvened in 2029 when the Mars rover project debate was heating up, to consider using the poles as launch sites for the rocket sleds."

Shelly tapped to close the video. "They wanted to use the poles as airports to send large numbers of people to Mars." She sighed at the very thought of millions of people tramping all over the Arctic and Antarctic, destroying the habitats of the polar bears, penguins, and walruses.

George shook his head in exasperation and moved to the 2030 terminal. "Let's hear more about this polar airport."

Shelly lowered her head and followed him. Something about this whole thing was making her feel queasy. She had rather hoped that the murder was not about the polar region and that no one had committed murder to destroy that last protected place on the planet. She tapped the screen at their new computer station, and when a new list of dates came up, she typed in "polar region development" and waited.

"In 2032 the renewed call for a polar port to evacuate people to Mars began to heat up when the hurricanes destroyed most of Florida and the Gulf region of the

United States. The American government was already hard-pressed to come up with some way to save the people already being decimated by floods, famine, and drought in the middle of the nation, but the hurricanes made it imperative that they find a way to evacuate citizens to somewhere safe from the ravages of a climate already altered by global warming."

George and Shelly both cringed at the thought of the world being so plagued by climate change. Shelly had been hearing about these issues her entire life, and there was a part of her that had always prayed that it was all just talk and that it would never come to anything harmful for the people of the earth. Yet here they were listening to a report that seemed to lay out in plain English how the world would have to evacuate to Mars when the entire planet went to hell.

"Many people recalled in the 2032 debates how their predecessors in earlier years had decried the idea of polar development, but their voices were silenced by the stronger committee members from China, Russia, Canada, and Australia who saw no hope for the Americans if a way off the planet was not found. In 2032 the committee decided to build the terminals to Mars at the poles, but some still denounced using the poles for such development."

Shelly tapped the screen to pause the video and drummed her fingers on the wall behind the terminal.

"I bet one of the people who originally denounced development was the former president of the United States," George said. "And after someone went back and killed him, there was no one strong enough to stand up to the rest of the committee, which meant they gave the green light to using the poles as airports to Mars."

"Wow." Shelly touched the terminal again, and the narration resumed.

"The committee finally assigned the development project for the building of terminals on Baffin Island and on the Antarctic ice sheet. The Canadian government, in consort with the Americans, took on the Baffin Island project while the Antarctic project was taken on by a consortium of British, Brazilian, Chinese, and Russian financial companies."

George reached over and tapped the screen. "So it was the Antarctic project that was given to private companies, which means someone made a whole lot of money on it."

Shelly pulled up the main screen and typed in "Antarctic project financial backing."

They waited a moment, and when the screen went blank, they were shocked. George glanced around and saw the young historian who had helped them earlier. "Excuse me, my good man, why would the screen go blank like that?"

The young man walked over to them and squinted at the blank screen. "Depends on the question. Sometimes if your question is too specific or you are asking something that is outside public knowledge, then the terminal shuts down."

"Outside public knowledge?" Shelly was suddenly feeling very angry. "You mean something someone does not want us to know about."

"That is usually what it means. There have been a lot of limits put on what people can access, and if you put in the wrong inquiry, the government can arrest you." The young man tapped the terminal and brought the main screen back up. "What were you asking about anyway?"

"We asked who backed the building of the polar launch terminals," said George. Shelly could tell that he was trying to sound disinterested in the subject, but he could not keep the edge out of his voice.

"Oh," the young man said, nodding his head, "that explains it then. Financial questions cannot be answered without the prior approval of the central authority, and they rarely give it."

"Even information about something built before 2040?" George asked, shocked.

"They will only open that material to the general population after one hundred years have passed." The young man turned off the terminal. "They want to protect the developers and the financial institutions."

"Protect them from what?" Shelly could not believe what she was hearing.

The young man stood and stared at her for a moment. "You know, I have never actually understood that myself."

Shelly was shaking with indignation and fury. It was hard enough to gain knowledge about financial institutions without the government denying access to even the most basic information. She wanted to scream, stamp her feet, and demand to see someone in authority, but she had no idea who to ask for. They were strangers in a strange land without a library pass.

George grabbed her hand and headed for the door. "Come on, girl. I am tired of this trip into the past. Let's go shopping and get something to eat." He pulled her from the building, and the two of them stood on the sidewalk.

Shelly pulled herself free from his grasp. "Something to eat? Are you joking? They have slammed the door in our faces, and we have nowhere to go."

"Well, our friend in there had no answers, and he had no one he could ask. If you caused a scene, all you might manage to do is get us arrested and taken to some bureaucratic wasteland from which we might never return."

Shelly's shoulders slumped forward as if she had suddenly lost all the air in her body. "All right, what do you suggest we do?"

George stood there a moment, considering that question. "You are the newspaper woman—who would you ask if the government closed all the doors to vital information?"

Shelly considered that thought, and for the first time in days, she realized that she needed another source. "Emmett told me that there once had been a black market for government information—hackers—but most of them were arrested in early 2020 when the government was able to track a number of leaks back to their source."

"Black markets have always been a source for things and information," George chuckled. "All we have to do is find the one in this time period and figure out what to ask."

Shelly glared at him. "You are suggesting that we look for someone outside the realms of official information and ask him or her for something we were just told is protected by the government."

"Yes, I am," George said, smiling at her. "We have come this far, and since we look like a couple of fruits, it is time to dice it up and make a salad."

"That makes no sense."

"In this crazy world, what does?" He headed down the sidewalk, and Shelly fell in step beside him.

"George, where are we going to look for this black market?"

"Actually"—he stopped and glanced around—"first we are going to find a hotel. Then we will begin to ask some discreet questions that will get us either arrested or pointed to the right people who can help us."

Shelly shook her head and took his arm. "Sounds like fun."

CHAPTER 25

They found a hotel, and when they registered as Mr. and Mrs. Smith, the front-desk clerk giggled, likely because of their age difference—not to mention that the only luggage they had was a bag from the store where they'd clearly bought the clothes they were wearing. The situation made George feel odd, and he blushed when the man typed their names into his computer without asking for any form of identification. The clerk was probably used to rendezvous in his hotel, but George Marsh had never done anything like that in his entire life, and here he was fifty years in the future, checking into a hotel with a beautiful girl on his arm.

He was sure that Shelly could tell he was uneasy about checking into the hotel, and he would have preferred to ask for separate rooms, but they had no way to know how long they would need to be in the future or how long the money they had been able to obtain would last. They had to be frugal in a place that did not seem to understand the word. No one they met seemed to believe in being invisible either, considering the bright ridiculous clothing that they wore.

George sat in a chair by the window, and Shelly sat on the bed, staring at a blank screen on the wall. It seemed to be some sort of television, but no matter what buttons she pushed on the remote, she could not get it to turn on, so she gave up even trying. "All right, Mr. Smith," she finally said, "what do you suggest we try?"

He looked up at her and smiled uneasily. "Well, I have heard that if you ever need something illegal at a hotel, you ask the concierge."

"I have heard that too, but what do we ask for?" She leaned forward, her eyes suddenly glowing.

George scratched his head and shifted the bright orange shirt on his large frame. He felt like a clown in this suit, but it seemed to be the clothing of choice in this land. "Well, we have to be careful that no one guesses the real reason for our journey."

"You know that today in our time, there were those WikiLeaks geeks who were squashed." She smiled knowingly.

"How do we get to that information?" George pointed to the screen across from the bed. "You can't even get that thing to turn on."

She lowered her gaze in defeat. "I would hate to have to ask someone for help with simply turning it on, but we may have no choice."

"All right." George rose to his feet. "I have an idea. I'll pretend that you are in the shower and I will call down to the front desk. I will tell them that you had it on, and I pushed some damn button, and it went off, and I can't get it back on. I'll tell them I would rather not look like an old fool in front of the missus."

"You would never look like a fool to your missus." She squeezed his arm and headed for the bathroom.

George smiled at her and shook his head. He already did feel like a fool with this young woman. He picked up the phone and waited for the front desk to answer. He explained his predicament, which received a rather off-putting giggle, but the attendant did say he would send a technician up to their room right away. George then paced the room, listening to the shower running in the bathroom. The idea of her being naked in the next room made him uneasy.

The technician was a beautiful young woman in a glowing yellow uniform that George was convinced could have been seen from the moon, but perhaps that was the idea. She smiled at him and picked up the remote. She pressed some buttons and pulled up a screen. "There you go, sir. You can get anything you want now."

"Thank you," he said, his eyes on the floor. He really did feel like a fool, but that had been the point, and it had worked. The young woman giggled and left the room.

He did not want to lose the screen, so he opted not to touch anything and to wait for Shelly to join him. He had never been very good with technological things, and he did not want to do anything to lose their connection to information. He knew enough to plug in the codes at the museum, and he'd thought that was enough, but now he had to wonder if perhaps he needed to learn more about computers.

Shelly came out in a lime-green bathrobe, her hair damp from the shower, and glanced at the screen on the wall, which was now on a home screen for the hotel. "All right," she said as she picked up the remote. "Let's see where this can take us."

She sat on the edge of the bed, and George sat down beside her. She surfed through some basic channels until she came to an Internet access menu that said that it would give them access to the local news and weather feeds. "I think this is where we can start."

George sat rigid, his eyes on the screen. He knew it was stupid, but he could not seem to focus on anything but the warm smell of her freshly washed skin. She suddenly smelled of lilacs and roses, and it made him want to run and sit across the room, as far from her as he could get. He wondered what he would do if they had to remain here and had to share this bed for a night. That thought scared him more than the fact that they were fifty years in the future.

"We seem to have access to the World Wide Web." Shelly stared intently at the screen and the images flashing by at lightning speed. She was a child of the Internet age, and this was something she knew about even if it made her companion uneasy. "All right, this is a site called Crawler Information, and they seem to specialize in the seedier side of the world."

"Is that what we want?" George looked at the pictures of people in black clothes and Gothic attire. "It looks like they are the opposite of the people we have met."

"Every culture has its counter groups, and if this world has gone rainbow, it stands to reason that the counter to that would be Gothic."

"So they have rebelled against the rainbow clothing craze. That does not mean that they have information about financial builders."

"George," Shelly said as she reached over and patted his leg, "it is a place to start, and they might have some knowledge about who would have access to the information we need."

"Fine." He tensed under her touch and rose to his feet. "You keep looking, and I will take a shower."

ଓଓଓ

Shelly watched George leave the room and then turned back to the screen. She had sensed his unease but assumed it had more to do with his lack of computer savvy than anything else. She did not want to think about his possibly being uneasy with her being naked under the lime-green robe. She returned her focus to the Gothic site and its membership. She had to find something in their world that would help her and George discover who had made a killing in the killing of the penguins and seals. She was so engrossed in the effort that nearly an hour slipped by without her noticing.

"Have you found anything we can use?" asked a deep voice.

Shelly jumped. "What?" She turned to see George seated in the chair across the room, freshly showered and wearing his orange suit again. She had been so intent on the images on the screen before her that she had not even seen him emerge from the bathroom. "I think so, if you are willing to risk a trip to the darker side of London at night."

"Do we have a choice?" He got to his feet and moved over to the bed again. "Where are we going?"

"There is a coffee shop where the more Gothic members meet every night and discuss the day's events, and actually, it is only a couple of blocks from here."

George looked at her lime-green robe and the orange suit he wore. "We do not exactly look Gothic right now."

"No, we don't," she giggled, running a hand over her robe. "But the clothes we were wearing when we landed in this wonderland will do just fine. They'll get us in the front door if nothing else."

CHAPTER 26

After changing back into the more discreet clothes that they had arrived in, they used the stairs to slip quietly out of the hotel and into the dark of the night. The streets were lit up in a panoramic rainbow of neon that fit the day world of rainbow, which made them feel uneasy in the jeans they now wore. The pair walked in silence, keeping to the shadows so that the people wandering into the restaurants and nightclubs would not notice how ill-suited they were to this Lite-Brite world. Shelly was right: the coffee shop where the Gothic group met was only a couple of blocks from the hotel, and within ten minutes they were walking into the café.

George quickly realized that he felt more comfortable in this place than in the Technicolor world of the hotel. People were wearing black jeans and the drab colors he had worn his whole life. No one even looked up when he and Shelly took a seat in the corner of the room and ordered some ale. "This feels like home," he whispered to her.

"Yes, it does," she agreed. "So it might be easier to get information out of these people than anyone else on this planet. At least we seem to fit in."

As they sipped on their beer, they watched the groups of people talking in animated tones. Shelly realized that this reminded her of the university students she had interviewed just a few days ago. It was hard to wrap her head around the fact that all of that had happened decades earlier and they were actually in the future. Out in the bright rainbow world, it was easier to remember that this was not their London, but in this place it seemed as if time had stood still. She shuddered at the thought and took another sip of the beer.

"We can't sit here all night," George said, taking a long gulp of his drink. "We need to ask someone something."

"All right," she sighed. Picking up her drink, she rose stiffly to her feet. "Follow my lead."

Shelly walked over to a table and started listening to the conversation, just as she had done with the students. She was looking for a place where she and George could jump into the conversation.

"The whole thing bloody well stinks," said a middle-aged man as he sipped on a whiskey sour. "They want us to pay for the new launches when the people going could easily pay for their own trips."

"Philip, you know it is not that simple," his companion said, patting his hand. "Not all of the new Martian rovers are rich cats looking for adventure; some of them do have legitimate reasons for wanting off the planet. Look at what is happening in the subcontinent."

"Fine," Philip said, rolling his eyes. "Some of the people in Karachi and India have real reasons to want to be on the ships, but those paying for first-class seats do not need my tax dollars to fund their excesses."

George wanted to laugh. The more things changed, the more things remained the same. Fifty years later, and the people in the pub were still complaining about how the government was using the tax money that the working people turned over day after day. This was his chance to join the conversation. "Excuse me," said George. "I overheard what you were discussing, and I was telling my young friend here that I actually have to agree with you, sir, about the rich not needing the public monies. But I do have to wonder, has the government funded all of the expeditions? I thought the first trips were privately funded." He sipped at his beer nonchalantly.

"Give me a break," Philip snorted. "Even the first trip was heavily subsidized by the government."

Shelly sighed at the thought. She wanted to appear bored with her man's political interests, which would give them an out should they need it, but she was just as interested as he was. "Do we have to talk about this again?" she said.

"Oh, sit down, girl." George pulled out a chair, and Shelly fell into it. "I am always willing to talk to someone who disagrees with the government's use of taxpayer money."

The woman nodded. "So few do nowadays," she said as George sat down beside Shelly. "Everyone is terrified of the central authority."

"I keep telling her that it was not always this way." George winked at his companion. "I told her that before the launch there was a more open form of government and that they actually provided information on these projects. Then the central authority took over and shut down all avenues of information to the public."

"That was over forty years in the past," the woman said, sighing heavily. "Long before this girl was even born."

"I was young," George said, snorting at the memory, "but my father talked about the days when the government allowed public access to information about things like who funded the launch pads in the Antarctic." He knew that he had to be very careful about what he said, or these two might guess that he and his companion did not fit into the roles that they were playing.

The woman leaned forward and whispered, "You know, I think it was the launch that shut down the access to information. It was as if they did not want us to find out the names of the people involved in the building of the terminals, which makes no sense to me."

"Nothing makes sense to you," Philip said, waving the server over and ordering another round of ale, "but I am here to tell you it makes perfect sense."

"Why do you think it makes perfect sense?" Shelly could not help herself now. She was genuinely interested in the tone of the man's voice.

"Well ..." Philip glanced around to make certain no one was eavesdropping on their conversation. "My old man told me that when the launch terminals were funded, there were some odd negotiations surrounding the whole thing. He told me that forty years ago the government shut down access to information without any real input from other nations or from the public."

Just then, the server approached and placed four drinks on the table. When she was gone, George said, "So whoever won the right to build the terminal also got some concessions from the government on access to the information." He tapped his fingers on the table. "I wonder what that cost them."

"Those were deep pockets, my friend," Philip whispered.

"A lot deeper than mine," the woman giggled.

"A lot deeper than all of ours," Shelly said, nodding.

The woman sipped at her beer. "You know, something I have long believed is that whoever won that contract made a killing on the costs of the trips, which is why some of the fat cats today are able to head to Mars."

"Who?" George pressed. "Who made that sort of killing?"

The woman shrugged her shoulders. "God, I have no idea. I wish I did."

"Please, Lillian," Philip said, laughing out loud. "Everyone knows it was Carl Peterson and his coconspirators who made the most money on that whole thing."

"Peterson." Lillian said the name with a tone of reverence.

"Lillian here thinks that Peterson is a god who can do no wrong," Philip snorted. "But there are those of us who know that he made his fortune on the backs of the poor slobs who needed to go to Mars to get away from the climate catastrophes that were unfolding here."

"Well, he does help a lot of people," George said, winking at Shelly. He decided to play along and see what he could learn about this man who appeared to elicit divergent responses.

"He helps only those who make him look good." Philip slapped his hand on the table. "Anyone who thinks anything else has been blinded by the light."

"He opened the ships to those who could not pay," Lillian said, her voice shrill with indignation.

"Oh my God, listen to you." Philip glared at the woman. "We all know that if the poor could not pay their way, Peterson made the governments pay for it in grants, access, and new contracts. Hell, by the time he was done blackmailing the world's powers, he was the only power left."

Lillian lowered her gaze and seemed to be contemplating the color of the table. "You have no proof of any of that."

"I have no proof that the sun will someday die, but there is enough evidence to make it a fact."

A silence now engulfed the group. Lillian was still contemplating the table; Philip was drinking his beer with deepening anger; and George and Shelly stared at each other, wondering how they could find out more about the enigmatic Carl Peterson.

Philip downed his beer in one long gulp and got up from the table. "Come on, I want something to eat."

Lillian looked up and smiled at Shelly. "I guess it is getting late."

George and Shelly watched them head into the pub's dining area and felt a mixture of sorrow and giddiness. They had not meant to cause such heated division between their new drinking partners, but they had needed the information. "They will be fine," George said as he shook his head and gestured toward them. "I know a lot of couples like them. They argue about politics and actors for a moment, and it is all forgotten in an hour."

For a moment George thought about heading back to the hotel, but he also wondered if there was something else they could learn. Rising from his chair, he nodded at Shelly, who followed him. Carrying their beers into the dining area, they took a table next to Philip and Lillian and ordered a round of fish and chips from the waitress. George wanted to ask something more about the man Peterson, but he had no idea where to take the conversation without seeming too pushy.

"George, you have to admit that Peterson was one of the first to really see the potential of the Antarctic development." Shelly sipped at her beer and smiled at her companion.

George winked at her, thankful that she at least knew how to open up this conversation. "Oh sure, he saw the potential, but that did not make it right."

"No kidding," Philip chimed in. "There were many who disagreed with any development at the poles, but their voices were drowned out by the big corporations."

"Philip," Lillian said, her voice rising in mild anger, "there were a lot of people suffering who needed a way off the planet, and the launches were the only way to do that."

"Did they have to mess up the ecosystems of the poles to do that?" George groaned, subtly glancing at Philip and Lillian. He had no idea whether environmental issues were still a hot-button topic like they had been fifty years ago. Perhaps no one cared anymore about penguins and polar bears.

"I understand all of that," the woman moaned under her breath. "But we had to consider the lives of millions."

Philip pushed his food around his plate. "And a bunch of flightless birds in the Antarctic did not matter when matched with all those people."

As the waitress set their plates in front of them, George looked at Shelly and shrugged his shoulders; this line of conversation was getting them nowhere. These were things they already knew. What they needed was some more information directly tied to the man Peterson. "I often wondered about Peterson, though," George said, taking a bite of his fish. "I mean, where did he get his funding?"

"God only knows," Philip said with an uneasy smile, "because no one else is allowed to ask."

"I heard he started out relatively poor and built his empire from the ground up," Shelly said, taking a guess and repeating a common story.

Philip shook his head. "Everyone has heard that story, and maybe it's true, but what no one can figure out is who his partner is. All anyone knows is that the man's name was Zack Lords, but there has never been a picture of him, and everyone I know thinks he is the real power and Peterson is just a figurehead." Philip whispered the last statement as if he was afraid to let anyone hear him speculate on the man. "Or maybe Peterson made the man up to take the speculation off him when there were problems in the early days of the launches." Philip stabbed at his meal in a fury. "A lot of us have often wondered about the appearance of Lords in the news when the original launches were delayed due to faulty materials."

"I honestly believe that," George said, keeping his eyes on his meal. "I think Peterson is playing all of us."

The rest of the dinner was eaten in relative silence, with George and Shelly exchanging knowing glances. They knew that Philip and Lillian had no more to give them, but they couldn't run out without arousing suspicions, so they ate the fish and chips, slowly savoring the familiar tastes. At least some things would not change in fifty years. When they were done, they bid their companions good night and headed back to the hotel, keeping to the shadows as best they could, which was made difficult by the shimmering disco lights of the streets.

When they reached the hotel, they sneaked in the side entrance and made their way back up to their room. They sat on the bed and looked at the screen, which still showed the address for the café they had just left. Shelly grabbed the remote and pulled up a search engine, into which she typed the name Carl Peterson. The screen went blank and then shimmered onto the shining face of an older man whose smile made both of them cringe.

CHAPTER 27

George read the introduction aloud. "Carl Peterson, cofounder of the Vesper group of companies, is a philanthropist and innovator of many of the polar launch vehicles that are still in use today. In other words he is a great man."

"According to Lillian he is," Shelly said, frowning at the image. "But that could all be just a great PR job."

George leaned forward. "Does it give any information about his cofounder, Lords?"

Shelly scrolled down the screen, and her frown deepened. "You know something—it does not seem to say, which makes me wonder about him and his role in the company. Philip may have been right about him being a made-up scapegoat for when things went wrong."

George rubbed his ear. "Or they made damn certain no one ever found out who Lords is."

Shelly turned and stared at her partner. "You know, if murder was how they founded this company, then it stands to reason that whoever did the actual killing would want to remain in the shadows. Perhaps our friend Carl Peterson here is just a figurehead, and the real money and brains behind Vesper lives in the shadows."

"But why even say that there was a cofounder if you do not want anyone to discover his identity?"

Shelly was silent for a moment as she pondered this odd question. She then suddenly brightened and turned back to the screen. "Perry once told me that in order to keep a secret, you need to bury it among facts so snow-white that no one would ever even look at them."

"Now you have lost me."

"Don't you see?" She typed furiously on the remote. "If there was a cofounder, the real brains behind Vesper, then in order to keep that information out of the realm of public interest, you would need to create a bright, colorful figure like Peterson, who would hold the attention of the public. But if your bobblehead got into any trouble, he would have to be able to divert attention back into the shadows by saying that those issues had been caused by the cofounder that no one knows anything about."

"Sounds like a double-edged sword," George said as he watched information jump onto the screen. "What are you looking for anyway?"

"Mentions of Peterson in the news," she said as she continued to type. "I'm looking for places where he mentioned his cofounder in order to backpedal, and I think I just found what I was looking for."

George studied the picture on the screen of Mr. Peterson looking rather gloomy and forlorn. The text read, "A malfunction of the Mars rover launch today was attributed to an overheated coil in the original specs, which Peterson said was a result of his cofounder sending the orders to an American firm rather than to the Russian one he had wanted to use."

"What does any of that prove?"

Shelly giggled and pressed a button the remote that she hoped would take the screen back to the hotel homepage.

"Don't you see? I think Philip's original assessment that there is no cofounder was correct. He was a creation of Peterson to take the blame when anything went wrong. We don't have any real proof, but it does make sense."

"Like overheated coils." George began to laugh too. "So now we know the name of our quarry."

Shelly clapped her hands together. "I think we do. So can we now leave this Rainbow Brite world and head home?"

George laughed at her enthusiasm. "What? You no longer want to share a hotel room with me?"

"Don't be daft," she giggled. "I am thoroughly enjoying this adventure, but I also want to get home to someplace that makes more sense."

"I have to agree." He rose to his feet. "But we have to wait until the museum is actually open, so we do have to stay here one night."

"Oh." Shelly's face fell. She had not thought that they would be in this world for more than a few hours, and now they were actually going to be spending the night.

"I will take the floor," George said as he grabbed one of the pillows and pulled at the blankets.

"Oh, for heaven's sake, George Marsh, do not be silly." She grabbed the pillow from him. "The bed is big enough for the two of us, and if you promise not to hog the covers, I will stay on my side of the bed."

George stood there staring at her for a moment, his heart pounding. How could he explain any of this to Clancy or the rest of his mates down at the pub? He was about to spend a night in a bed with the most beautiful woman he had ever met, fifty years in the future. No one would ever believe him; he did not believe any of it himself.

He was a middle-aged security guard who had never done anything with his life, and now he was traveling through time, spending the night with a lovely woman, and deciding how to deal with a murderer.

ᏣᏣᏣ

Having changed back into the lime-green bathrobe, Shelly crawled under the covers and felt a shiver pass over her tiny frame. She was not scared to be in bed with this man. Actually, George was probably the only man she trusted 100 percent. He was the sweetest person she had ever met, and if she could find someone like him closer to her own age, she would be the happiest woman in the world. The problem was that she was still terrified to be jumping through time with a stupid amulet as their only road back to their own world. She had not said anything to George about it, but she was worried that they would never make it back to 2020. The thought that they might be stuck in 2070 scared the wits out of her.

Neither of them slept that night. They both lay in the large bed staring up at the ceiling, both afraid to move for fear of disturbing the other person. It was a large bed, and it would have been easy for them to toss and turn without actually touching, but the terror kept both of them still as rocks. The morning found them dressing in complete silence, unwilling to really look at each other in case the fear was written in their eyes.

CHAPTER 28

They walked to the museum, the silence between them growing more and more strained. Shelly was not certain why she was afraid to say what was on her mind. Why could she not tell this man that she was terrified? She had been able to talk to him about everything else, but the fear in her soul was something she wanted to keep to herself. As they neared the museum, she noticed that George seemed to be walking a little slower.

"Are you okay, George?"

"Are we certain that Peterson is the man we think killed the president?"

Shelly spun around and glared at him. "Have you lost your mind? We just spent an entire night in the year 2070 to find out that man's name, and now you are having second thoughts?"

"We have to be sure before we take the next step."

"What the hell is the next step?" Her voice was quivering in anticipation. She had feared this moment almost as much as she feared being stuck fifty years in the future.

"I am not sure," he whispered. "I assumed that once we found out who did the deed, it would be easy, but it just seems more complicated."

Shelly grabbed his hand and headed to the main entrance of the museum. "I do not care how complicated it seems to you. All I know is that I want to go home to my own time. We will figure it out when we reach 2020."

They had to get back before they were stuck in this world forever, lost in time and space permanently. They paid their way into the museum and headed for the mummy room. They glanced around and saw that the place was almost deserted. Fifty years in the future, no one seemed to care about the dead and the world that had been left behind. Or maybe it was just that world had fewer people, so there were fewer people around to pay their way into the hallowed halls of the famed museum.

Shelly could feel the tension in George, but she assumed it was the same terror that now consumed her. Would the medallion now take them back to their own time and to the flat they had left yesterday? The closer they got to the mummy wing, the more fear filled her soul. "What date are you going to say when we open the door?"

"We should make it as close to the time we left as possible so that no one will notice we ever left," he whispered as they passed a couple staring at one of the mummies. They were actually the first people George and Shelly had seen since entering the building.

"What time would you say that was?" Shelly looked around the room, her eyes darting back and forth.

"September 14, 2020, 1200," he said in a deep baritone.

The couple looked over at them, an odd expression on their faces. Shelly could feel their eyes boring into her, and it made her want to run and hide. "Come on." She grabbed George's hand and headed to the end of the room where the door stood that would lead them back to the world she knew.

She slipped the medallion around her neck and in a hushed tone said the words: "Open to protect the pharaoh." When the door shimmered and opened, she repeated the date and time George had given her. The room before them began to shimmer and glow.

CHAPTER 29

The moment they made it through the door and back into his flat, George walked over and sat at the table, his head in his hands. He watched out of the corner of his eye as Shelly took off the necklace and placed it in the box that still sat on the table. She then sat down opposite him and waited. It was a long wait. He sat there with his head resting in his hands for what seemed like forever. Shelly seemed to become restless and walked over to where the cat sat on the windowsill. She petted the tiny creature and listened to the deep, contented purring.

George finally looked up at her standing in the light streaming through the window and sighed. He really did love her and wanted her to be a part of his life forever, but he knew that was an impossible dream and one he really needed to stop thinking about. It was time to look for some form of reality in this bizarre situation. "Is there any way we can find information about Carl Peterson today?" he asked.

Shelly looked over at him and smiled. "The Internet would probably be our best bet. We could go over to my place and use my computer since you seem to be in the Dark Ages about these types of things."

"Very funny." He got to his feet, grabbed the medallion's box, and stuffed it into his pocket. "I just never had use for one until now." He then stopped and looked at Shelly, who was still petting the kitten. "But I think we should change before we head out. Wearing these clothes might get us some odd looks, don't you think?"

He went into the bedroom to change while Shelly grabbed the bag containing her clothes and headed for the bathroom.

ᏈᏈᏈ

As Shelly slipped back into her jeans and blouse, she thought about her reliance on the Internet and realized that perhaps she did rely on it a little too much. Emmett had warned her on her very first day on the job that online research would never replace boots-on-the-ground interviews. She had initially told some of her college friends that she thought he was too old-school to really teach her anything; how wrong had she been about that? The truth was that she had known nothing about interviews, reporting, or working at a newspaper before this job.

ᏈᏈᏈ

As they drove across the city, George came to the startling realization that he was about to step into this young woman's private dwelling. He had not been invited into a woman's flat in more years than he cared to admit, and it scared the hell out of him. What if he said something stupid or sat on some flimsy, girly little chair and broke the damn thing into a million pieces? Considering the insanity racing around them and the presence of a time-traveling medallion in his pocket, he realized that his worry about breaking this woman's furniture was a ridiculous thing to be obsessing over, but those were the thoughts that plagued him as they parked across from her building.

She had not seemed to have any reaction to being in his apartment, but he was becoming completely unglued at the very idea of entering her world. He shook his head, and as he stepped out of the car, he braced himself. He wanted to appear calm and collected around her even though inside he was quivering like a bowl full of jelly. That image made him want to laugh, and as he caught his reflection in the car window, he stopped and stared. He was a large, overweight man with a fat face and a blob of a belly to match, so who was he really kidding? Someone like Shelly Jenkins was never going to look twice at him.

Shelly unlocked the door to her walk-up and waited for the large man to follow her. He hesitated and could sense that his unmanly reaction was making her uneasy. After all they had been through, he was still acting like a shy schoolboy around her. She finally smiled at him. "Well, are you coming, sweetie, or do I have to come drag you in?"

He knew she was pulling his leg, but the joking actually did not help his disposition any. He did not want this girl teasing him; he wanted her to take him seriously. So he shrugged his shoulders and followed her into the flat, a frown on his usually jolly face. Shelly sighed and closed the door after him, probably wondering if things would ever get easier between them.

George glanced around the tiny stylish flat, trying desperately not to compare it to his drab quarters, but how could he not? She had floral prints on the walls, brocade curtains on the windows, and lovely covers on all the chairs. He had been right to worry about breaking something in this sweet little place, and as he took a seat, he could feel his weight straining the chair's small legs. He was even certain that he heard the distinct creak of wood that was about to give way and send him crashing to the floor. He cringed and waited for that embarrassing moment, but when it did not come, he relaxed a little. He pulled the box out of his pocket and placed it gingerly on the table.

Shelly sat down opposite him, and together they stared at the object as if neither had ever seen it before. She opened her computer and typed the name Carl Peterson into a search engine. Right away, an article popped up concerning some start-up company. "He is only twenty-seven years old," she said.

"That makes sense." George leaned forward with growing interest. "When we saw his picture in 2070, he looked to be an old man, so today he would be a young man."

"I had supposed, from the vague description you gave, that the assassin would have been an older man." Shelly sounded defeated.

"Of course," George said, peering at the website. "But the killer came back in time, so it was an older version of this man, but not as old as the man we saw in 2070. You are going to have to keep your time periods straight on this little caper, my dear."

"All right." She leaned in with him and continued reading from the website. "According to this, he is from here in London and grew up on the west end. He went to a business school but dropped out to start his own company, specializing in odd building contracts in remote locations."

"Like building launch pads in the Antarctic," George laughed.

"But not why he would want President Carlson dead." Shelly closed the computer. "We can't assume that the younger version would be involved in all of this."

George knew that she was right; Carl Peterson in 2020 might have no idea why they would knock on his door, asking him about the death of the president. The guard shook his head and picked up the box again. It was just so confusing. "So what do you suggest we do?"

Shelly leaned back in her chair and stared up at the ceiling. "I could go and interview him about his start-up. Those people are always demanding that the paper give them some ink, so it would seem normal to him."

"So that gets you in the front door." George rose to his feet and began to pace around the room. "But still, how can you ask him about the president since he has yet to know about the medallion? He will not know about the murder at this stage of his life."

He felt defeated, and frankly, so did Shelly. He sat back down, and together they resumed staring at the box in the middle of the table. They had their suspect, but there was not one question they could ask him that would really make any sense to Carl Peterson. Minutes ticked by, and the pair continued to stare at the box.

"All of this makes me wonder why this even works." Shelly turned her head and gazed out the window. "Why would protecting the pharaoh mean opening a door to a museum when the mummified pharaoh is long dead and so are the men who would have protected him?"

"Our friendly little curator, Carl told me that ancients actually thought they had to protect the dead as well as the living."

"God, that is so much rubbish." She let out a snort. "As if that mummy even cares about those idiots."

George laughed unexpectedly, causing Shelly to jump. "It had nothing to do with what the mummy or the pharaoh believed. It was about what the person wearing the medallion believed."

"I was wearing it, and I can tell you that to be honest, until that door opened, I did not believe." Shelly sighed. "And there is a part of me that still thinks this whole thing is just a bad dream."

George reached out and patted her hand. "Well, I can tell you, there is only one way to be sure that we have the right one, and that is to go talk to him. Ask Mr. Peterson how he views the president's untimely death."

"I know you are right." Shelly let out another long breath. "I am just a little overwhelmed by all of this."

"I can go with you if it will help." He saw relief blaze across her intense eyes, and he finally understood that she never would have considered going to see Peterson on her own. It rather pleased him to know that she might actually need him.

"I thought that was understood, but who would we tell Peterson you are? I have a press pass, and you do not."

George laughed; he could not really envision himself as a reporter, let alone a reporter working alongside someone like Shelly. Yet wasn't that exactly what he was doing? "I could be a colleague of some sort, I suppose."

"Or my boyfriend." She smiled at him with a look that made him feel special and angry all at the same time.

The smile from his own face faded. "No one in their right mind would ever believe that I am your boyfriend.

So we tell him that I am your supervisor tailing you to see how you do on an interview."

"We never do that," Shelly said, her face dropping into a frown. "But I guess it makes some sense."

"Can I have a beer or something?" he asked nervously, not even certain she would have beer. When she nodded, George rose to his feet again and went over to the fridge. He then turned back to where Shelly sat at the table. Shrugging his shoulders, he tried to smile again. "So if I am your supervisor, do I look the part?"

Shelly rose stiffly to her feet and appraised him with a critical eye. He fidgeted under her intense scrutiny and began to bounce back and forth. He knew that with his tired old blue jeans and scruffy jacket, he looked like a homeless person. Honestly, George had never cared what he looked like or wore, but today, for the first time in his life, he did care.

"I think we are going to have to go shopping before we visit Mr. Peterson," she finally said with a wily grin on her face.

George smiled timidly down at her. "I was afraid you were going to say that."

CHAPTER 30

Flo Miller watched the pair come into the shop. The young girl breezed in, her eyes laughing as she tugged on the arm of the lumbering man who stumbled as he crossed the floor to the men's suits. Flo smiled and shook her head at the sight. At first she thought they might be father and daughter, but she quickly realized by the way the young girl touched the man's arm and the way he blushed that this was a couple on the verge of something new and intimate. They were not there yet, but they soon would be.

Flo had seen a great deal in her five short years in the retail market. She might be only twenty-five herself, but she had seen plenty of couples come into the shop—the woman seeking to make over a man and the man fighting it every step of the way. She knew the look, and she knew that it was a disaster waiting to happen. She watched them and laughed as the girl pulled suits for her man to try on.

The girl forced him to try on a dark suit, but for some reason, when he came out of the dressing room wearing it, he looked just as disheveled as he had in the jeans and white shirt. Flo smiled and suppressed a bizarre urge to giggle.

"Well, that is not quite you," said the man's young companion, shaking her head at the sight.

"It is still better than that odd orange thing I was wearing yesterday."

"Actually, that odd orange thing looked better than this suit." The girl walked around him and appraised the man more closely. "Perhaps what you do need is a little color."

"Oh God, you are not thinking of putting me in some awful color." He flopped into a chair and stared at himself in the mirror. "I look enough like a fruit as it is."

Flo wondered what they were talking about. The comments about the orange thing he'd been wearing seemed a little odd, but it might be an inside joke that only they would understand. Some people were like that—talking in codes particular to them. Flo had learned very quickly not to ask for clarification on the more intimate aspects of conversations. She could see that the young woman was suppressing the urge to laugh at the man, who was obviously uncomfortable in the dark suit, which if Flo was honest, she had to admit really did not do anything for the big burly man. He sat before the mirror looking utterly miserable. Flo could tell he was trying to be positive for his companion, but it was no use—he would never be happy wearing that outfit.

"Sir, may I make a suggestion?" she called from behind them, her eyes on the mirror and a tailored sports jacket in her hand.

They turned to look at her, and the girl's smile faded into a scowl; it was obvious that she did not want Flo to take over this shopping expedition. Flo knew enough about human interaction to know that this woman saw it as her task to find the right style for her man. Flo was an intrusion and one that was not appreciated.

The middle-aged man tried to smile, but his face fell into a deep frown as well. "I doubt there is anything you can put me in that would make any difference. I am a slob, and that is the way it is going to remain."

"Now, sir," Flo said with a knowing grin, "everyone has a style. It is just a matter of finding the right one for you."

He groaned and glared at the two women, who now were engrossed in finding the right style and size of sports coat he should be wearing.

Flo was determined to help the couple mainly so that she could make the sale but also because despite their odd behavior, she actually liked both of them. While the man was in the dressing room for what felt like the millionth time, the young woman chatted excitedly on her cell phone. When he came out, she said, "George, we are all set to meet with him tomorrow morning at ten."

"Peterson?" he quietly asked.

"Yes," she said, nodding. "I just set up the appointment. So we have to make certain you look the part." She looked at his latest outfit with a critical eye. Flo had placed him in a pair of dark jeans, a pale blue shirt, and a sports jacket with a soft plaid pattern. It actually did look decent on the man; he looked put-together without looking too dressy.

"Well, will I pass as a journalist?" he finally asked.

"I think we finally have it." The young woman nodded her approval.

Flo laughed as George put all the new clothes on his credit card. She had seen this before—a young girlfriend making over her older man—but for some reason this pair seemed slightly odd. It was as if neither wanted to admit that there was any form of attraction between them, but it was there for the entire world to see. Flo had never seen anyone as intent on denial as these two were.

"Have a nice day," she said as they left. "And please come again." Once they were gone, she sighed and put away the fake sugary smile. She doubted that she would ever see them again. She realized that she actually never *wanted* to see them again either, and she had no idea why. They seemed like a nice enough pair, even if they were an odd match. However, somewhere in the recess of her mind, the clerk had never felt so ill at ease or wary of a couple.

That night as she tried to explain it to her boyfriend over cocktails, all she managed to do was confuse him, which made sense because she was really confused herself.

CHAPTER 31

The next morning, Shelly drove over to fetch George so that they could head to the 10:00 a.m. meeting with Peterson. She had told his assistant that they were doing a piece on young entrepreneurs with innovative ideas. He was actually excited at the prospect of being singled out by a major publication and could not wait to meet with her. She felt a tad dirty lying to the man like this, but it was really the only way that they could get in to see him.

A part of her still did not accept that this young man held any resemblance to the old man they had seen on their journey into the future, mainly because she could not accept the fact that they had been in the future; after all, time travel was impossible. This part of her still thought that the entire trip must be part of some insane dream and that soon she would wake up to find that the US president was even still alive and she was just another struggling reporter, begging for that first byline. However, there was another part of her that realized she was being very self-centered and petty considering what other people were dealing with at this moment in time.

The president's wife had made her first public appearance that morning, looking twenty years older than she had before seeing her husband shot in front of her and her three children. She had made no statement but had allowed the secretary of state to announce that the first family would be escorting the president's body back to the United States on Air Force One that afternoon. The woman's dark eyes had remained focused on the ground, as if she was hunting the earth for her lost earring, or maybe she was praying that this was all some terrible joke and tomorrow she would wake up and life would have returned to normal. Shelly had watched the news conference from her kitchen, her eyes never leaving the woman in the dark suit who stood behind the podium, refusing to answer the questions the media threw at her. The reporter in her wished she had been there, but the humanity in her cringed at the unbearable grief in the woman's bent frame and dark eyes.

George was waiting for her outside his flat in his new clothes. The fact that he had allowed her and the salesgirl to talk him into wearing the sports coat told her a great deal about the man; he would do almost anything for her. It was a thought that made her smile, and as he sat down next to her in the car, she reached over and squeezed his arm. "You do look wonderful in that jacket."

"I feel like a bloody fool." He scowled as he adjusted his seat belt. "I will tell you this much—I will never wear it again."

Shelly's smile faded as she pulled out into traffic. "That is really too bad because you could win many a lady looking like that."

George looked over at her, and the scowl on his face deepened further. "Just drive."

They did not speak again until they were parked at the office building where Peterson held court. It was a tall nondescript building, unkempt and shabby. She had thought it would be one of the more spectacular glimmering towers of the financial elite, but it was more in keeping with someone just starting out, and it reminded her that this man was not the rich man who would rule the world in 2070. Shelly sat for a moment, uncertain as to what her first question to this man should actually be; after all, this was not a typical interview. Hell, it was not even a real interview.

George looked over at her and shook his head. "Come on, girl. We do not have all day."

They walked into the office building, and Shelly flashed her press pass. Peterson had informed the front desk to expect their arrival, and they were soon escorted into the man's outer office, which was not as opulent as they had thought it might be. The young man came out of the inner office into the empty outer room where a secretary should have been. Peterson extended a hand to George and then to Shelly. "I am so pleased that someone in the press is taking an interest in my little company." He was obviously in his twenties with his messy brown hair and ill-fitting dark suit. "Come in, and we can talk about what I hope to accomplish in the next few years."

They followed him into his office, and as they sat around his paper-strewn desk, George made a mental note to keep the image of the elderly man who had damaged the Antarctic in his mind—because if he didn't, he might actually begin to like this man. Right now he was just a hardworking fellow who was just trying to make a living. He certainly did not look like the slimy, evil government blackmailer that Philip had railed against in 2070.

"I wanted to do a feature on new start-up companies," Shelly said as she pulled out her phone and placed it on the desk. "My superiors are not totally sold on the idea, and with so much going on right now, they are not exactly ready to commit too much space to the story."

"We are willing to allow her to test her interview skills, though," George said, leaning forward. "After all, she has to learn these things somewhere."

Peterson's smile faded, and he sat back heavily in the well-worn leather chair behind his desk. "Are you telling me that this article may never see the light of day?"

"No." George smiled and tried to look a little more enthusiastic. "If her skills are not up to the task, then I will take over the interview. But no matter whose name is on the byline, when the news of the world has calmed down, this story will be told—of that you have my guarantee."

Peterson studied George for a moment and then rose to his feet and headed to the side table, where a pot of coffee waited. He poured three cups and set them on a tray, which he carried to his guests. George and Shelly accepted their cups with thanks, and Peterson returned to his seat behind the desk with his coffee. "I have never taken guarantees on face value, but since I really have nothing to lose in this case, I do not see the harm in talking to the two of you today."

George glanced at Shelly and gave her a sly smile. He had to wonder if they might indeed be of some harm to this man, but for now there was no need to give him any reason to doubt their intentions. This really was just a fact-finding mission.

Shelly leaned forward and pushed a button on her phone to start recording the interview. "Mr. Peterson, what made you drop out of college when you did?"

Peterson stared at her for a moment. "You have done your homework."

"That is part of the job," Shelly said, beaming at him.

Peterson sighed and leaned back. "I thought I was being smart when I dropped out of college, but to be honest, I wish I had finished those last years of higher learning. I always feel as if I am running to catch up to the Harvard, Oxford, and Cambridge types."

"You feel as if they know something that you should," George said, nodding in understanding.

Peterson stared at him. "You know that feeling?"

"More than you might think." George gripped his cup a little too hard and noticed his knuckles turning white.

Shelly cringed at the statement before she continued. "Mr. Peterson, what did you do when you dropped out of college?"

"I actually went to South America for a while and worked on some construction crews. I helped build roads and dams. It was real hands-on education."

George shuddered. He had so wanted to dislike this man—in fact, he had wanted to hate him on sight—but this was not a brain-trust, silver-spoon idiot; this was a man who had worked for a living.

Shelly could see the indecision creeping into her companion, and it worried her, so she tapped her hand on the desk. They needed to keep to the task at hand. "So you're not one of these people who inherited a business."

"God no," Peterson said, letting out a snort of laughter. "My mom was a single parent, and she never told me who my father was. And actually, I never asked her because it did not matter one way or the other."

George sighed heavily, and Shelly glared at him as she asked Peterson another question. "Would you say your mother is proud of you?"

Peterson sighed too. "I doubt it. She wanted me to finish college. Hell, we have not really spoken since I left college to head to Brazil. I know that is really my fault, and if I had to do it over, I might change how we left things, but you can't travel back in time, so I have to live with my decisions."

George choked on the sip of coffee he was taking, and Shelly pressed her hand to his knee. "We all have things we would like to change in our past, Mr. Peterson, but since no one has a time machine, we have to accept those things. What did you do after South America?"

"Well," he said, leaning back in his chair, "I actually enjoyed construction, so I decided to become a builder in my own right. I put up everything I had to fund a small project in Ecuador, which paid off quite well, and that led me back home, where I am building up capital to fund some mega projects in Africa and Asia."

"Can you afford mega projects if you are not one of the elite?" Shelly fidgeted with her cup.

"You want to know where I am getting the billions for this project—is that it?"

"Yes, Mr. Peterson, that is it." Shelly leaned forward. "You have to admit that your rags-to-riches story is impressive, but there are some major holes in it."

George nodded his head in agreement.

Peterson's smile faded into a deep scowl. "All right, I did sugarcoat some of the things I did in South America, but you have to understand that those countries are not England, and some of the things we do here do not work over there. I had to play by their rules, and I played the game really well."

Shelly drummed her fingers on the desk. "What does that mean?"

"I did not hurt anyone," he said with a grimace.

Shelly sighed and drummed her fingers on the table again. "All right, let us forget about that for the time being. You have begun building in some remote locations in Africa and Asia. Why in those areas? Why not here in England?"

The man glared at her for a moment and then closed his eyes. He leaned back into his chair and sighed. "Well, Miss Jenkins, let us say that it is easier to get past the regulations in Africa and Asia than here in England."

"Where would you like to build next?" George asked, jumping in. "Where is that dream location for you?"

Peterson opened his eyes slowly and looked at George as if he had not really seen him before now. His face was suddenly beaming. "Well, sir, if you must know, a couple of years ago while I was down in South America, I took a trip to the Antarctic, and it occurred to me that someday people will be building there. I want to be that pioneer."

"The Antarctic," Shelly said, her voice going up an octave. "What about the environmental impact?"

"My God," Peterson said, rolling his eyes. "Every time anyone wants to build anything bigger than a bird feeder, we have to do an environmental impact assessment. Do you have any idea what those things have cost us in terms of progress?"

George could see Shelly biting her tongue and tapping her toe nervously. He did agree with her that people like Peterson were dangerous to the environment, but she had told him during their morning drive that at this point in time, they could not afford to take the man to task for his opinion about impact assessments.

"So what do you think about the environmental concerns about building in the polar regions?" George emptied his coffee and set the cup on the desk.

Peterson leaned across the desk until his eyes were level with George's. "I am saying one report on the region should be enough. We do not need a dozen on the same spot every time we dig a hole."

"You think the South Pole will be the next target for building?" Shelly pushed her thigh against George's leg.

"Yes, I do," Peterson said, leaning back into his chair, "if the international committees do not get in the way."

"International committees," Shelly said quietly. Here was the motivation behind the death of the American president. "You are talking about the Polar Expeditions Oversight Committee."

"Yes, that is exactly what I am talking about," Peterson said, folding his hands into his lap. "They are the ones we have to convince in order to be able to build anything at either pole."

"Do you think the recent death of President Carlson will change the tone of that particular committee?" Shelly asked. It was time to find out this man's real agenda. "After all, he was slotted to head that committee, and he had made it clear he was against any negative impact on the poles."

There was a moment of silence as Peterson weighed this question. Shelly studied the man thoughtfully. He was obviously worried about how he should proceed with this line of questioning. If he stated that he was even a little glad that the man was dead, it might derail some of the deals he had in the works, but he had already made his view of polar development clear, and so backpedaling now would make him appear weak.

"I disagreed with some of the president's hard-line opposition to polar development," he said slowly, "but had he lived, I am certain we would have come to some form of understanding. We would have been able to work together. His death was a tragedy, and I would never applaud such an action just to green-light polar development."

Shelly and George exchanged a smile and subtly nodded at one another. They really did not need to ask him anything more, but it would have been impolite just to get up and leave. So over the next forty minutes or so, they discussed development in Africa and Asia, including Peterson's take on African politics and the latest innovations in building codes in China. No one mentioned the Antarctic or the president's death again.

George became listless and bored with the whole thing, but he waited for Shelly to finish the interview. After they were done, they said their good-byes and headed to the car, neither of them talking.

CHAPTER 32

Shelly climbed into the driver's seat and leaned forward, resting her head on the steering wheel. George stared at her for a moment. "Are you all right?" he finally asked her.

"No." She did not even bother lifting her head. "He must have thought I was insane, asking him if he thought the death of the president would make it easier for him to get his development deal past the Polar Expeditions Oversight Committee."

George let out a long sigh. "You had to ask the question. It was the reason we came to this meeting."

"You do not have to remind me why we came to this meeting." Shelly finally raised her head and glared at the man seated next to her. "I remember all too well why we are here."

"So why are you beating yourself up over something you had to do?"

"We had to do it," Shelly said, starting the car, "but I do not have to like it." She pulled out into traffic and nosed the car into the ongoing rush of vehicles. She pushed down on the accelerator and uncharacteristically cut in front of other cars, dodging through lanes and heading across the city at a speed George had never seen her travel before.

George grabbed for the dashboard in front of him and held on, wondering if she was trying to kill the two of them so that they would not have to deal with the issue at hand. What were they going to do now that they had met the young Mr. Peterson?

The car skidded to a halt in front of George's flat, and Shelly slumped forward in the driver's seat, resting her head on the steering wheel once more.

Her companion glared at her for a moment, his hands still gripping the dashboard in front of him. "All right." He finally let go and allowed his hands to fall to his side. "Now that you are done with the steeplechase, can we discuss this a little more calmly?"

Shelly sighed heavily and then began to laugh. "Calmly, he says—calmly, as if this is all so normal."

"I know that none of this is normal, but we have to make some sort of plan."

"Plan to do what?" She looked up and stared out the window. "What do you suggest we do now that we have met the man?"

"I don't know," he whispered under his breath. "But it is clear to me at least that he would have orchestrated the deed if he had the means."

"You don't know that for a fact," she cried in an anxious voice. She turned her head and stared at George. "He may have been against the president's goals for the Antarctic, but that does not mean he would want the man dead. I am against the prime minister's European Union goals, but that does not mean I would hire a gunman to kill him."

George sat for a moment staring at the front door of his apartment building. Everything had made so much more sense when they had traveled through the time door to 2070 to look for a killer. But now they had him in their sights, and none of it seemed so cut-and-dried anymore. The young man in the office building had no idea that he had been involved in the assassination that had taken place three days earlier. How could he?

"We can't accuse him of this crime," Shelly said, sighing once more. "Hell, he would have us locked up as raving maniacs, and he would be right."

"But we are right." George opened his door and stepped out onto the pavement. "He will be involved in the future. Sometime in the future, he will be the one to step through a door into the museum, and he will kill that man sure as I am standing here."

"You really do have no proof of that, George." She leaned across the seat and glared up at him. "It is all rampant speculation based on some wild time-travel theory we could never prove in a million years."

"Theory!" He turned back to face her. "You were there. You saw the same things that I did. How can you call it a theory?"

"Easy," she said, her voice suddenly a whisper. "It was a delusion, and that was all it was. None of it was real. How could it have happened?"

"You are looking for a way out," George said, shocked. "You do not want to have to deal with this now that Peterson is a real person and not some name on a computer."

"You don't understand." Shelly leaned back into her seat. "He is the only thing that is real about any of this."

George bent over and leaned into the car. "You listen to me, girly. I will tell you about real—the blood on the floor of the mummy room, the body of a man who was breathing one moment, laughing with his wife and children, and dead the next; those things were damn real. You seem to think we made those things up to sell newspapers and gain you a byline, but to his family it is far too real."

"I know that." She closed her eyes. "I know a man is dead."

"And you wanted to keep the byline, didn't you?" He was suddenly mad, furious even, that this girl was no longer willing to take the next step with him. "It was never about finding the truth or justice for the president and his family. It was all about extending your career and keeping your name in the paper."

Shelly's bottom lip quivered, and her hands gripped the steering wheel. "I don't think you are being fair to me or to Peterson. The man we met today has no idea what you want, and neither do I."

"I want to stop a murder," his said, his voice suddenly low. "If I can, I will use the medallion to go back and stop it from happening."

"That is not possible."

"I have it." He pointed at his front door. "You left it in there, and if I need to, I will go alone, and I will stop Peterson before he can kill the president. I will not have that man's wife and children see him shot before their very eyes, not if I have the means to stop it."

Shelly glared at George for a moment and then turned the car back on. "Fine. Then you will go alone because I am not convinced Peterson is the killer."

ଔଔଔ

As George stood up and slowly turned to walk into his building, Shelly sat in her vehicle, shocked that he was not going to agree with her. He had been so accommodating about everything. She had assumed he would fold like a cheap suit and blindly follow her wherever she wanted to go, just like most men did. All her adult life, men had simply done everything she had asked of them; all she had to do was smile that cute little imp smile, and the deed was done. This middle-aged security guard had been the easiest man to manipulate that she had ever met. She had done very little, and he had led her to the greatest story imaginable. Now he was running in a direction she did not want to go, and he was not willing to listen to her.

She put the car into gear and pulled out into traffic, driving a lot more slowly than she had on their trip from Peterson's office. All the way home, she debated the way they had handled that interview and the possibility that at some point Peterson would commit murder, but mostly she considered the possibility that she was losing the sexual edge that she had once had over most men.

When she pulled up in front of her own flat, she wondered what she would say to George the next morning. She would go to see him, and together they would come to some compromise; they would find something to agree on, just as they had throughout this crazy story. She had no reason to doubt that. He was still her friend and someone she could talk to about anything. Tomorrow everything would return to normal.

CHAPTER 33

George knew that Shelly was upset with him, that she was angry that he had not agreed to give Peterson the benefit of the doubt. Yet how could he give the man a free pass on a cold-blooded murder? The problem was that he knew she might be right. They were looking at this young man as a murderer in the distant future, believing that years from today he would discover the secret of the amulet and use it to open a door to the mummy room so that he could alter history.

The security guard sat at his kitchen table where he and Shelly had discussed the medallion and brooded over the oddity of the situation. After a few minutes, he got up and put the kettle on to boil. He did not really want a cup of tea, but he also did not want to be sitting there all afternoon staring at that box, second-guessing himself. The cat padded over to him and curled his small little body around George's foot. George looked down at the cat and smiled. "I wish my life was as simple as yours."

The problem was that he was not a cat, and nothing was ever going to be simple again. He held the key to the future if he had the stomach to use it. The problem was he had never been a brave man; he had never been a risk taker. He walked back to the table and picked up the box, carefully rotating it in his large hand. He was still staring at the box when the kettle whistled. He let out a sigh, put the box back on the table, and went to the cupboard for a cup and the tea.

Minutes later, he again sat at the table staring at the box, the tea growing cold. He had always kept tea in the house, first for his dear departed mother and then for mates who never actually came around and who, when they did, preferred a beer. He still had the tea in the cupboard more out of habit than anything else because although he knew it was not a very British thing to say, he really did hate the stuff.

An hour later he had poured the tea down the sink and was seated in front of the television with a beer in his hand, watching an afternoon cricket game but not really paying attention to it. He remembered that he had laid a bet with someone at the pub about this particular match, but for the life of him, he could not recall who he had said would win. It was odd, but he no longer seemed to care about these things, nor did he want to head off to the pub to watch the match with the gang that was gathered there. What would he say to any of them about the murder at the museum? They would ask, and he would shake his head because there was nothing he could tell them that made any sense.

He knew who the killer was, but he did not have one bit of evidence that a court would believe. This frustrated him, and the fact that the one other person who knew this had run out on him only added to his level of frustration. George had assumed that once they met up with Peterson, it would be only a matter of figuring out how to use the medallion to correct the mistake the man had made, to return the time line to its true course. He knew that might mean killing the man, but what other choice did they really have? Carl Peterson had used time travel to murder the US president, so it was only right and just that they use it to kill him before he could actually commit that act.

George turned back to the box still resting on the table and stared at it. The cat lay on the table beside it, sound asleep. "So, fella, what do you think?" the security guard asked the sleeping cat. "Do I take a risk and commit a crime for the betterment of all, or do I allow sleeping cats to lie there undisturbed?"

The cat looked up at him and gave a rather pathetic meow that made the man smile.

"I guess that answers that question." George picked up the box and opened it. He stared at the medallion for a moment and then gingerly picked it up. It seemed to shine in the afternoon light, winking at him. "God, do you really think this is the way it was meant to be?" He stared at the cat still lying on the table. "Am I really meant to do this all on my own? I thought that she would be with me, helping me make this decision, but who the hell was I fooling? Did I really think she was going to be here with me?"

With the necklace in his hand, George suddenly stopped and looked down at the kitten. "I am talking to a cat. That shows the world how far off I am." He placed the amulet around his neck and stood facing the wall. "But it is the only place I need to be." He took a deep breath and in a low voice muttered the words: "open to protect the pharaoh." As the door fluttered into existence once more, George closed his eyes and considered the date that would best serve his needs.

If the idea was to change the events that had caused the death of the president, he would have to go back a week prior to the murder, and it would be best to choose a date when the earlier version of himself would not be at the museum. That always had been the best course, and he saw no reason to alter that now, so he spoke a date two weeks in the past and stepped back into the museum.

As he walked through the building in a daze, he wondered about the turns his life had taken in the last two weeks. This day in the past was his day off, and George was off to a football game in Manchester with some of his mates from the pub. That version of him would be drinking, laughing, and yelling at the players all afternoon as his team lost another match, but that was the life of a football fan in premier league. The odd part of all of those memories was that now he realized that none of those things really mattered to him or to anyone else. It did not matter if his team won or lost because there was always next year, and even that was nothing when compared to the long-term effects of global warming and death on a global scale.

He shuddered at the thought that his life had been that empty and useless. All he had ever cared about was football, cricket, and a pint at the pub. "I really am a pathetic lout," he sneered to himself as he walked out into another drizzly morning in London. He headed to the tube and a place where death was waiting for him. He never could have imagined these events two weeks ago as he watched that game. Now he was thinking about life and death and what would happen when Peterson discovered the truth about the medallion.

George wondered where the man had found out the truth about the medallion and how he had come to the earth-shattering decision to use it to commit murder. He and Miss Shelly Jenkins had stumbled onto the words by accident, so perhaps that was how Carl Peterson had found out about the medallion's hidden secrets too. Maybe he had put on the necklace one stormy afternoon while strolling through the museum and had somehow cracked its code. That scenario did make some sense, but the theory had some flaws as well since it relied on a builder knowing hieroglyphics, and that made about as much sense as a security guard knowing how to read that ancient Egyptian language. Also, how would he even have come to look at that medallion, and how would he have acquired it? The only reason George had paid it attention was that it had been found in the rubbish bin. Those were questions George could not answer.

The security guard stared out the window of the tube as the stops rolled past. He ignored the people standing on the platforms, the signs indicating the stops, and the sounds of people chatting, laughing, and musing about the world. He was in a daze as he went through the possibilities in his mind and tried to find the one that would best explain what he had seen in the museum the day the president was shot.

He stepped out of the station a few blocks from Peterson's office and started walking down the street, but every step made him feel sick. Feeling the urge to throw up, he darted into a restaurant and sat down at the counter, bracing his hands against the countertop. When the waitress wandered over to him, he ordered a cup of coffee and a biscuit, neither of which he actually wanted, but then again he did not want to be near that office either. He sipped at the coffee and looked out the window at the people passing the little diner. They were all briskly running as the dreary rain pelted their turned-up collars and umbrellas. He scanned every face, praying one moment that he would see Peterson and the next moment that he would never see the man again.

Shelly had been right about one thing: thinking about murder was not an easy thing to do. So how had Peterson leaped to that unrelenting idea? How did anyone suddenly decide to take another person's life? George downed the coffee, paid the waitress, and headed out the door, determined to find Carl Peterson before the day was over. He had to ask him. He had to find out how any of this had happened.

As he walked toward Peterson's office building, his mind was a jumble of disconnected thoughts. What if Peterson had not come in to work that day? How would George find him then? George knew he would never have the nerve to get into the tube and head to this part of the city again. It was now or never, so he headed into the shabby lobby of the building, praying that the man was there. He stepped into the dilapidated old lift, pushed the button for Peterson's floor, and braced himself against the wall.

He knew it was ridiculous to pray that Peterson would be in his office, but that was exactly what George did during the entire ride in that lift up to the tenth floor, where he and Shelly had interviewed the man. George was not a religious individual, so he had never considered asking for God's help for anything, but asking God to help now seemed even more bizarre and almost antireligious. "God, this is not what I ever thought I would ask, but today you must know that Peterson used that medallion to go against your will. Please allow me this one thing, and I will take my punishment like a man. I will go to prison with a song in my heart if that is your will." As he quietly spoke the words, George looked around the lift for a camera and found nothing. It was an old building, and that technology had not been installed. "Is that a good thing or a bad thing?" George wondered aloud as the elevator came to a stop and the doors opened.

He had not even considered trying to get away with the crime he was thinking about committing. In his own mind he was already in custody, awaiting trial for the murder of Carl Peterson. He had even wondered how he would explain something that his mates would say was completely outside his normal behavior. The press would head to the pub where he drank and push cameras into their faces, and those men would be hard-pressed to come up with some reason that made any sense. Even he would not be able to explain his actions in a way that made sense to anyone. If he managed to do it—to kill this man—then George's very reason for killing him would no longer exist. The president would not be killed. The president would be alive, and George would be in a lunatic asylum with a medallion around his neck.

He walked without hesitation to the office door and pushed it open, expecting to see Peterson's secretary, even though he and Shelly had not seen her when they had come to interview Peterson. He figured the day of their interview might have been her day off. But there was no assistant in the office today either.

"Peggy, is that you?" Peterson's voice called out from the inner office. "I thought I told you to take the day off and get some rest. I am going to need you fresh as a daisy tomorrow." Peterson came out of his office and stared with a mixture of anger and confusion at George, who stood just feet away beside the secretary's desk. "Who the hell are you?"

George stared at the young man who had been so nice and accommodating when he thought George was a reporter, or at least some reporter's supervisor, but that interview was in the future, and this man did not know him. George briefly thought about what he could say, but no words could make this any easier, so he simply picked up a heavy lamp seated on the secretary's desk and stepped forward in one swift motion, smashing it into Carl Peterson's temple.

Peterson let out a gasp. The moment was so shocking that the man seemed to forget to even scream. Peterson fell back against the desk, sending papers and pens flying to the floor, and then crumbled into a ball beside the desk, where he lay moaning. George leaned over him and hit him again and again with the lamp until the moaning stopped. The last word Carl Peterson spoke was "Why?" and it was the one question George could not answer for him. How could he explain it to the dead man when he was struggling to explain it to himself?

George calmly unplugged the heavy lamp and walked out of the building with it, but not because he knew it bore his fingerprints. He was not thinking clearly enough to consciously take away evidence; he just wanted to keep it in his hands a little longer, to feel its weight as a stark reminder of what he had just done.

Oddly enough, no one stopped him. No one even seemed to notice him or pay any attention to the man walking to the tube station with a brass lamp in his hands. He did not consider that the lamp might have blood on it, but as it happened, the force had not broken skin but simply smashed the man's skull in. So why would anyone notice him and what he was carrying? It was just a lamp, with nothing really remarkable about it. It was not large, but it was heavy, and he felt it with each step that he took, but he knew that he could not put it down. On the train he sat with it on his lap, as if it was a child he needed to protect. An elderly woman wearing a scarf over her head stared at the lamp for a moment, but then she turned back to the book she was reading, not giving him more than a passing glance.

As George walked into his flat, with the lamp still in his sweaty hands, he wondered if he was about to get away with murder. The thought left a lump in his throat and made him feel queasy inside. He had not wanted to get away with it, and for a split second he had thought about sitting beside the body and waiting for the police. Yet in his dazed mind all he could really think about was getting home and putting the medallion back in the museum where it belonged. The only way he could do that was by stepping back through the door into his correct time. Besides, there was another George Marsh who at this moment was at a football match in Manchester. How would he explain that to the police—or to anyone else for that matter?

He put the lamp down on his kitchen table and placed the medallion beside it. If anyone were to ask, Clancy would be able to tell the police that George had been at the game all day with the rest of the gang from the pub. However, George was sure that no one would connect him to or contact him about the death of some obscure businessman, so he was worrying over nothing. He pulled an ale from the fridge and sat down at the table, pouring it into a glass. He then looked at the lamp and traced his finger over its edge.

He turned and looked at the cat, who let out a soft little meow and curled himself around George's feet. The guard knelt down and rubbed the little animal's back. "Promise me, you stupid cat, that you won't tell me that I was here today with a murder weapon." He glanced at the lamp and wondered for a moment what he was going to do with it. He decided it was fine in his flat for now and it would be a reminder of what he had done.

He knew that he had to go through the door before this day's version of him got back from the match, or the world would explode or implode or do something equally terrible. He picked up the medallion, put it around his neck, and once more said, "Open to protect the pharaoh."

The door shimmered into existence, and George stated the date and the time in the afternoon when he had left. A moment later, he opened the door and stepped back into a world he hoped he had changed forever. He looked around the museum and sighed at the sight of the mummy room. He had always hated it, and now he hated it more than ever. He looked intently at the displays and wondered for a fleeting moment which of the wrapped corpses the medallion was meant to protect. It was the one question no one seemed to want to ask, or perhaps it was a question to which no one knew the answer.

He smiled for an instant and then headed for the main floor. If he had not changed the course of events, then the American security team would jump him, but if he had succeeded, he would be able to walk to his desk and go back to work as if nothing had ever happened. It was a risk, but considering he had just committed cold-blooded murder, it was a small one and one that he was willing to take.

"Afternoon, George," said one of the assistants, greeting him with a nod of her head. She was one of the people Harry called the brush squad, the people who worked at cleaning artifacts with tiny little brushes day in and day out. If she was back in the building, then either the Americans had allowed the museum to reopen, or it had never closed.

"Afternoon, Katherine," he said, smiling back at the middle-aged woman. "Has it been busy today?"

"Typical for a Wednesday," she muttered as she walked past him.

George felt his entire body go limp as the tension left it—typical for a Wednesday. If it was a typical day, then that meant nothing unusual had happened recently to put the place into a tailspin. He took a deep breath and headed for his desk. He was out of uniform, but that was not always a problem for the people in charge. He had a spare one in his locker, and he could change quickly enough if need be, but if this was a typical Wednesday, he was supposed to work only until noon anyway and have the afternoon off.

"You heading home then?" Harry called to him across the floor. "Or to the pub?"

"Either one," George said with a smile. "Nothing doing here."

"There never is," Harry said with a nod as he headed back to his monitors.

"There never is," George muttered under his breath and headed to his locker.

CHAPTER 34

When Shelly awoke early the next morning, she knew that sleep had been a useless idea. She felt more tired than she had when she lay down, but now she really did have to go in to work and at least touch base with Perry. She dressed slowly in a pair of jeans and a blue T-shirt, which she knew Perry would scoff at as far too casual, but perhaps that was the idea. Maybe today she wanted him to yell at her over something, anything. She felt so wrong after that interview with Peterson and how she had reacted that she wanted someone to chastise her for it, even if that person had no idea why she was feeling so wrong.

The office seemed unusually quiet, which only added to Shelly's feeling of dread. Days had passed since the US president's death, but an event like the assassination of a world leader should have had this place running at full steam for at least a month, if not longer. She walked over to her desk and glanced at the computer screen to see what notes Perry had left for her on the interviews she had done with the students, but there was nothing. Did that mean he liked what she had written, or was he scrapping the entire article?

She looked up and saw Perry at his desk furiously typing at his computer. She took a deep breath and walked over to him, wondering what she would say when she got there. "Sir, is there anything you need me to do today?" She closed her eyes and waited for him to answer.

Perry looked up at her and hesitated for a moment, as if he was trying to recall her name. "Miss Jenkins, we are in the middle of the G-20, so just help Gary with research on the leaders and try to keep yourself out of the way."

Shelly opened her eyes and stared at her supervisor for a moment. "What about the president of the United States?"

"Emmett put James on that aspect of the conference, so don't worry about him," Perry said, sighing with contempt. Shelly had noticed that he didn't seem to like James Keller. "You help Gary get background on the rest of the world leaders."

Shelly nodded her head in dumb wonder and stumbled back to her desk. She put her head down and muttered under her breath, "God, George, what did you do?"

It seemed the entire world had forgotten that just a few days ago the American president had been assassinated, leaving her with a memory that made no sense. But if that event had not taken place, why did she recall it with such stark clarity? She cringed at the question and its implications. She then pulled her head up and stared at her computer, wondering if it could provide some of the answers. Perry expected her to be trolling online for something they could use, so she decided it was a place to start. She typed the name Carl Peterson into a search engine and held her breath as the results came up.

"Businessman Killed in His Office by Unknown Assailant," the headline blared out at her. Shelly put her head back down on her desk and felt her stomach lurch. "George, what did you do?" she muttered again.

"Why are you looking at that case? It is two weeks old." Her colleague Gary stood next to her desk, glancing over her shoulder. "It is a dead end; the police have no leads."

"They have no idea who may have killed this man?" Shelly stared up into the handsome face. "Weren't there any witnesses?"

Gary smiled at her and gave her an odd wink. "Nary a one, but that is not unusual in these cases." He sat down on the edge of her desk. "I covered that one myself. They believe that Peterson surprised a burglar, who bashed him over the head with a brass lamp, which is the only thing missing according to Peterson's secretary."

"A brass lamp," Shelly repeated. She really did feel that she was going to be sick.

"Yeah, the police have looked everywhere for it with no luck." Gary looked suddenly deep in thought. "Why are you interested in this case anyway?"

She knew Gary. She knew that he was overly protective of his crime beat and would fight tooth and nail to remain the main criminal case reporter. So she mustered up all the courage she could and flashed a coy smile. "Oh, come on, Gary. I was just keeping up with your byline."

He studied her for a moment and then flashed his winning smile back at her. "It is an interesting story, and I did a pretty good job on it."

Shelly sighed and smiled; appealing to a man's vanity worked every time, and Gary was a vain man when it came to his writing skills. "Do you think the police will break the case?"

"It is not exactly top on the list, and since they have no leads, I don't see them working it too hard." Gary stood up and headed back to his own desk. "But you never know what might happen in the future."

Shelly laid her head back on her desk and coughed. "I do know the future, or at least I thought I did," she whispered. Her mind was whirling with an image she did not want in her head, an image of her friend George bashing a man over the head with a heavy brass lamp. She had considered him a friend, but now she was not so sure about that. There was only one way to find out for certain. She grabbed her car keys and headed for the elevator. She thought she heard a voice call her name, but she did not care. Her job no longer mattered to her; finding out whether someone she considered a friend had committed murder was much more important than being a reporter.

Shelly started toward George's flat, but as she drove down the busy street, she realized that if the world had returned to normal, then it was possible that George was back at work, minding the front door of the museum. So she quickly made a left turn and headed toward the British Museum instead, praying that she wasn't right. A small part of her was still hopeful that what had just happened at the newspaper was all a dream and that the museum was still locked up. But the moment she drove past it, she knew that her world had changed while she was sleeping—the massive doors were open, and people were entering the ornate structure once more.

As Shelly walked up to the door and entered, she could feel her heart pounding in her chest. She knew George would be there working at his desk, but she was not really certain that she wanted to see him. What could she say to the man who she knew in her soul was guilty of cold-blooded murder? With each step, her heart raced and she felt more nauseated. Past the front lobby where she paid to enter, she could see the security desk and the man who sat there, a man she had thought of as her friend, a man she did not want to talk to. But she knew that she had to say something to him.

She waited until a group of Japanese tourists moved off with a tour guide and then stiffly walked over to the security desk. George smiled at her, but when he saw the misery written in her eyes, his smile faded. "Shelly," he whispered, "I had to."

Shelly glared at him, tears shimmering in her eyes. "You expect me to accept that, to accept the fact that you bashed a man's skull in with a lamp, to carry on as if nothing happened?"

"No." He solemnly shook his head. "But everything has changed. The world has changed. So Peterson must have been the guilty party. Since the president is alive today and his children did not see their father killed, that means that I made a difference."

Shelly's eyes went to the floor. He was right about one thing: the president was alive and well. He was at the G-20, and the world leaders were arguing over some stupidity that made no sense in the long run, so Peterson must have been guilty of the murder. George had killed a man who in the future would have discovered the secret of the Bastet amulet, so why was she so angry with him? "Just because you were right does not mean I have to like it," she finally whispered.

"What did you want me to do with the information?" George muttered in exasperation. "Pretend it did not happen? Allow the man to get away with murder?"

Shelly was crying now, and she had no idea why. What had she expected from this man? "So the president is alive. That does not mean that the Antarctic is safe from development. That one man may not really have made a difference in the history of the planet."

"I think there is a way we can check on whether the president made a difference."

Shelly looked up at him, her eyes the size of saucers. "You are not seriously thinking about what I think you are thinking about."

"We are both thinking it." George smiled at her and winked. "We could put on those colorful outfits one more time and head back to 2070."

"You have lost your mind!" she exclaimed, attracting the attention of everyone on the main floor of the museum. She glanced around at the people staring at them and then lowered her voice. "Do you honestly expect me to walk through that door again?"

"If you want to answer the question of whether killing Peterson was worth it"—George held his breath for a moment—"then it is exactly what we have to do. I was going to go after I finish work today. You are welcome to join me if you want to."

Shelly thought about what he was implying, and it made her feel sick inside. She was the one who had said she enjoyed the adventure of 2070. She had laughed at the man as he struggled with wearing a bright orange suit, and she had been the one to suggest they go to that bar where they met Philip and Lillian. Now she was terrified to head back to that place, not because it meant going back to that colorful world but because it might prove that George was right. "I do not want to wear that purple outfit again." She turned and headed for the door, her fists curled into tight little balls.

George sighed and shook his head. "If you change your mind, meet me outside the front doors at five," he called after her.

ଓଓଓ

"Who was that girl you were talking to?" Harry asked him once Shelly was gone.

"My cousin's daughter," George said, falling back on the lie, although in his heart he still wished that she was something else, something more.

"Sure," Harry said, before heading back to his cameras and his little dark office.

George dragged his feet when five o'clock finally came. He was almost afraid to head out the door, afraid that Shelly would not be there waiting for him. However, there was another part of him that was afraid she would be there and he would have nothing to say to her.

The moment he passed through the door, he saw the lovely young woman waiting by the main steps, and it made his heart skip a beat. "Shelly," he whispered as he walked up to her. That name had become almost a prayer to him and one that he hoped he would still be allowed to say at the end of this day.

"All right, I am here," she growled. "So what are we about to do to prove that you killing a man was the right thing to do?"

George sighed and shrugged his shoulders. "I told you, I am heading back to 2070 and the depository outside the museum."

"You are simply going to ask who now holds the Antarctic launchpad development?"

"It is much easier than that," he said with a smile. "I am going to ask where the launch pads are. If the president is a man of his word, he will have made certain that the launch took place somewhere away from the penguins. And if that is changed in the future, maybe the government crackdown on information is changed too—at least I hope it is."

Shelly nodded her head solemnly. "That sounds simple enough," she said. She fell in step beside the man, and they walked to her car in complete silence.

As they neared the car, George glanced at the silent young woman. "Did you bring your purple outfit? Because you will need it in 2070."

"It is in the car," she said, her voice barely above a whisper. "I was not about to wear that on the streets of London."

George laughed at the thought of the two of them wearing those colorful outfits anywhere except in the futuristic mod world of 2070. "It would be a sight."

"I do not find it funny," Shelly said as she pressed the button to unlock the car doors.

"Of course." George bit his lip and opened the passenger door. "We will change at my flat and then head to the future."

The drive to George's home was silent and riddled with tension. He wanted to say something to ease the young woman's mood, but he had no idea what he could say to make things easier. He had never considered that killing Peterson would upset her so much. He had done what he thought would remove the pain for the president's family, and now it seemed all he had managed to do was cause his new friend pain.

The two walked into the flat, and Shelly headed into the bathroom to change into her purple outfit while George grabbed his orange suit from the closet. As he changed, he wondered for the first time that day why it was still there if Peterson had not actually killed the president. He finished dressing and looked at himself in the mirror. He had not even considered the fact that everyone else seemed to be unaware of the change in the time line—everyone but Shelly and him. When Shelly came out of the bathroom, he was still staring at his own reflection.

Shelly finally smiled at him. "I still say that orange suit looks good on you."

"If you say so," he said with a smirk. "But that is not what has me so confused."

"A lot of things have me confused, sir." She sat down at the table and folded her arms across her chest.

"Like why do we remember the president being killed and everything that happened after that when no one else does?" George asked as he sat down across from her.

Shelly bolted upright and placed her hands on the table in front of her. "You're right. No one else at work seemed aware that the president had been killed. All they were talking about at the paper was the G-20 leaders' summit."

George shifted uneasily. "If no one else is aware of the change in the time line, why are we?"

The two sat there for almost five minutes, neither moving. They stared out into space, trying to come to terms with the fact that they were seemingly the only people on the planet who knew that a change had been made to the time line. Finally, George pulled the amulet out of the box on the table and studied it for a moment. "Maybe this silly thing is the reason we know about the shift."

"How did you come up with that theory?"

"You and I are the only people who have walked through that door." George turned the medallion over in his hand. "Perhaps that changed us as well as the time line."

"You, me, and the future Carl Peterson." She spat the name with a trace of venom in her voice.

CHAPTER 35

George and Shelly walked through the door and entered the year 2070 one last time, having chosen a date and time four months before their last trip to 2070, so that they would not meet themselves or anyone who had already interacted with them. It all made sense in a time-traveler kind of way, but in some ways, neither of them really understood what they were doing. They passed through the mummy room, left the museum, and headed for the library—or what the people in the year 2070 called The Depository of Knowledge.

George and Shelly were not really talking to one another; they were barely even acknowledging each other. George was afraid to say anything that might set her off, and Shelly was too angry to even think about talking. George bumped into a man in a lime-green suit and purple shirt. "Sorry, sir," he mumbled before continuing down the street. The year 2070 was the same as they had left it, but the two of them were decidedly different.

They walked into the depository and headed to the bank of monitors at the back of the room. Shelly sat in front of one marked 2030 and woke up the computer. She tapped her foot nervously as she waited for the screen to pop up asking her what she wanted to know. Without even looking at her companion, she typed the words "Mars launch pad." The images came up, and George heaved a sigh of relief. Shelly could see what made him so relieved. It was obvious from the holographic images that none of the shuttles were leaving from the Antarctic.

Shelly began reading the article aloud. "The first Mars shuttles left in the year 2037 from bases in the Gobi Desert and the Sahara Desert. Although some had argued that polar launches would make orbits a little easier to maintain, the environmental impact of building such massive structures on already fragile ecosystems made those projects unfeasible."

Shelly shook her head and stiffly rose to her feet. "I guess you were right after all."

"I know you do not like to admit that killing Peterson was the only answer." George reached out to pat her shoulder, but Shelly pulled away from him. "However, even you have to admit that we saved the world a whole lot of pain by removing him from the equation."

"You do not know that!" she screamed. "Someone else could have easily stepped in to make those deals. Someone else could have made those billions on the launch pads just like he did; the only difference is that they built the pads in the deserts instead of the poles."

"Shelly," George whispered, trying to keep his voice level and hoping this would calm her down, "all we have to do is ask, and perhaps this machine will provide some of those answers."

"Why should it?" She sat back down. "It froze us out last time, remember?"

"That was a different 2070." He pointed to the machine. "Peterson was not alive to ask them to keep the financial backing a secret from the public, so maybe the information will be there."

Shelly knew he had a point, but she was still loath to admit how right he had been. She stared at the terminal for a moment, wondering what to ask to gain the information they wanted. There seemed to be no way to frame the question that, if the same issues did still exist in this 2070, would not get them booted off the system again. She tapped the screen, took her seat again, and waited. She then typed her question: "Who backed the launch pad building in the deserts?" She held her breath and waited for the machine to freeze them out.

Quickly, the machine beeped, and an answer popped up. "Financial backing for the launch pads in both the Gobi and the Sahara came directly from government sources across the globe. Money was funneled to the African and Asian governments so that they could build the pads on their own with help from some private companies, but the major funding came from the governments that needed to get their citizens away from the natural disasters affecting the planet."

"See?" George said smugly. "There were no private companies making billions on this deal. It is not like it was before."

Shelly wanted to scream. She wanted to slam her fist into something. But she had no idea why. She sat there watching holographic images spiral into a mess of little black dots that only she seemed able to see. She slowly rose to her feet and braced herself on the table. She thought it was altogether possible that she was about to be sick. "George," she finally muttered, "I want to go home."

The young man who had helped them the last time they were in this building now came over to the terminal and smiled as George gave Shelly his hand. "Did you find everything you were looking for today?"

"Yes," George said, smiling back at him. "She wanted to know who financed the desert launch pads."

"It is a truly interesting part of our history," the young historian said as he turned off the machine. "There were rumors that in the beginning someone wanted to build both launch pads in the polar regions, but the committee overseeing polar development said no. They were obviously worried about what it would do to the environment, and considering the problems we were already experiencing from climate change, they did have a point."

Shelly was shaking as she listened to this academic explain a history that was years in her future. "Do you know who was in charge of the committee?" she asked, though she knew the answer without asking the question.

"Of course, everyone knows it was President Carlson of the United States." The man's smile grew as he launched into another explanation of events. "He took the post with the committee after his term in office was up. Many believe that he is the real reason the ice caps may be rebounding, since he was the one who put so much pressure on environmental cleanup and protecting the poles from development."

"He was an important figure in world history," George said, gently squeezing Shelly's arm. She pulled away from him and headed toward the door. Shrugging his shoulders, George followed her. The young historian shook his head and headed back to his workstation.

George caught up to Shelly, who was almost running down the street toward the museum. "Shelly, where do you think you are going? You can't get home without me. I have the medallion."

She stopped outside the front door of the museum and waited with her back turned to him. George walked up to her very slowly, and for the first time in his long life, George was actually afraid of a woman. She was so angry, and all of it was directed right at him. They walked into the museum, headed to the mummy room, and walked through the door without one word passing between them. George did mutter the necessary words to open the secret door and take them back to their time, but that was all he said.

Once they were back in his flat in the year 2020, standing in his kitchen, he took off his orange suit jacket and stared at the young woman in her purple outfit. "Shelly, tell me what you wanted me to do."

"I don't know." Her voice was barely above a whisper. "I just thought I knew who you were, and I did not think you were the sort of man who would bash someone over the head with a heavy lamp."

George sat down at the table and placed the medallion back in the box. He sat there in silence for a moment, and then with a heavy sigh he slumped forward. "You do not know me at all, Miss Jenkins. Hell, you have really only known me for a few days. You know nothing about me."

Shelly stared at the man seated across from her, and for the first time in the days since they met, she had to admit that she did know nothing about him. She did not know anything about his family, his friends, or his life. All she really knew was that he lived alone, worked in the museum, had a cat, and enjoyed Monty Python. She knew more about Emmett White, and that was a man who never allowed anyone near him except perhaps for Jillian Parker.

"I thought we shared something." She closed her eyes and remembered that night in 2070 when they had shared a bed. "We traveled to the future together, so I thought that meant something."

"I thought so too." George tried to smile, but it felt phony, so he simply shook his head. "But let's be honest, Miss Jenkins. We are two very different people. You are a reporter looking for a story, and I am a working stiff who saw a man die, killed right in front of his wife and children. We were in this thing for very different reasons."

Shelly flopped into the chair opposite and glared at the large man in his orange suit. "Why do you think I was in this thing?"

"Originally, to get a juicy story and have your name on a byline." He placed his head in his hands and leaned on the table. "You have to admit it, Miss Jenkins—that was the only thing that kept you coming to the flat of this middle-aged security guard."

She cringed, and for the first time she noticed that he was no longer calling her Shelly. He was calling her Miss Jenkins, as if he was trying to distance himself from her already. "I suppose that might be true, George." She placed a great deal of emphasis on his name, trying to maintain the familiarity that they had enjoyed over the last few days. "But it became something more than that, and you know it."

"All I know is that I wanted to save that man." He closed his eyes, and the memory of the president's children flashed into his mind once more. Those youngsters might not have that memory any longer, but he did, and it was something he would remember for the rest of his life. "You saw it as a story, but I only knew one thing: I had to save those children from the agony of seeing their father killed."

Shelly felt another shudder pass over her slight frame. Were they really that different? Was she all about the story whereas he was all about saving the president and his children? What did that say about her and the things that motivated her in life? Perry had told her that a real reporter would sell her soul for the story, give up everything for the truth. Was that what she had become?

She stared at the man sitting across from her, and for the first time since they met, she really looked at him. He did have a kind face, but there was a hardness to his deep blue eyes that she had never seen before. This was a man who had lived a lot longer than she had, and he had seen things that she never would have thought about bearing witness to. Maybe that was the point; maybe he was an entire generation removed from her experiences, and he knew more than she would ever think of knowing. Gary had once called her naive, and here was the proof laid out before her in stark colors.

"You really think that I would not have wanted to save the president?" Her voice was quivering. "Is that what you really think?"

"I am not sure what to think." George picked up the box holding the medallion and turned it over in his hand. "Ever since you walked into the museum this morning, all I have gotten from you is anger. So, Miss Jenkins, tell me—what has made you so angry?"

Shelly stared at the box in his hand and thought about what he was asking her. Why was she so consumed with rage? Was it what he had done to Carl Peterson, or was it something more fundamental than that? "I guess I believed that the time line was sacred and that we had no right to alter it."

"Peterson had already altered it," George said, putting the box back down on the table. "The moment he walked through that door with a gun in his hand, he put things in motion that we had to stop, one way or another."

"You honestly believe that, don't you?"

"Shelly," he whispered, "I am a man who believes that things happen a certain way for a reason. And God, or whatever higher power there is in this crazy mixed-up world, showed me that medallion and showed me the truth of what it was capable of doing. God showed me all of that because he expected me to make a difference and set things back the way they were meant to be before Peterson opened that door."

"God?" Shelly shook her head. "You actually think that God called on you to kill Peterson?"

"No." George lowered his gaze to the floor. "I know that I committed a mortal sin the moment I picked up that lamp, but it was something I had to do. I had to make things right, and it was the only way I knew to make things right again."

Shelly was shocked. She had never thought about God in all of this insanity, mainly because she had never really believed in God or a higher power. It had never even occurred to her that this man might believe in something so basic as God. She slowly rose to her feet and headed for the door. "George ..." She stopped and looked back at him. "I am not sure what any of this means, but I do know that I cannot accept murder as a means to an end."

"You might be right, but I think it was the one thing I could live with."

"I can't." She opened the door and left him sitting alone with the box before him.

CHAPTER 36

George Marsh was seated at his usual place at the security desk, watching as a group of teenagers filed into the building. He smiled, knowing that the day was going to be noisy and unruly, just the way he liked it. He had been given advance warning that a group from one of the schools was going to be taking a guided tour, so he was prepared for the assault to his routine. He had sent warnings to all the department heads and had told Carl to watch and be sure that those little hands did not move any of the displays.

He always felt a wave of horror wash over him whenever he had to speak to the academic, and it had nothing to do with the man himself or worry that he might find out that George was the one who had placed an Egyptian medallion in the trash of the Roman display. George had done that simply because he liked the idea of some form of continuity in the time line, even though in reality it made no sense. He disliked talking to Carl only because the name brought back too many violent memories—memories of the man George had murdered five years earlier when the world had stood still for a moment and he was the only one who could put things right. He knew that the name Carl would always haunt him and that he would always cringe whenever someone was introduced to him as Carl. Unfortunately, he had the same reaction now to the name Shelly.

He watched the students plod in as if the museum was the worst place they could think of being, but he knew that by the end of the day, they would all be chattering about the wonders that they had seen; the mummies and the odd statues would fill their imaginations for days to come. "All right, everyone, stay with your group leaders," a familiar voice called out, and George felt his heart skip a beat. It could not be possible, but there she was, leading the youngsters toward his desk. Shelly Jenkins was one of the group leaders.

She was wearing a plain white blouse and a mid-calf-length skirt with simple shoes—a typical uniform of teachers, he had determined years ago. This woman who had come into his life as a reporter was now acting as a teacher to these students. As she walked over, he wondered what if anything he could say to the woman he had not seen since the day she walked out of his flat wearing a bright purple outfit.

"Miss Jenkins." He nodded his head to her, but she did not even bother to smile at him.

"Mr. Marsh" was all she managed in reply.

He sat up a little straighter. "You are no longer working for the newspaper?"

"I gave that up the last day I saw you." Her bottom lip quivered slightly. "I knew right then and there that I was not cut out to be a reporter. I did not have the determination needed to go after a story at all costs."

"I see." George smiled a little, trying to make her feel more at ease. "So now you are a teacher."

She nodded her head and glanced over her shoulder at the group of students assembled in front of the main staircase. "I went back and got my teaching certificate. I have been teaching at the middle-school level for the last two years."

"I am happy for you," he whispered. "I mean, I am happy that you found something that means something to you."

"And you are still here," Shelly said. She cringed slightly. "And where is the medallion?"

"In the display case where it belongs," he said with a grin, "where no one else can get to it or understand what it is capable of doing."

"Someone did once," she said, her voice cold as ice. "Someone in the future figured it out, and maybe someone else will too."

George felt his heart grow cold. She was right about that. Peterson had discovered the secret of the amulet, so it was possible that someday someone else might uncover the truth. "I know you're right," he said, "but for now it is under glass, and no one touches it."

ଓଓଓ

Shelly turned and walked away toward the group of students. She had wanted to say more to George. She had rehearsed a thousand speeches in her head since this field trip was announced, but the moment she saw him sitting there, all those words had vanished. All she could really remember was the anger and pain that she had felt the last time she saw him.

George Marsh had altered everything about her life five years ago. He was the reason she had left the world of journalism without so much as one world of explanation to Perry, Emmett, or Gary. Perry was especially flabbergasted by her decision to just up and quit when he had told her that she had some potential that just needed to be cultivated. Yet there was no way she could explain her reasons in a way that would make any sense to them; that would have required her to tell them about the time line shift and the death of a world leader that none of them remembered. They would have called in a team of psychiatrists to check her into a loony bin.

The one story she could have used to create a real buzz about her ability as a field reporter was the only one she would never be able to tell anyone. Perhaps that was the real reason she had called it quits. Holding that secret was too much for her, and it made her feel like a hypocrite—not to mention the fact that she knew the identity of a murderer, and it was just one more secret in a long line of secrets that she could never actually tell. There would have been just too many questions asked by the paper and the police about how she had come to know that George Marsh was guilty of the murder of Carl Peterson. What type of reporter kept secrets like that?

"Do you know that security guard?" Helen Forster asked as Shelly rejoined the mob of students fidgeting near the staircase. Helen was a science teacher on duty with her today.

"I used to." Shelly pulled a clipboard from her briefcase and began to tick off the names of the students. "Back when I was in college." Shelly was not sure why she told that lie, but it made more sense than trying to explain that she had interviewed him in another reality back when she was a reporter.

Helen nodded and didn't ask more. Over the last few years, she had learned not to ask Shelly Jenkins too many personal questions.

ଔଔଔ

George watched the group move up the stairs and knew from past experience that they were heading to the mummy room. It was always a good place to begin with younger people because it really grabbed their imagination and pulled them into the world of ancient mysteries. He typed some information about the group into his terminal and settled back into his chair to await the calls he was certain would come from someone upstairs who was upset that those same children had knocked over a display or had set off an alarm on one of the cases. It happened every time. In some ways he looked forward to the panicked voice calling him to help deal with the unruly student who was messing up some long-dead mummy or trying to open a display case to get a closer view of a pretty little bauble. It made for a lively afternoon instead of the usual long boring day of sitting there doing nothing.

His mind then drifted to Shelly Jenkins and the last time he had seen her five years ago. The anger was still there, and it had radiated off her the moment she had walked into the building. He had been thrilled when he heard her voice and pleased when she walked over to his desk, but the moment she spoke to him, his heart had dropped like a stone. "How could she hate me that much?" he whispered under his breath. "I did nothing to her."

A part of his heart had died the day she walked away from him, and he had no idea why. It was not like they were destined to be a couple, but he had prayed that they would be able to remain friends. He had thought she would have at least some understanding of why he had committed the murder, but he also understood her response. He was loath to admit it, but a little piece of his soul had left him when he brought that lamp down on Peterson's head.

George caught sight of her a couple of times during the day as she ran after the mob of teenagers, but she would not even look his way. Actually, she appeared to be avoiding eye contact with him. By three in the afternoon, the group was heading into the museum gift shop, and he saw Shelly plop down onto a bench near the entrance. He smiled and walked over to her. "They have worn you out, haven't they?" he laughed as he sat down next to her.

"Yes, they certainly have," she said, nodding in agreement. "For a bunch who did not want to come here, they really have run me ragged."

"Typical kids." George watched as she leaned back and closed her eyes. "They never would say it out loud, but most of them enjoy this dusty old building. The mummies and mysteries fuel their imaginations just as much as the video games do."

Shelly opened one eye and let out a low chuckle. "I guess some things never do change."

George wanted to ask her something, anything, about what had happened five years ago, but he was terrified of the answer. "So do you like teaching?" That was all he could think to ask.

"Actually, I do." She sat up and smiled at him. "I never would have expected this about myself, but I find it very fulfilling."

"We all end up where we are meant to be." He sighed and found himself gazing across the floor to the security desk. "When I applied for this job, it was more because of a dare than a desire to be here. I actually hated this place back then, and for a while all I wanted to do was find something, anything, else to do."

"Why are you still here then?"

He chuckled and turned back to the young woman's smiling face. "Because somewhere along the line, I came to the realization that I was meant to be here, and once, five years ago, it made a difference."

Shelly froze and glared at him. "You think it made a difference to actually kill a man."

"Miss Jenkins, you may still hate what I did, but you cannot deny that the right man is alive and making a difference in the world. The poles are safe because the president is sitting as head of the Polar Expeditions Oversight Committee, where he was meant to be. It might not totally save the world from the climate change to come, but it was the right thing to do."

"Who were you to decide which time line was right?" Shelly said through clenched teeth.

"Who was Peterson to do so?" George shook his head in frustration. "He was the one who used the amulet to put in motion a shift in the time line. I just put things back the way they were meant to be. I made certain he did not use it to change history."

"What do you know about history?"

"I sit here every day leaning on it, learning from it." He passed his hand through the air. "Your students may see only the barest outline of it, but I live with it. Five years ago, I came to understand that history is a living, breathing thing, and it is not to be used as a tool. Peterson tried to change the fabric of time and space for financial gain, and history made use of me to prove him wrong."

Shelly stiffly rose to her feet. "I am not going to sit here listening to someone talk about history like it is something alive, telling him to commit murder. That is ridiculous, and if you were half the man I thought you were when I met you five years ago, you would not believe it either."

George sighed heavily and then stood, towering above her. "Five years ago, I told you that you do not know me; you never did. And personally, I knew nothing about you either. I never thought you would become a teacher, but that proves we really were not in step with each other, then or now. You can hate what I did all you want—you can believe it was the wrong thing to do—but it does not change things, and even if it were possible to walk through that door one more time and change what I did, I doubt that I would."

Shelly looked shocked. "You would not change any of it?"

"No." He smiled down at her and then turned to walk away. Suddenly, he stopped and shook his head. "And quite frankly, I don't think you would either. As much as you hate it, in your heart you know it was right thing to do."

ଓଓଓ

Shelly stood there for a long time watching him as he resumed his seat at the security desk. She wanted to scream at him that she did not agree with anything he had just said, but what was the point? She was not about to go into that mummy room and steal the necklace to change what had happened. She was not going to try to go back and stop him from killing Peterson. How could she? The reason she had become a teacher was that she was not really a woman of action, comfortable hitting the streets to obtain a story, nor was she the type who would crash through a door to stop a murder. George had taken that step, the step she was too afraid to even consider.

She heard her students chattering in the museum gift shop, and she knew it was time to get back to work. Helen joined her at the front of the store to monitor the mob as they tried to decide whether they should spend all the money in their pockets. "I am so glad this trip is almost over," said Helen.

Shelly smiled at her. "What, you do not enjoy history?"

"It was never one of my interests," Helen said, sighing heavily. "I would rather go to the Museum of Natural History than this place."

"I am so sorry that ancient history does not thrill you," Shelly finally said, letting out a low laugh. "But it is a part of their education, and maybe it will inspire at least one of them."

"I noticed you remained in that room with the ancient Egyptian jewels for a long time," Helen said, bracing herself against the door frame. "What could have been in there that was so intriguing anyway?"

"Just a necklace." Shelly's mind drifted back to what it had felt like to wear the Bastet amulet. "I thought it was rather beautiful."

"If you say so," Helen said, shaking her head. "I would never be caught dead in any of that old jewelry. Still, those who did wear it are long dead, so what difference does any of it make?"

Shelly shook her head and entered the gift shop to round up her charges. It was time to go home. She would never agree to come on another outing to the museum; she would never risk seeing him again. She could not bear to think about the man or the questions he asked of her.

CHAPTER 37

Shelly sat in her car, watching the rain come down over the cemetery, and realized how much she hated places like this. No matter how beautiful people tried to make them, they were still places filled with death. She had considered remaining at home, but she had to be there to see his funeral.

The day she saw the notice in the newspaper of the death of George Marsh from a heart attack, she had told her husband, Kenneth, that she would be taking a day off from work to attend the funeral of an old friend. He was shocked to hear the friend's name because she had brought up the name only once before, and that was when their son was born. Shelly had wanted to name the baby George, but Kenneth could see no reason for that since neither of them knew anyone personally named George other than a prince who would one day be king.

"There is no one in your family named George," he had argued when she suggested the name. "Why would you want to name our boy George? I told you I want to name him Gerald after my father."

Shelly knew he was right, that it was illogical to give her son the one name that reminded her of the worst moments of her life. The only name that would have been worse was Carl. She was not even really certain why she had made the suggestion; it was as if some unseen force had compelled her to state the very name she had refused to speak out loud for years. She had finally given in, and their son was named Gerald.

Kenneth and Gerald both read the obituary, which mentioned that George had been a long-time security guard at the famed British Museum.

"How did you know him?" Kenneth asked, staring at her in disbelief.

"God, Mom, you won't even go near that museum, so how did you ever meet the guard?" Gerald chuckled at the idea of his mom knowing anyone they did not know. His mother was so nervous around strangers that he had once teasingly said that she had his friends checked out by Scotland Yard before he was allowed to play with them. Her husband and son were right about the schoolteacher: she was a little wary around new people and never allowed anyone to really get close.

"Seriously, love, when did you meet this man?" asked Kenneth.

Shelly hesitated for a moment. "Long before I ever met you," she finally said. "That year I worked on the newspaper."

"Mom worked for a newspaper?" The ten-year-old was shocked. He had never heard this piece of monumental news before. Like most children, the boy thought he knew everything there was to know about his parents, and most of that was boring. His mother taught school, and his father worked in a bank, refusing to give people loans.

Shelly tussled the boy's blond hair and handed him his schoolbooks. "I did have a life before you were born, you know."

Kenneth laughed, and like so often, Shelly knew he was confused by her secretive side. He offered to go to the service with her, but she told him that it would be all right and that she just wanted to pay her respects.

Shelly knew that Kenneth would not press her because a part of him was afraid of the answers to his questions. She had never told him why she left the paper or why she made such a point of never taking part in school field trips to museums. They had met fifteen years earlier, when she had walked into the bank to open a new account. He had been drawn to her immediately, but there was something closed-off about her now, and he would never know all of it. Still, he had fallen so completely in love with her, and when he had asked, she had agreed to marry him, even though there was always going to be a part of her that remained closed to him.

As the world's climate shifted into uncharted waters, Shelly had chosen to say nothing about it. She knew where it was heading. Floods, famine, and drought were coming, just as the time line had predicated. The unfolding world events filled her with doubt, and when her son was born, she cried for him and the uncertainty of a future she knew all too well. Would Gerald be one of the people heading to Mars one day? When talks began about the evacuations, she shuddered and held on to Kenneth, her entire being trembling. He had no idea why she was so afraid, and like always, he chose not to ask.

On the day of George's funeral, Shelly sat outside the cemetery's chapel, staring at the line of cars, and realized that there were a lot of people at this service. She looked at herself in the mirror and cringed. "Bloody hell, girl. Did you think you were going to be the only one at this thing?"

She pulled out her lipstick and applied a fresh coat. "If you had really wanted to honor the man, you would have worn that stupid purple outfit," she muttered. It still hung in the back of her closet, where it had been for years. She had told Kenneth that it was an old fancy dress outfit she could not bear to part with, and he had accepted that explanation, just as he had accepted a lot of things she had said. She opened the car door and stepped into the rain, wondering why she had not brought her umbrella.

Inside the memorial room, Shelly sought the relative safety of a corner chair. She did not want to talk to any of George's friends because they would ask who she was and how she had known the man they had come to bury. What could she really tell them? The group assembled, and everyone quieted down as the minister began the service. He spoke the usual words about God and a life rewarded; Shelly barely paid any attention to it. She thought about George and the last time they had spoken at the museum. He had been so certain that God, or at least history itself, had meant for him to be there, that he was a part of some infinite plan to protect history.

"George was a man who had a great capacity for life," said an elderly man with thin gray hair who had gone up to eulogize George. He bent solemnly over his cane as he spoke. "He could make all of us laugh as he went on and on about Manchester United as if it was the only team worthy of his time and effort. He would sit in the pub and toast their success and their failures, as if he and he alone could make a difference in the outcome."

Everyone in the assembled group laughed at the memory except the woman seated in the corner. She had never heard George even mention sports, let alone drone on about his favorite team.

"He complained endlessly about the boredom of his job, but no one loved the museum more than George. He would laugh at the children as they ran in terror from the mummy rooms, but to be honest, he often told people that those things gave him the creeps too." The man gave a throaty chuckle. "He once told me that he was convinced that they one day would leap up from their sleep and attack all of us. I was never quite certain if he was having it on with me or if he really believed that one."

Shelly sighed because that was one feeling they had shared. Neither one of them had wanted to be in the mummy room longer than necessary.

"George loved a good joke and was never happier than when he was making other people laugh. We were all witness to his attempts to recreate some of the classic Monty Python sketches, and he was especially fond of the one that began with 'wink, wink, nudge, nudge.'"

The entire group responded with the required "Know what I mean?" Shelly did not join in. Her mind drifted back to the night they went to see the movie *And Now for Something Completely Different*. It was a wonderful evening and something she had thoroughly enjoyed. The problem with that amazing memory was that it made her unable to watch those old movies without thinking of George, so she had never watched the Python troupe again.

"George's bizarre sense of humor touched all of us, and I am certain that some of you saw that ridiculous orange suit he would often pull out to wear on Halloween." The crowd laughed, but Shelly felt her body go limp. She may have kept the purple outfit she had worn in the future, but it had sat in the back of her closet untouched. How could he have thought to put that on, even as a joke?

The group continued the stories and jokes for well over an hour, with many people getting up to reminisce about the man she had barely gotten to know before she said good-bye. The more they talked about his stories and jokes, the more she felt like a fool for being there because it was obvious that he had been right all along: she really did not know him.

A short little balding man walked up to the microphone and cleared his throat. "My name is Carl Kettle, and as far as I could tell, George Marsh was an odd man, and I did not always understand him."

Join the club, Shelly thought. At the same time, her stomach did a little lurch, as it often did whenever a man told her that his name was Carl.

"He often came to me and spoke of history as if it was something alive, with moods and emotions," the man continued. "I thought it was silly, and as a historian, I would tell him he was being ridiculous. However, he once said that as much as we thought we knew about the artifacts in our charge at the museum, there were a great many things we would never know. I had to admit that intrigued me, and it always made me wonder what sitting at his desk had taught him."

There was a general nodding of heads around her, and Shelly caught glimpses of people smiling at the idea of the security guard knowing more than the archaeologists and historians.

"He seemed to have a genuine curiosity about the world of our museum," Carl continued, "and I have told many that if everyone took as much interest in our artifacts as George did, our attendance would not be dropping. The world would still care about mummies and antiquity. George might never have believed it of me, but I will miss him."

The group all nodded in agreement, and then the minister led them in a moment of prayer before they all rose to walk to the cemetery. Shelly sat in her seat for a moment, lost in thought. A spindly old gray-haired man with a cane stumbled over to her. "Are you related to George, Miss?" he asked in a gruff voice.

"No." She looked up at him and realized that for the first time that day, there were tears in her eyes. "I only met him once or twice, and after listening to all of you talk about him, I realize that I did not know him at all."

The old man gave her a puzzled look. "Why would you come to the memorial for a man you did not know?"

Shelly rose to her feet and shook her head. "I am beginning to ask myself the same question, Mr. ..."

"Clancy Jasper. And who are you anyway?"

"Shelly Tunstill." She offered him her arm, and together they walked out the door and into the rain toward the cemetery. "I really did meet him, but it was years ago, and I guess I never gave myself the chance to get to know him."

"You should have taken the time," Clancy said, smiling knowingly. "He was a delightful fellow, our George."

"So it seems." Shelly tried to smile at the old man but found it difficult.

"Why did you not give him a chance, if you don't mind my asking?"

"Something happened that made me angry with him, and after that I could not forgive him."

"George did something you couldn't forgive him for?" It was clear from his expression and voice that this was not something Clancy had ever considered possible.

"It was a long time ago, and to be honest, it was not the sort of thing that was easy to forgive. No matter how hard I tried, I could not get past it." Shelly's voice wavered under the strain. She had never told anyone even this much about her time spent with George Marsh.

"George never said anything to me about someone being that angry with him, and I have known him forever."

Shelly gently squeezed the old man's arm. "I think we both made an agreement to never talk about what happened. I have never even told my husband about George."

"I am a little confused by all of this, Mrs. Tunstill." Clancy stopped and looked at her with intense interest. "My old mate was never one to keep secrets."

"Some things are meant to be kept secret, Mr. Jasper, and what happened to George and me was one of those things. He had done something monumental, and the more I thought about it, the more it frightened me."

Clancy's face was contorted in deep thought. "George did tell me that he had once changed the world, but that was on a night when we both had drunk a lot more than usual."

"That might have been what he meant." She sighed, and they continued walking to join the group assembled around the grave site. "I was not one to want to change the world, so I ran away."

Shelly knew that Clancy was staring at her, but there was nothing she could say to explain her relationship with George. They had not been friends in the strictest sense of the word; they had barely been acquaintances. What they had been to each other was as much a mystery as that stupid amulet that now sat in the museum, waiting for someone else to realize its magical powers. George would no longer be there to watch over it to make certain no one put it on and saw the glowing pictures on the wall.

After the burial, Shelly sat in her vehicle, staring at the rain hitting the windshield, and wondered what she could have done differently. "George, I wish you would have said something to me," she cried, her voice rising an octave. "Told me what you were planning on doing that day." But would she have stopped him? She had no answer for that question either.

She leaned forward and put her head on the steering wheel, tears rolling down her cheeks, and for the first time in her life, she understood what it meant to hate and love at the same time. She hated him for what he did, mainly because she had been falling in love with him. She had wanted so much from him, and when he committed that act of murder, he had somehow become less of a man in her eyes.

Shelly thought of her husband and her son waiting for her at home and pulled herself together. She sat up straight and drove out into the afternoon traffic. "Kenneth," she whispered. She suddenly realized that she had lied to him all those years ago when he asked if he was the first man she had ever loved. She had said he was, but now she knew that was not true. Before she met him, there had been George Marsh, a middle-aged security guard who had broken her heart.

Shelly went home and made a nice dinner of pork chops, potatoes, and peas for her two men. When Kenneth asked her about the funeral, she told him it was fine.

After that day, she never mentioned George Marsh again. He was in the secret place in her heart that even her husband would never know about; it was the place she would go in her dreams. And years later, when she was lying on her deathbed, the last word Shelly ever said was the name George.

"Mom," her son whispered as he held her hand, "who is George?" But it was too late. The secret was gone, and it would remain a mystery forever.

Printed in the United States
By Bookmasters